BEYOND ESCAPE

BEYOND ESCAPE

A Novel

Deborah K. Jensen

BEAVER'S POND
PRESS

This book is a work of fiction. Names, characters, places, and incidents either are products of the author's imagination or are used fictitiously. Any resemblance to actual events or locales or persons, living or dead, is entirely coincidental.

ISBN: 978-1-59298-438-1

Library of Congress Control Number: 2012915093
Printed in the United States of America
Book design by Ryan Scheife, Mayfly Design
Typeset in Filosofia
First Printing: 2012

16   15   14   13   12   5   4   3   2   1

Beaver's Pond Press, Inc.
7108 Ohms Lane
Edina, MN 55439-2129
(952) 829-8818
www.BeaversPondPress.com

To order, visit www.BeaversPondBooks.com
or call (800) 901-3480. Reseller discounts available.

For Jim
Thanks for always believing in me.

CHAPTER ONE

Kim set the receiver of the antique-looking phone gently back in its cradle, although she felt more like slamming it down. She sat for a minute staring at it, the one thing she insisted on keeping when she and Alex split their personal property, the accumulation of stuff they had acquired over the past twenty years. Kim reached for her throat, feeling first a swelling ache and then the tears, tears that she didn't want to shed. They streamed down her face as she sobbed uncontrollably.

After a few minutes, she lifted her head, pushed a strand of blond hair behind her ear, and wiped her hands across her face, drying her wet eyes. She cleared her throat and focused on the conversation she had just had with Kathleen Woods, her attorney.

"The papers are all signed," Kathleen had said in a hushed, monotone voice. Kim sat in silence as she listened to the words. "Alex hired a good attorney," Kathleen continued, "one even better than me. I may be known as the Dragon Lady, but his lawyer is ruthless—and good at it, too." *That's it; it's finalized,* Kim had thought as she listened to Kathleen's voice. While she hadn't gotten Kim her fair share, Kathleen reassured her it was the best they could do.

Alex made a respectable wage as a financial planner and the last few years had been good ones for her. She and Alex had enjoyed some luxuries they hadn't been able to afford in the past. She was going to miss the lifestyle she had become so accustomed to. She was going to have to make some changes in her spending habits, and those frequent getaway trips were now a thing of the past.

Kim got up from the couch and looked around the tiny apartment she had rented only eight weeks earlier, when she filed for divorce. "I'm divorced," she said softly to herself. The thought of it was bad enough, but saying it out loud made it real. *How did it get to this point?* This was not what she envisioned when she had fantasized about her wedding, marriage, and children so long ago when she was a little girl. She had gotten the marriage, but not the children, and in the end, she got nothing.

Kim went into the kitchen and took a stool from the small closet next to the refrigerator. She had bought it soon after she moved out on her own. She had always had the convenience of Alex's tall statue to retrieve things that were out of her reach, but that was a thing of the past. She set the stool on the floor in front of the stove, spread the legs apart, and climbed to the top step to reach the cupboard overhead. She stood on tippy toes and stretched her fingers out, trying to find the sacred bottle of wine she had been saving for a special occasion—only that occasion was supposed to be with Alex, not to mark the finalization of their divorce. But somehow she felt she needed to drink the wine to get rid of memories of happier times.

The average temperature during December in Raleigh usually hovered around the fifty-degree mark, and it rained only eight to ten days during the month. But that year was unseasonably cold and rainy, with some days of snow, which really put the city in a frantic state. For the previous few weeks, the cold drizzle and dreary days had added to Kim's sullen mood; she needed a change of pace. She was sick of the weather, sick of her job, and right now, she was sick of her life.

After finding the wine and taking her best cut-crystal glass from another cupboard, Kim stood in front of the small living room's window, looking through the blackness of the night at the scattered streetlights below. What had started as light showers during the day had turned into sheets of rain that made thumping sounds as they fell against the windowpanes. *I only wish the rain would wash away my feelings as easily as it washes away the remnants of whatever is on the sill.*

Kim turned away from the window and suddenly blurted out, "I need to escape."

Kim was the youngest child and only girl of Jack and Nita Whitman. They now spent their winters in a retirement village in south Texas. Visiting her parents seemed to be her only option. It wouldn't necessarily be a luxury getaway, but it would be an inexpensive vacation. Kim was very familiar with south Texas. As a child, she and her family often visited her grandmother Sadie, who spent her winters there. The trip from northern Maine to south Texas was a long one, but Jack and Nita made sure they visited Sadie at least once a year, usually over the children's spring break. Then there was the short stint Kim spent there as a young adult, the memories of which were stored away in the back of her mind somewhere.

Kim's job as a sales representative for an athletic clothing company, Wicked International, afforded her the luxury of having time off for most of the holiday season. Manufacturing usually halted in December, so the company closed down for most of the month, giving every employee, from the receptionist to the president, a vacation over the holidays.

Kim turned back to the window and stared at the rain for a minute before picking up the bottle of wine she had set on the table next to her. She poured the deep red liquid into the glass, looked at the label, and sighed, remembering when she and Alex had bought the vintage wine at an auction. She lifted the glass toward her mouth and stopped to trace the "T" that was etched on the side with her finger. The wine glasses were a wedding gift from Phil and Peggy Thompson, Alex's parents. They were so happy to finally have a daughter in the family and were equally pleased that Kim was taking Alex's name. The wine glasses solidified that fact.

As a young couple, Kim and Alex had had visions of a long life together, a life filled with excitement, fun, and "getting ahead." Although she didn't know it at the time, getting ahead had meant something different to Alex than it did to Kim. Kim squeezed her eyes shut at the thought of the night she first found out about Alex's affair. The memories came tumbling back as if it had all happened yesterday. She usually fought hard to squelch those thoughts but tonight, they came streaming back beyond her control.

It first started with the traces of red lipstick she found on his collar, a color close to her own shade, one she didn't wear any more. Then reality really set in when her coworker spotted him with the other woman. Hearing about that night knocked her whole world down.

"They were sitting in a very intimate, dark corner table," she was told, "and it definitely was not a business meeting. She was beautiful, brunette, very tall and athletic," her confidant said.

That stung Kim particularly hard, since Alex always said that blondes were his weak spot. This woman sounded like she was the total opposite of Kim. Was that bit about blondes just a line he had told her, or had his preference changed? If they had, was it due to her? Kim jerked away from the window and shook her head. *No; I am not going to let him make this about me.* She looked toward the table next to her. "Now you can make me numb," she said, picking up the bottle again, looking at the label once more, sighing, and setting it back down. She took a sip of the merlot, paused for a moment, then swirled it around in her mouth. Before she even swallowed it, Kim decided that she would regroup in Texas.

Before the next sip of wine, Kim thought she'd better call her parents to tell them about her plans.

"Mom, are you going to be home for Christmas?" She knew the answer; of course they were going to be there, but she thought she'd better find out if a month with their beloved daughter would be okay with them.

"Yes, we'll be home." Her mom's voice sounded hurried on the other end. Then there was a pause, as if she was remembering something. "How are you doing? I've been thinking about you all day." Kim was surprised at the question. Nita Whitman was not one to pick up the phone to converse, and this day was no exception, even though she knew it was the day Kim's divorce would be finalized.

"I'm fine, Mom," Kim said. "I'm going to come down for Christmas?" she quickly added, eager to change the subject.

"Of course; we would love to have you."

"Actually, I won't be coming just for Christmas. I'd like to spend about a month with the two of you," she said, pausing to hear a response. When she didn't get one right away, she squeezed her eyes shut and grit her teeth, waiting for an answer.

"Yes, that's just fine," Nita finally replied. "I'll be working, you know, and I do have my dancing. Your dad has golf . . . and bowling . . . and oh, yes, he just started running the shuffleboard league. He really enjoys it and he's working on getting everyone back on track."

Kim relaxed her jaw and shook her head in silence. *Maybe this was a bad idea.* "Mom, you don't have to entertain me. I just want to get away and think—or no, not think," Kim promptly added. "I'll stay out of your hair. You don't have to worry about me." Kim cringed at the tone in her voice, feeling like she was being disrespectful. Then added, "I just think some warm weather and family is what I need right now."

Nita's response was more comforting. "I think that is just perfect. I do agree it's what you need, and your dad will be pleased. When are you thinking of coming down?" With that question, Nita's usually hasty tone was back, and Kim heard her sigh on the other end of the phone. Kim felt like ending the conversation right then and there. She slowly closed her eyes and took in three deep breaths.

"Mom?" Kim said, breaking the uncomfortable silence.

"Yes, dear?"

"If it's going to be an inconvenience, I can go else-where over the holidays."

"Nonsense," she said, the slight edge still in her voice.

Their busy retirement life and Kim's hectic work schedule meant that Kim and her parents, especially her mom, interacted infrequently. They had never had that wonderful mother-daughter bond that most of her friends had with their mothers. Nita and Jack loved their children, and their children loved them—no question about that—but Kim always felt that she was interrupting something when she spoke to her mom.

Chris and Allen, Kim's brothers, never seemed to understand when Kim tried to explain how she thought that Nita felt more like living her life doing entirely her own thing rather than spending time with her children. With Jack, it was a different story. Kim was his little girl. This was quite obvious to those both inside and outside the family circle.

"We close up the first week of December, and I don't have to be back to work until after New Year's. I'm going to see if I can get a flight out around the eighth. I'll call you when I make the reservations and let you know my itinerary."

"Okay, dear; just let us know."

Kim heard a click on the other end and stood a min-ute before hanging up the phone. *This is a bad idea,* she thought again. She contemplated calling her mom back to tell her that she had changed her mind, but then she thought about her dad. It really would be good to see him. Kim walked over to the tiny desk situated between the window and the couch. There was not any room in the apartment for an office, let alone much else, so she had to make do with this setup.

She wedged herself behind the couch, sat down on the wooden crate she used for a chair, and opened her laptop. An hour later she had booked a flight and printed her boarding pass. She would leave North Carolina in two weeks. Suddenly, a strange feeling came over her, one she hadn't felt for quite some time. Was she finally starting to relax?

Kim jumped as the buzzer from her intercom blared throughout the quiet room. "What the heck?" she said under her breath. Kim quickly glanced at her watch as she walked toward the door. "Nine thirty! Who would be here at this hour of the night?" she said a little louder.

She pushed the button on the intercom box. "Hello?" she hesitantly called out.

"Hello."

Her stomach lurched when she heard the voice on the other end.

"Alex, what are you doing here?" Kim demanded. She cringed when she heard the quiver in her voice, mad that she didn't sound more controlled.

"Can I come up?" Alex asked.

"What for? We have nothing further to say to each other." Her voice was now stronger. "I don't want to see you or talk to you. It's over, Alex."

"Please," he pleaded with her.

Kim pressed her forehead against the wall and closed her eyes. *What am I doing?* she thought as she hit the button to let Alex in. A few minutes later, they were seated on her couch, Alex facing her, his face drawn and pale. She noticed how he had aged over the past several months. She also could smell the hint of whiskey on this breath. *He must have been drowning his sorrows. .*

"I just wanted to say I'm sorry," Alex said. "I didn't set out to intentionally hurt you. I got caught up in something, and the next thing I knew, I thought I had fallen out of love with you."

"How nice. That's what you came all the way over here to tell me?" She straightened her back and sat up, hoping she looked defiant and not defeated.

"No, Kim; that's not what I meant. I wanted to explain to you that I was happy . . . I mean with us. I was not out looking for something else. If I could do it all over again, I would." He stopped before continuing, as if he were trying to formulate the exact words he wanted to say. "I've been thinking all afternoon since I left the attorney's office. It didn't hit me until today that this is finished. Our marriage is over."

"And you didn't know this until today?" The sarcasm in Kim's voice melted over the room. "It's been over for a long time, Alex, in case you haven't noticed."

"I know it's not been the best between us—"

"The best?" Kim interrupted. "It was horrible, and then it got worse."

"Like I said, I got caught in something I didn't mean. Kim, should we have tried more before we just threw everything away?" Kim looked sideways at him. What was he trying to say?

"I thought I had fallen out of love with you, but the reality is, I still do love you. I don't think I want this to be over," he said, looking into her eyes.

"I think it's a little too late for that, don't you? Alex, it's over. I can't go back. I don't think I could ever forget and so I don't think I can forgive, either. I'd always be wondering if you would get caught in something again. Alex, I really do think it's over and the divorce was the best thing to do. We have to go our separate ways now, lead our own lives."

He looked defeated as she spoke the words. Then he slowly got up and started for the door in silence. When he put his hand on the knob, he turned back to the couch where Kim was still sitting. "I do still love you," he said, then pulled the door open and walked out, shutting it quietly behind him. Kim sat frozen on the couch, trying to comprehend what had just taken place.

She picked up her glass of wine, took a sip, and thought about what he said. *He still loves me.* She cared about him and what was going to happen to him, that she knew for sure. She took another sip, stopped, and then shook her head. No; she was sure she didn't love him anymore. The first book of her life had been written. Now she needed to proceed to book two, the rest of her life. And that book's first chapter was going to start with a quiet month in Texas with her parents.

CHAPTER TWO

The next morning, Kim arrived at the building of Wicked International at the same time as she always did. As usual, the commute around Raleigh had been relatively effort-less—its traffic was unlike the congested traffic of other cities the same size—so she was able to gauge her morn-ing drive almost down to the minute. Kim pulled into her usual parking space, grabbed her umbrella, and walked into the building.

The company's home office was situated in the out-skirts of downtown Raleigh, close to the warehouse dis-trict. The twelve-story brick structure was in remarkably good shape, even though it had been built in the early 1920s. It used to house a bank, then a gentlemen's club, and then various retail companies before Wicked Manu-facturing bought it in 1981.

The massive lobby was relatively untouched from when the building had been a bank. Most of the ornate pillars were original, as was the gray and black swirled marble floor. The gold-flecked ceiling vaulted far above the first floor, stopping eight feet above the open stair-case on the second floor. The heels of Kim's boots clicked on the marble as she quickly crossed the lobby to the elevators. She hastily pushed the elevator button, waiting impatiently until the doors opened, and rode it up to the seventh floor.

When she stepped out of the elevator, she went straight to the break room. Her only thought at that moment was getting a nice strong cup of coffee and heading to her office to avoid her coworkers who would stream in at any moment. They all knew how her life had unfolded over these past several weeks. She assumed she was the topic of more than one conversation.

Jim Peterson was the first to walk into the break room after Kim had poured her coffee. He was a team lead for the marketing department and had become a good friend to Kim. Jim was a very insightful man and had a quirky but enduring look on life. His frame towered over almost everyone and everything, including the coffee pot in front of him. As he grabbed the handle of the pot, he looked like a scientist hovering over his experiment, hunched in anticipation of what he might find.

"Everything okay?" He did not look at Kim as he spoke but put all his attention to filling his cup with coffee.

"I'll be fine," she responded. "Thanks for asking. I appreciate it. But I really don't want to talk about it, if that's okay."

"You know where to find me if you do."

Connie rounded the corner and wedged herself between the two of them, grabbing the coffee pot from Jim. As usual, her vibrancy had entered the room ahead of her. She knew it, as did everyone else, including Jim. He rolled his eyes and gave her a quick wink.

Not only was Jim a good friend of Kim's, but he was also one of Connie's confidants. She had revealed to Kim on more than one occasion how much she admired Jim for his wit, cleverness, and downright niceness. She could ask him advice about anything. Jim's feelings for Connie, however, went much deeper. He had told Kim that he secretly wanted to move to a different level with Connie, and asked Kim if she thought it would be a good idea to ask Connie out. When faced with his question, Kim was torn: She did not want to encourage him, since she knew Connie would not be the least bit interested in that kind of a relationship with Jim, but she also didn't want Jim to get hurt. She successfully dodged the subject every time he brought it up, usually responding in a nonchalant way, asking him why he wanted to ruin such a good friendship. He seemed to be satisfied with that.

"Christ, you look like hell, girl," Connie said as she searched the cupboard for her favorite pink coffee mug. "I know you'll be fine. You're just that type of person, always looking at the glass half full." She found her mug and poured herself a cup of coffee, then set the pot back on the burner. Connie Ellingson was a fellow sales representative and Kim's best friend. "That's why I admire you so," she said as she blew a kiss in Kim's direction.

"Thanks, dear," Kim said, the corner of her mouth curling up slightly as she turned, walked out of the break room, and headed toward her office. Connie's tall, sleek figure followed behind her, strands of golden curls cascading over the red blouse that fit tightly around her breasts. The clacking of her matching heels on the marble floor echoed off the walls. Connie's choice of attire was way out of the normal range for the line of work they were in: selling athletic wear.

"Whatever!" Connie told her fellow employees whenever they commented on her dress. One colleague, a fellow sales rep named Joe, had once said to Kim, "Perhaps that is why she continually is in the top third for volume."

"It's her style," Kim had said, coming to her friend's rescue and giving him a scornful look that ended the conversation.

Kim put her hand on the doorknob of her office and turned to Connie. "I am heading south in two weeks," Kim said and waited for a response.

"South—girl! Good for you. Some romantic beach? How appropriate," she said, laughing.

"Not quite, honey. I'm going to a retirement village. How do you like that?"

"What?"

"I'm visiting my mom and dad down in Texas. I'm going to wrap myself with some love and warm weather. It's like a time warp down there, all those senior citizens shuffling through their lives without a care in the world, except I suppose hearts, health, and achy bones. I like going there. I have fond memories from my childhood and I always feel like a celebrity when I visit. My dad has to make sure everyone knows I am there and how proud he is of me. I even get announced at bingo!"

"Sounds like fun . . . I suppose." Connie hesitated. "Is your mom okay with you spending a month there?" Connie knew about Kim's frustrations with her mom, and when she saw the hurt on Kim's face, she quickly added with playful sarcasm, "Well, the warm sun can't be beat and I guess with you being in your forties and all, you have to start checking out where you will retire."

"Ha, ha, very funny," Kim said, walking into her office and closing the door behind her.

—— •••• ——

Connie stood and looked at the closed door for a minute before walking to her own office. *That felt like a slap in the face.* But she knew it had nothing to do with her. She sat down at her desk, put her hands to her forehead, and cradled her head as she shook it from side to side. She hadn't told Kim about her own plans for the next month and didn't want to. She wasn't even sure it was what she wanted to do; to reveal the plan would only make it real, and that scared her. Connie always had the comfort of friends and lovers around her, so venturing off on her own scared her immensely.

CHAPTER THREE

Packing for a month is a nightmare, Kim thought. Developing yearly business plans, forecasting, and crunching numbers were daily routines for Kim. But trying to pack four weeks of clothes into one suitcase was well beyond her organizational skills. She sat on the bed, looked at her bulging suitcase, and laughed. She threw herself face down on the bag, trying to get it closed. After a few more attempts, she finally zipped it shut.

The last two weeks had gone by fairly quickly. Kim had contacted all of her clients, mostly small to mid-sized athletic stores all along the Eastern seaboard, and then wrapped up her year, finishing final paper work and preparing for the coming selling season. She set appointments with her customers, formulated new sales presentations, and prepared reports. In spite of accomplishing all that, she felt as if she'd moved through the past weeks in a state of numbness, putting thoughts of her divorce behind her and concentrating solely on the present, not thinking about much of anything except work. And then, finally, she was ready to embark on thirty days of doing virtually nothing: no thinking, no work, and no divorce.

Connie had wanted to meet Kim for drinks to say one last goodbye before they parted ways for the company's winter shutdown. Earlier in the day, she told Kim she would miss not seeing her for a month. After all, Kim was her rock and support; she kept her grounded. Kim laughed when Connie told her she was actually afraid not to have her close by in case she needed her to get her out of whatever situation she found herself needing help getting out of.

Kim's plane wasn't going to leave until eleven o'clock the next morning and everything was ready, so drinks that night fit perfectly into Kim's schedule. After she finished packing, she set off to meet Connie at Bulgios, their favorite wine bar.

The unseasonable temperature had changed the rain into snow, making Kim's flight the next day that much more of a welcome getaway. She hugged her coat close to her as she stepped out the door and headed down the stairs. Just as she reached the last step, her foot slipped and she pitched forward. She instinctively swung out her arm, catching herself on the stair's railing. As she did, her purse tumbled to the snow-covered sidewalk.

She bent down to retrieve it, and as she stood up, she caught sight of a young couple holding each other closely. They were both bundled in heavy jackets and scarves, but their steamy embrace would have been enough to shield them from the cold. The girl had her back to Kim and her companion had his shoulder against the wall of the flat next door. The young man looked down at her, caressing her cheek as he moved his finger down the side of her face. He lifted her chin toward his and bent down to give her a soft, kiss full on her lips.

Kim's heart started to pound as she stood looking at the two lovers. She missed a man's touch; she hadn't known how much until that moment. Even though she had moved out of the house she shared with Alex only eight weeks earlier, the marriage had really ended years before that. The lack of intimacy, both in and out of the bedroom, had become routine for both of them. They had become used to it and moved through their lives that way.

Kim quickly turned away from the lovers, panting, trying to catch her breath. Alex's words from the day she last saw him rang through her head. Even though she had told him it was over, the finality of the divorce and the realization that she was truly alone hit her hard at that moment. The couple in front of her reminded her of what she had lost, and this realization made the scene she had just observed oddly depressing.

Bulgios was only a few blocks from Kim's apartment, and it had been one of her favorite spots for quite some time. In fact, she had found her apartment building one evening on her way to meet Connie at Bulgios. Kim had been the one who wanted to leave when she and Alex decided to get a divorce, so she had felt that she should be the one to move out and look for a new place to live. The available apartment hadn't really been what she wanted, but the price and convenience were right at the time. She had needed a place quickly and she didn't want to sign a long-term lease, so the apartment fit the bill. It would have to do for the short term.

When Kim arrived at Bulgois, Connie was already seated at a tiny table, looking exquisite as usual. She wore a tight, low-cut black sweater that showed off more cleavage than Kim felt comfortable with. Even though Connie was not one to frequent a gym, she had a figure that most women would kill for; full breasts, a tiny waist, and legs that didn't quit. Her shoulder-length blond hair was always meticulously styled. Kim preferred a longer, sleeker style for her own hair, a look that Connie often suggested she change. "Add some curl," Connie would tell her, but Kim always ignored the suggestion, saying that she liked her style just fine.

"Are you all set?" Connie said, looking up as Kim slid into the chair across from her. A candle flickered between them and Kim gazed at its flame before she answered.

"I guess as ready as I can be. I jammed thirty days of clothes into a suitcase I swear was meant only for a weekend retreat."

"So how are you, really, honey?" Connie inquired, still looking at Kim when the waitress came over to take their order. The waitress, a short, stocky twenty-something girl who looked like she'd feel much more comfortable in a pool hall rather than a quaint venue such as Bulgois, stood next to Kim and asked their order.

"I'll have the house chardonnay," Kim told her.

Connie's eyes narrowed as she looked at Kim, then she turned to the waitress. "I'll have the Rombauer cabernet." She looked back to Kim and said, "House wine!"

"Expenses," Kim replied. "I have only one income now and I have to watch my spending."

"Girl, when you come back, I'll treat you to a big night out, a whole evening without a single glass of house wine. Okay?" Her smile faded. "How are you doing?"

"Oh, you know. I'm surviving."

"That's what it looks like from the outside, but how do you really feel? I know Alex hurt you and you can't just push that under the carpet. You have to deal with it, Kim."

Kim contemplated for a moment what she was going to tell Connie. She was not sure she wanted to let Connie know she had had a visit from her ex-husband. Connie frequently let Kim know how much of a jerk she thought he was. Connie had not cared much for Alex before the affair, and his indiscretions only confirmed her contempt for the man. His visit would be the icing on the cake for Connie, confirming that he truly was a scumbag.

"Alex stopped by the other night," Kim blurted out.

"What?" Connie asked, her tone loud and sharp.

"Shh . . . you'll have the whole bar looking at us," Kim said, putting her finger up to her lips. She continued in a hushed voice. "He wanted to tell me that he was still in love with me and that we should have tried harder to work things out."

"Jerk."

"I didn't want to tell you because I knew you would gloat over the fact that this was one more idiot thing he would do."

"Well, you're darn right; it's confirmed. He *is* an asshole," Connie said, smiling.

"I'm done with it—the divorce and Alex. I'm now going to dive into the life of the retired," she said and smiled, "if only for a month." Kim paused and her smile disappeared. "I just saw a young couple on my way over here, a very attractive young couple, kissing, intertwined in an embrace." Kim drifted away in thought. "I guess I never realized how much I missed intimacy. It has been a long time since I felt, even for a moment, what I just saw them experiencing fifteen minutes ago."

Connie's brows drew tightly together. "Just because Alex cheated and hurt you doesn't mean that you'll never find happiness again, Kim. You're a very attractive forty-three-year-old woman. Heck, you look like you're in your thirties. You'll soon have men swarming all over you, just wait."

"Oh, and this coming from a girl who swears off relationships. By the way, thanks for the compliment."

Connie was a woman who knew only the slightest of details about romantic intimacy. "To get too close to a man will only hurt you," she always claimed. At this point in her life, Kim understood exactly what she meant.

"Yes, but I know you . . . you need it."

"Need what?" Kim asked.

"You need the closeness, and you deserve to have it."

"Deserve it? What are you talking about?"

"You're not like me; you need to have a stable relationship—kids and all that stuff. That's what you deserve; it's not a bad thing, it's just your destiny."

"And you don't deserve it?"

"It's different for me. I don't care."

"Okay, let's talk about something else, like where you are going over the holiday break."

"You have to stop calling it that. It sounds like we're back in school. Look at it as if we're on a sabbatical. Now that's more romantic, don't you think?"

"So where are you going on your sabbatical, then?"

"I decided last week to book a beach house in San Diego. I didn't tell you because I didn't want you to get depressed and all, me being in a luxurious beach house and you in retirement hell." Connie flashed a quick smile toward Kim. "I found this great deal online; the photos look fabulous and it's right on the beach," Connie explained.

"No need to worry about me. But you . . . you make sure you keep safe. Stay out of the bars, won't you?"

"Of course not. I'm going out there to get lucky. If I stay out of the bars, I won't accomplish my goal. Don't worry; I'll be safe. I have a truckload of condoms being delivered the first day," Connie said as she winked.

"Ha, very funny. But really, you tend to go beyond the extreme and get in all kinds of terrible situations. Be careful."

"I will, but I won't live a boring life."

"Whatever," Kim said, smiling an exasperated smile at her friend. She took a sip of the wine the waitress had set before her. It tasted unbelievably good. Even for house wine.

CHAPTER FOUR

Looking around the cabin, Kim figured that the average age on the plane had to be eighty. The airline she had chosen was a popular choice for the "winter Texans," since it scheduled direct flights right into the valley. Her flight companions next to her were a lovely eighty-something woman and her elderly husband. The woman, who was obviously the healthier of the two, attended to her husband's needs throughout the flight, all the while carrying on a conversation with Kim.

They talked about family, the weather, and Texas. At one point, Kim found herself revealing just a bit too much information about her personal life. Her elderly seatmate did not seem to mind, even giving Kim a knowing grin. Kim had smiled to herself and imagined what indiscretions the old man may have had in his past life. *But then again*, she had thought, *perhaps it had been his wife?*

An hour into the flight, Kim closed her eyes to rest for a while. Her thoughts drifted off to the past, back to when she was eighteen years old. Her impending arrival in south Texas, she was sure, prompted these thoughts. Twenty-five years earlier she had been a naïve young woman living in a small town looking for anything that might come along that was better than what she had at that moment. How ironic. Kim smiled to herself at the memory and at the fact that, just as she had back then, she was now stepping into the next chapter of her life.

Texas had played a big role in Kim's young adult life and now she was headed there again. Would south Texas help her find what she needed? Searching for clues to the answer, Kim sank further into her thoughts.

———•••———

It was a hot summer day in the late seventies. One of Kim's grandmother's nephews was visiting her family in Maine. He had traveled from south Texas, and was passing through on his way to his hometown to wrap up some family business. "Nephew" was a loose term for the young man, since he wasn't related to Kim's family by blood. Kim's grandmother had divorced and married a man who had a brother. That brother had two sons and a daughter, and upon Sadie's marriage, they became her niece and nephews. The two families became close and the children grew up together.

Sadie and Peter Carson had met through mutual friends at a neighbor's picnic when she was still married. She had been a very attractive woman. Her children were grown and she had become bored with her life; she needed more attention from her husband than she was getting, and she felt restless. One day, when she was attending a neighborhood picnic, a friend took her by the arm and said she just had to meet this widower who was a kind and gentle sea captain.

Sadie knew the minute she saw him that he was what she was looking for. And that started a feverish love affair. She had been divorced from her husband of twenty-five years only a few months when she and Peter married. Divorce in the late fifties was unheard of—even shunned—and Sadie became the disgrace of her family and friends, but she didn't care. She had finally found happiness with this man, and she wasn't going to pass it up.

Peter had been a true seaman. He had captained a fishing boat off the shores of Maine. When he retired from sea life, he bought a resort with his brother in Bridgton, Maine. After they were married, Sadie joined the family at the resort, working side by side with Peter, his brother, Art, and Art's wife, Violet.

Kim grew up in Augusta, Maine, which was only an hour and a half away from the resort, so the family was close enough to frequent Bridgton often. Her dad, Jack, owned a small pizza restaurant in Augusta, and over the years had developed a staff of employees he could trust, which allowed him and the family the freedom to spend more time at the resort.

As Kim got older, she and her brothers would stay with Sadie for weeks at a time, helping out with chores while enjoying the resort life. Kim's responsibilities consisted of household duties, like cleaning cabins and helping with the laundry, while her brothers worked the dock area, assisting guests and fishermen with their boats and cleaning their freshly caught fish. Seeing her brothers outdoors, working in the sun and fresh air, she always felt jealous; she would have loved to have been able to hang out by the water, listening to all the interesting stories the older folks had to tell.

One such sunny day, when she was delivering box lunches to the dock boys, she found herself alone by the harbor. The boys were off putting away the lawn mowers before they broke for lunch. When she reached the water, she saw a fisherman come through the channel and head straight for the gas dock instead of his usual slip. As he got closer, she could tell from his pale face that he was upset; something was terribly wrong. "Run and call for help!" he shouted to her. "I spotted him! He's floating over by the narrows west of Star Island."

It took Kim a moment to catch on to what he was saying, but then she realized he was referring to the drowning that occurred earlier in the week. A fisherman had gone out in rough waters and his boat had overturned. The boat turned up, but not its captain. Search crews immediately started dragging the area where the boat had been found, but they found nothing. They halted their search after a few days, knowing that the body would eventually come to the surface.

Kim ran up the long stairs to the top of the hill to find her grandmother. She hastily spat out the words between gasps for air as she tried to catch her breath. She eventually got out the message for Sadie to call for help.

That single incident had been traumatic for Kim. She became afraid of the water and stayed away from the dock area. Throughout that summer, she had nightmares of drowning that would often wake her up in the middle of the night. On one morning following one of her nightmares, Mark overheard Sadie talking with Kim, trying to comfort her. When Mark realized that Sadie was not being effective, he stepped in to help.

Kim was sitting on a high stool at the counter where lunch was served at the resort. He put his arm around her. "The water is our friend," he told her in a soft and gentle voice. Kim looked up at him, and her eyes narrowed in a puzzled look. Mark continued, "The water is there to help us live. Without it, we would die. But we must respect it; *she* can take us in an instant if we aren't careful."

Kim looked at Mark, surprised at how mature and philosophical he sounded. His arm was still around her as he gave her a gentle squeeze and leaned his head into hers. From that moment, Kim looked at Mark in a different way, not fully understanding her feelings until the next summer, when she developed a schoolgirl crush on him. Up until that point he had just been a family friend.

But the feelings were only one sided. His intentions stayed the way they had always been toward her: She was this pudgy little girl who was six years younger than he. Mark was more interested in girls his own age, many of whom would frequently visit him at the resort. There were always girls stopping by, and when they did, he would stop what he was doing, flash his wide smile as he flirted. Eventually he would take the girl by the hand and run off to some hideaway along the beach.

One of those girls was Alison, a beautiful, tall, black-haired beauty with American Indian ancestry that gave her a soft brown complexion. Her legs were lean and long, which made the short shorts she often wore seem that much shorter. Alison's favorite top to accompany those shorts was made of two triangle bandannas that tied behind her neck and joined at their ends to tie behind her back. She didn't have much of a chest, but she didn't need one; the bandanna gaped to show off the sides of her small, firm breasts, and that seemed to be enough for Mark.

Kim longed to be able to wear a top like Alison's. She went shopping one day to find one, but when she tried it on, all she could see were the rolls of fat bulging where the top wrapped below her breast and tied around the back. She thought of how beautiful Alison was and knew she had no chance with Mark.

Mark and Alison became inseparable, rarely spending any time apart. Kim found herself jealous about the time Mark spent with Alison. She had seen a number of Mark's girls come and go, but never had he been this serious about any of them. When Mark and Alison started talking about marriage, Kim's heart sank. She knew she might as well give up her crush on him.

Mark and Alison's marriage happened rather quickly. Some of the family feared Alison was pregnant, but Mark quickly dispelled that myth. "I love her and I know she's the one. Why should we wait?" he explained to friends and family. Mark did not have patience for anything and when he wanted something, he found a way to get it. This marriage was no different.

The wedding took place on a hot summer day at the resort under a big oak tree by the lake not far from the beach. Alison was dressed in a long white gauze dress with spaghetti straps that held the draped bodice around her tiny breasts. A small red ribbon was draped just under her bust and she wore her hair in a loose braid that hung to the middle of her back. Mark was dressed in a white tuxedo, white shirt, and vest, with a red bow tie to match

Alison's ribbon. They were a gorgeous couple.

During the time Mark and Alison were dating, they had set up a small shop nestled among the pine trees on the resort's property; there they created handcrafted candles in countless shapes and sizes. Mark's dream was to strike it rich and at that moment, he thought candle making was the answer.

Soon after Mark and Alison were married, Kim's step-grandfather died. Sadie inherited Peter's share of the resort and a few years later the three of them decided to sell. Art and Violet wanted to move to a warmer climate and headed south. Without the resort to keep her busy, Sadie followed them and found an apartment in Mission, a small southern Texas town. Mark and Alison soon joined them. They took their candle-making supplies and inventory to continue their company in the south.

Then that hot 1970s summer, the summer Kim turned eighteen, Mark took a short trip north. The family was anxious for his arrival, since they had not seen him in five years. The last time Kim had seen Mark—the year he moved to Texas—he had been nineteen and she thirteen. When Kim and her family visited Sadie during those five years, they would occasionally see Mark's family, but never Mark; he was usually doing some type of business deal somewhere.

The summer Mark came to visit, he and Alison were no longer married. Kim found out later that Alison had left Texas two years after they arrived. She told Mark that she was just too far from family, was lonely, and wanted to go home. Later, the truth came out that she was concerned about the lifestyle Mark was living and she wanted out.

When Kim and Mark saw each other again that summer, the years had changed them both. He had matured
into an even more attractive man and she had become a
desirable young woman. They were equally surprised when
they laid eyes on each other. Kim was not prepared for her
provocative thoughts and Mark was not prepared for her.

Catching sight of him across the room, Kim was
struck by Mark's wide white smile. Still very charm-
ing, she found it even more appealing against his dark
tan. He was quite a bit taller than she remembered, and
blonder; the sun had bleached out his thick hair, giving
it streaks of gold. The white T-shirt he wore conformed
closely to his shoulders and chest, revealing a very well-
defined body.

Kim found herself first staring at the thickness of his
arms, her eyes moving upward to the base of this throat
where his Adam's apple heaved up and down as he spoke.
He was talking to Kim's parents, and alongside him was a
young Hispanic woman Kim assumed was his new wife,
Maite. When Mark had called Kim's family to let them
know of his visit, he had told them how he had met his
new wife in Texas and they had just celebrated their first
anniversary. Kim noticed that Maite was about her height,
but maybe twenty pounds heavier. Given the fact that she
wasn't joining in the conversation, Kim wondered if she
even spoke English.

Mark threw his head back in laughter at something
Kim's father said, and as he did, Kim saw the flash of his
ocean green eyes and couldn't help but notice a hint of
sunlight in them. Mark noticed her staring at him and
her heart skipped a beat when he winked at her. She gave

him a weak smile back, but didn't move, not able to take her eyes off of him.

His gaze fell upon her body as if he were examining a painting in a museum. The past few years had changed her physique quite a bit. She had lost all of her baby fat and had developed curves in all the right places, from her breasts to her shapely hips. She wore her blond hair straight; it hung to the middle of her back. That, combined with her hazel eyes against a lightly tanned face, gave her a particularly alluring, even mysterious look.

That summer, Kim had been in a state of total confusion about what to do with her life. She had just finished high school but had not made a decision about what she was going to do next. Her parents had never pushed her to go on to college. Neither had been college educated, and they didn't feel that was an important goal for their daughter, either.

Kim found this strange; she thought they would push her to accomplish what they never did. Her brothers both pursued degrees at a local college, but Kim didn't have the drive or the desire to attend the same school they had. She had other things in mind. She hoped to leave Augusta. Kim's dream was to become a hair stylist in New York City. She really didn't know how that dream came about or how she was going to get there; she just knew it would be an exciting life, much more glamorous than the northern hick life she was living.

On the afternoon of his arrival, Mark was able to get Kim's parents alone to question them more about Kim and her plans for the coming year. They revealed to him her impending career choice and her plans to leave

Augusta. The knowledge of her budding hairstyling skills gave Mark an excuse to speak to her when he finally got her alone.

"Hey Kim, how about a haircut? I could really use one."

"I'm not trained," she blushed, surprised at his request.

"I don't care," he said, his green eyes twinkling. "Go ahead, do what you need to do. I trust you." Kim reluctantly agreed and told him to meet her outside. She then went to the bathroom, gathered what she needed, grabbed a chair and small table, and went to find Mark.

The sun was beating down on the driveway so intensely that it made the asphalt soft; Kim could smell the faint odor of tar as she set the chair down, and she saw the legs sink into the driveway as Mark sat down. She wrapped a towel around his neck, took the water-drenched comb from the glass she had sitting on the table beside them, and slid the comb through his thick hair, her hands shaking slightly.

With that simple gesture, all her childhood feelings flooded back. The old school girl crush reemerged, but this time the feelings were intensified, coming not from a child but from a young woman. He must have felt her unease, because right before she picked up a strand of hair to take the first clip, he turned around in the chair, smiled up at her, and gave her yet another wink.

His eyes lingered on hers for a minute before he turned back around and began chatting about his life in Texas. He talked nonstop about and how great Texas was, about all the opportunities there were, and best of all how the weather was fabulous. It only got cold about one month out of the year and even that was not cold compared to northern Maine.

"You should come down and visit sometime," he said.

"Oh, I don't know," Kim shyly replied. She knew she was going to go somewhere but Texas had not even been on the radar.

Still nervous, Kim concentrated on Mark's haircut, finishing fairly quickly and doing a decent job, if she did say so herself. As she was putting things away, she heard Maite scolding Mark for leaving her alone for so long. She spoke English loud and clear. Kim was starting to get the idea that this trip was an inconvenience for Maite. She didn't seem to like meeting strangers, much less having to stay with them. And Kim saw no sign of the usual newlywed romance. Instead, Maite seemed overbearing and controlling, intent on bickering. This new wife of Mark's was not at all like the beautiful, dark, complicated Alison.

Mark and Maite's visit was going to be a short one, since they were scheduled to be in Bridgton the next day to finalize some family business. Mark's father had died the year before and he needed to take care of some legal issues. His mother, Violet, now lived in the same town as Mark and had no desire to make the long trip north, so she sent Mark and his wife to take care of things.

Later that evening after dinner, Mark, Maite, Kim, and her parents sat in the den overlooking the new deck Jack had just finished building. Jack turned on the lights to reveal his newly dug backyard pond. He went on and on about the goldfish he just put in the pond and how they were going to grow to about the size of small perch. "Just about the size of the ones they used to catch in Highland Lake," he said. They laughed about the fact that a goldfish could really get that big. The only ones Kim had ever seen were in a small bowl the size of a rock. "Dad, are you sure?" Kim questioned.

"Really! They grow to the size of their environment," he assured her.

Mark was just as skeptical. "I can't imagine dropping a line for a goldfish. Would you filet them the same way?" he asked and smiled as Jack frowned back at him.

The conversation then turned to old times and to summers at the resort. Kim's two older brothers, Chris and Allen, came in and out of the room as the others reminisced, intermittently joining the conversation, adding their memories about adventures at the resort, cautiously sharing stories with Jack and Nita so as not to reveal too many details about their escapades.

Maite was clearly bored. Kim noticed that as she listened to the group talk about old times, she didn't say a word, but glared at the wall, occasionally shooting angry glances at Mark. At one point, she hit him in the leg, not able to contain her annoyance any longer. Mark ignored her completely and continued chatting away as if nothing was wrong, which made Maite even angrier. Then she got up, huffed loudly in a show of disdain, and walked out of the room.

After a while Kim got tired of the conversation as well, said goodnight to everyone, and went to her bedroom. Chris and Allen had already gone, which left Jack and Nita alone with Mark. When she got to her room, Kim flipped on the light, noticed something on her pillow, and picked it up. She stood by her bed holding the sealed plain white envelope, turning it over several times as she cautiously examined it. She sat down on the bed, put her finger under the flap, tore it open, pulled out a five-page letter, and began to read. The words on the paper appeared hastily scribbled with black pen on lined paper.

The ends were ragged from being ripped out of a notebook. As her eyes moved down the page, Kim could not believe what she was reading. It became very apparent that Mark had written the letter. Over and over she read expressions of love, expressions of love for her.

You have turned me inside out with your charm and beauty. I need you and want you.

It was a captivating and poetic love letter, revealing Mark's feelings and his desire to be with her. He invited her to come and stay with him and Maite in Texas. The letter stated that Maite would be absolutely fine with them having a relationship. *We have a very open marriage*, the letter stated. Kim could not believe the Maite she had met would be fine with anything remotely close to what Mark proposed. But she was just a naïve young eighteen-year-old. What did she know about the ways of married people?

She finished reading the letter and put it back in the envelope, not knowing what to do next. She sat on her bed and thought about what she had just read. She wasn't sure about the relationship, but did not discount the idea of moving to Texas. She could spend a few months down there before heading to New York.

Kim's dreams that night were filled with erotic days

and nights with a desirably handsome man who bore an astonishing resemblance to Mark. She tossed and turned, waking up several times. Each time she fell back to sleep, she resumed her ongoing dream of love and passion. In the morning, she was exhausted and confused.

"Good morning," Nita said, greeting Kim in the kitchen. "Did you sleep well? You still look tired."

"I slept fine," Kim muttered. "Where is Mark? Have you seen him yet?"

"No, not yet, but they will probably be up soon. They want to get going to the lake."

Kim shuffled back to her room to get dressed, thinking she would like to avoid him and everything else that morning. *Maybe I'll just sit here until they leave.* She thought again about Texas and what her parents would think if she left with Mark. She couldn't imagine they would have a problem with it. After all, it was Mark. She knew they would be happy and would probably think that her plans to go to New York would be over. They had tried to convince Kim that New York was not the place for her and consistently attempted to persuade her to stay in Augusta.

If she went to Texas instead of New York, she'd still be leaving, but in her parents' eyes Mark would be there to protect her and ease their minds, especially Jack's. From the moment Kim told him of her plans, he didn't want her to go. "I'm sure there are all kinds of hair cut places you can work at here in Augusta," he had told her. Jack adored his daughter, admiring everything she said and did, and Kim felt the same way about him. They had such a close relationship that Nita and he would often have words about who was more important to him. He would always assure Nita that of course it was she.

Kim heard her mom in the kitchen talking to someone and as she listened, she realized it was Mark. She heard the back door slam shut, then her mom's footsteps coming down the hallway toward her bedroom. Nita tapped softly on the door and Kim opened it slightly for her. Kim peered through the crack at her mom. "Mark wants you to go outside. He says he has something for you," Nita said.

Kim blushed and turned her head before slowly opening the door. "Okay, Mom." Nita paused and then went back to the kitchen. Kim slipped on a sweater and headed outside. *So much for hiding in my room.*

"Good morning," Mark said, looking up and smiling when Kim pushed open the screen door on the side of the garage.

"Hi," she replied, pulling her hair back in a ponytail.

"You look tired. Sleep well?" he said and smiled. He then turned toward the car and finished putting a suitcase in the back seat. "Did you find something last night?"

"I'm not sure what to say," Kim replied, looking down at her feet.

"Say yes," he said. "I think you'll like it there. I can help you find a job and I'm sure there are barber schools—or beauty schools or whatever you call them—in south Texas. From what I hear, you don't have a set plan. Your mom and dad are a little worried about you. Kim, I assured them I would take care of you."

"You told them?" Kim asked sharply, jerking her head up and looking at him.

"Relax . . . not everything. They said you were looking at going to New York and then I told them I would invite you to come and stay with us for a while until you found a job or a school."

"I don't know," she said and looked down again.

Three days later, Kim found herself sitting in the back seat of Mark's car, her entire life packed in suitcases and boxes beside her on the seat as she set out on the next phase of her life.

——•••——

The roaring of the plane's engine brought Kim back to the present and her eyes suddenly flew open. The cabin of the plane was quiet. She looked over at her companions who dozed next to her. Her heart started pounding and she was feeling closed in, gasping for breath as sweat started dripping down her back. The memories of her past came flooding back, bringing up feelings she had squelched for quite some time . . . until now. *I am a horrid, horrid person,* she thought. *I am a slut.* She suddenly realized that she was no better than Alex.

Alex had cheated on her with another women right under her nose while they were married. This other woman was a business associate of his whom he had known for quite some time. At first they were just friends; then it turned into something much more. "I got caught up in something . . ." he had told Kim.

Kim thought back to Mark. He had been a family friend and then she *got caught up in something. Oh God,* Kim thought and put her head in her hands. She stayed that way for a while before she got up from her seat and cautiously made her way down the aisle. Her legs and hands shook as if she were a stumbling drunk. Finally, she got to the lavatory door and pushed it open, finding her way into the tiny cubicle, barely missing the open toilet with her knee. She looked at her reflection in the mirror and saw a pale stranger. How could she not have thought about this before? Had she jumped too quickly to judgment when she chastised Alex?

So long ago, she had been the other woman in a broken marriage, and for all these years, Kim had separated herself from that part of her life. What had happened back when she was eighteen had happened quickly, and she had acted without much thought. She had been caught up in her youthful desires and Mark had been a more-than-willing participant. Kim had felt so confused and ashamed of her actions that she buried the memory so deep inside of her that she hadn't thought about it until now.

Kim filled the small basin and splashed water on her face, despite the desperate state of the sink. Her need for the cool water on her face was greater than her worry about the germs lurking before her. She didn't want to go back to her seat and continue to relive the love affair with Mark, so she continued to stare at her reflection in the mirror.

"Ma'am, are you okay?" the flight attendant asked as she knocked on the lavatory door.

"Yes," Kim responded. She grabbed a towel from the dispenser, wiped her face, then shoved it into the disposal, her hands still shaking. Kim made her way back to her seat the same wavering way she took to get to the bathroom. Her companions were awake now. As soon as she sat down, her elderly seatmate started chatting with her, picking up the conversation where they had left off. Kim welcomed the idle chitchat, which allowed her to escape from her thoughts.

The flight attendant's voice came over the speaker telling them to prepare for landing and Kim's thoughts turned back to the present. She had buried the memories again but this time Kim feared they were not buried as deep as before and would surface again soon.

— ••• —

Connie woke from a deep sleep, feeling the jerk of the plane's landing gear. Her eyes flew open and she looked around the dark cabin, getting a sense of where she was. The person sitting next to her was a large lady who was snoring loudly, apparently unaffected by the noise of the plane preparing to land. As she looked at her seatmate, Connie reflected back on her life. It seemed not that long ago that Connie, too, was overweight, unhealthy, and very much living a miserable life; not that she knew this woman was, but Connie assumed that she had an unhappy life, the same life that Connie once had had. Then Connie shook her head and squeezed her eyes shut. *I am so very happy that I am who I am now.* Connie was trying to convince herself of that fact.

CHAPTER FIVE

The warm, muggy air and smell of palm trees greeted Kim as she stepped off the airplane. A breeze blew through the open walkways and the smell permeated the building and swirled around, engulfing her. She took a deep breath and smiled. *What a wonderful smell.*

"Kimberly!"

Her mom waved from the bottom of the escalator, calling her by her given name. She usually used it when she was scolding Kim, but today there was a welcome cheerfulness in her voice. Kim instantly recognized her mom's smile, a smile that could light up a room. Despite how Nita acted toward Kim, others were drawn to her. People did not necessarily describe Nita as beautiful, but when she walked in a room, her friendliness and charm attracted people to her instantly, including the men.

Kim waved back and spotted her dad. *They look so healthy and vibrant*, Kim thought. Nita was dressed in her usual shorts and matching top, with huaraches Kim suspected were bought in Mexico. Jack had on his usual jeans and suspenders, which he wore no matter the weather. Mr. and Mrs. Whitman were not necessarily lean and athletic—far from it—but they certainly had a healthy glow about them. *Strange how they seemed to have gotten younger. An active retirement life must do that to you.*

Kim reached her parents and gave them both a hug—her dad first. He wrapped his arms around her like a big bear and patted her on the back, hesitating to let her go. Then she turned to her mom and bent down slightly to give her a hug; she squeezed a little tighter than she usually dared to. Nita hesitated before she responded with an embrace of her own. Kim instantly concluded she had done the right thing in coming; it felt good to be there, even if she was a little nervous about spending the entire month with her parents.

"The weather is just how you like it," Nita commented. "Too hot for me. I had to turn the air conditioning on this morning, but I know this is just right for you. You can go to the pool this afternoon before dinner and relax."

"I think I'll do that. Thanks, Mom. Now Dad, I hear you have been showing the old folks all about how to run the shuffleboard league," Kim said and smiled.

"Your mother talks too much," he said and waved his arm at her, gesturing the insignificance of it. "They just needed somebody to organize the league and keep everyone on track, that's all," he said. It was apparent that her dad didn't want to talk about himself; the look in his eyes had turned to sadness. She knew he was thinking about his sweet little girl being hurt by that no good son-in-law of his. Actually, Jack really liked Alex, at one time anyway.

"Honey, how are you?" he asked as he squeezed her arm.

"I'm okay, Dad, really." She narrowed her eyes at him, signaling she didn't want to talk about it.

Jack and Nita Whitman had retired after twenty-five years of running the pizza business in Augusta while they were fairly young. The two of them had made a great pair in business. Jack had cunning business sense and Nita was smart with the books. When they first came to the valley, they were the youngest members of their retirement group; the kids, they were called.

Not long after they arrived, they adopted their new friends' ways. Jack's only concern was whether they had enough string to wrap around the newspapers for recycling. And Nita, who had never had a hobby in her life, became interested in line dancing. Kim used to roll her eyes, teasing them about their new way of life, but then she realized this was just the life they wanted after all those long, hard years owning their own business. They wanted and deserved the worry-free chores and activities.

"Let's get your suitcases and get out of here," Jack said as he walked toward the baggage claim area. Kim was glad the airport was small and that they didn't have to go through all the hassle she usually did when she traveled. After a few minutes, the luggage started to barrel down the conveyer belt. When she spotted her suitcase, she motioned to her dad, then stopped. What was she thinking? She should pick up her bag, not him.

"Here, let me," she said as slid next to him. "I can get it."

"That's silly; I got it. Is that the one?" He pointed to a big black suitcase with a red silk tie around the handle.

"That's the one."

"I remember you always tied a ribbon around the handle." He smiled and grunted as he picked up the bag. "Did you pack everything you own?" He struggled a bit to get the bag over the edge of the conveyer belt and to the floor while Kim stood back and watched, feeling foolish but allowing him to take care of her.

"Okay. Do you see the next one?" he asked.

"I only have one."

"I thought you were staying a month."

"I am, but for some reason I felt that I needed to stuff everything into one suitcase." She smiled at him. "I can do laundry, you know."

The three of them headed toward the exit. As they got close, the sliding glass doors opened up to the bright sunshine and warm breezes. Instantly, Kim's hair whipped around and flew in her face, and her thoughts of dreary North Carolina and divorce quickly faded away.

The streets from the airport to Sunbeams RV Park were lined with strip malls, fast food restaurants, and convenience stores, the most prevalent being the restaurants. The whole town catered to the "winter Texans," since these seasonal visitors supported much of the economy. From what Kim heard, retired people didn't like to cook much, so eating out was a favorite pastime. They planned their days around where they were going to eat their evening meals. Each had their favorite places, and Kim was sure she would visit many of them over the next month.

"We're here," Jack announced from the driver's seat of his blue minivan as he turned into the park. He was very proud of his car and had called Kim the day he picked it up from the dealer. "It's a doozy," he'd told her. Kim looked out the window from the passenger's side and saw a big yellow neon sign that flashed SUNBEAMS RV PARK, A RETIRE-

MENT COMMUNITY. They took the long driveway lined with palm trees into the park. After they went through a white wrought-iron gate, they took the main road in, passing several street signs, each marking a block-long lane.

The streets, with names like Frontier Boulevard, Amarillo Lane, or Ranchers Drive, were all Texas related. They passed several streets before Jack turned the van right onto Longhorn Lane and went halfway down the block, eventually turning into the carport of the Whitman's park model. There were rows and rows of these modular homes throughout the retirement complex and they all looked alike. Kim was glad she spotted the small wooden sign painted with THE WHITMANS stuck in the ground in front of the house. She knew she was going to need it to help her identify the right house.

Nita opened the sliding glass door and Kim followed her as Jack got her suitcase out of the van. The room they stepped into held a small couch and a desk where Nita's computer sat. "This is the addition we added," Nita announced. "It gives us much more room." As she looked around, Kim couldn't imagine the house any smaller than it was now. To the left sat two arm chairs, side by side, with an end table separating them. In front of each chair was a footstool. On the end table sat a lamp and a small bowl holding a small colorful fish.

Kim stepped closer to look at it. "It's a beta fish," Jack told her when he came in. "I got it at Walmart." In front of Jack's chair sat a television and just beyond that was the kitchen counter that separated the two rooms. Past the kitchen was the bathroom on the right and straight ahead was Jack and Nita's bedroom.

The house was small, but it suited the Whitmans' needs during the winter months they spent in Texas. Kim set her suitcase in a corner of the living room, which was going to be her bedroom for the next month. "The couch pulls out to a bed," Nita told her. "We can move the table a little to give you more room." She walked to the back of the house, and when she did, Jack sat down at the table and patted the chair next to him.

"Now we are going to talk," he said.

"Talk about what?" Kim asked coyly.

"I want to know how you are doing and what your plans are. I know you always want to be the strong one and keep everything inside. Heck, I'm the one who taught you that, but being like me is not always the right way."

"I think it is," she said and smiled back.

"Kimmy, what went wrong?" he asked, using his pet name for her.

Kim had never let her parents in on all the details of her marriage or the divorce, and she really didn't want to talk about it now. But they deserved to know the truth, even if it was going to upset them. She didn't want them to worry about how bad their daughter had been hurt. And part of her didn't want them to hate Alex, even though she knew that was silly.

"Well, Dad, I found Alex with another woman." She paused, waiting for Jack's reaction. He sat next to her in silence, so she continued. "Well, not actually found them. I heard about a possible affair from an acquaintance."

"Then how did you confirm it?"

She stopped before she answered, hearing her mom in the back bedroom putting laundry away. It was uncomfortable speaking of this in front of her mom, so she didn't continue until she knew she was out of earshot. She wasn't necessarily hiding the details. She knew her dad would fill Nita in. She was just afraid of Nita blaming her somehow, thinking she had failed. When Kim knew her mom wasn't going to come in the room, she continued talking without looking directly at her dad. Instead, she looked down at her hands and twirled a piece of paper that was lying on the table.

"An acquaintance at work told me she had seen them in a restaurant together. I really didn't think much of it. I have lunch with men all the time—you know, business lunches." She briefly looked up to assure Jack of that and then put her attention back to the piece of paper. "Then there were different signs that showed he might be seeing someone else. Dad, we really were not getting along even before I found out. I didn't want to worry you and mom, so I never mentioned it."

"We could tell something was up. You never talked about him, and when your mother asked questions about how the two of you were doing, you were very vague."

"Hmm, trying to fool you guys is impossible, isn't it?" she said with a laugh. Kim heard Nita go out on the porch as the door closed behind her. "He seemed to stay out late a lot with no really good answer as to where he was. I started doing all the suspicious wife things, like smelling his clothes and checking his pockets. I never did find anything.

"One night, one of his friends from work called looking for Alex. He was supposed to be at a business meeting with this friend, and since this friend knew nothing about the meeting, I knew something was up. So I confronted him when he got home." Kim looked up again at her dad and could see the sadness in his eyes.

Then her heart started to pound and moisture beaded up on the back of her neck. As she revealed the horrible thing her husband had done, the memories that she revisited on the plane come forward again. *I am not any better than he is. How dare I criticize Alex?* She suddenly felt ashamed, so much so that she couldn't lift her head to look into her dad's face. She could barely speak.

"I am so sorry," Jack said, mistaking the waver in her voice for sadness rather than shame.

"I . . . I guess I am glad I found out. We could have gone on for years like that," Kim stammered, feeling very hot and uncomfortable, still staring at her hands. "I can start a new life, I guess . . . it must have been meant to be," she stammered, mustering up the words. She believed what she was saying, but the words did not come out with much conviction.

"Was this a one-time thing? Did he have a wandering eye and then act on it?" Jack asked.

Kim looked up at her dad. "Well, no, actually," she said, her voice firm. "When I confronted him about the woman, he told me it was an affair that had been going on for a while. He just didn't know how to tell me and didn't want to hurt me." She shook her head. "I asked him how he thought I was never going to find out and whether when I did, I'd be hurt even more."

"And what did he say?"

"He couldn't answer me." She shrugged her shoulders.

"Let's go out to the garden," Jack suddenly said and got up from his chair. "I want to show you my bougainvillea plant; it's just started to bloom." Kim could tell he had enough information from her and was done talking about it. She felt thankful for this; she wasn't sure how she was going to continue.

Kim was projected back to her childhood when she saw her dad's beautiful flowering plant. He loved these flowers and had admired them at his mother's winter home so many years before. The plant is considered wild in Texas. While up north they are scarce and priced at a premium, Jack still made sure they were in his garden in Augusta every summer.

"Hi there!" a voice said from the yard directly behind Kim and Jack. Jack turned around and when he saw who it was, a big smile spread across his face. "Annie!" he yelled and gave her a big hug when she got close. "Annie, this is my daughter, Kimmy." He put his arm around Kim. "Kim, this is my girlfriend, Annie."

Kim laughed. "Right, Dad. He is such a flirt, isn't he? Nice to meet you," she said, nodding to the tall, slender woman standing in front of her. She was a beautiful woman with short blond hair and appeared to be in her fifties. Kim was amazed at how young she was, a far cry from all the senior citizens who lived in the park; she was instantly curious.

Jack continued, "Annie's the youngster in the group."

Annie laughed and said, "And I keep you all in line!" She extended her hand toward Kim. "Nice to meet you. How long are you staying?"

"For a month, actually," Kim responded.

"Wow, how nice," Annie said and smiled.

"Where do you live?" Kim asked.

"Right over there." Annie turned around and pointed down the street. "I'm not as lucky as these old coots," she said with a laugh. "I still have to work. I don't have the luxury of the retirement life yet, but I like it here. Living alone is lonely enough and if I had a regular home, I would really be alone. This way, I have company and friends around all the time. And I really do keep them out of trouble," she said, smiling at Jack.

"Where do you work?" Kim asked.

"At a travel agency in town," Annie told her. "My main job is to arrange excursions, mainly with these senior citizens," she said and gestured toward Jack. "It pays the bills and I get to travel, so I enjoy it." She paused. "Except when these old coots get ornery and demanding, then I feel like a babysitter. Oh, but not you, Jack," she said and put her arm around him. "You would never put up a fuss."

She stepped closer to Kim, as if she was going to tell her a secret. "Your dad has to be one of the nicest men I have ever met. Too bad he's already taken." She laughed. "Well, I had better get going, off to work. I just wanted to come by and say hi," she said, looking first at Kim and then turning back to Jack. "Happy hour tonight?"

"You bet," he responded. "Four o'clock." He waved at her as she headed back down the street.

"Hey, Dad, I think I'm going to sit by the pool for a while, soak up some of this sunshine before dinner. Is that okay?" Kim walked into the house, grabbed a book and a towel, poured herself a glass of wine, and headed over to the recreation hall where the pool was located.

She needed some breathing room. *I'll try to relax with a glass of wine and divert my thoughts.*

A few minutes later, Kim settled into a lawn chair by the side of the pool. She glanced up at the clock; it read one o'clock. The thermometer below it showed seventy-five degrees. She looked around and noticed that she was by far the youngest person in the vicinity. She felt unusually out of place and could feel the glances of the park residents as they walked past her. She occasionally looked up and greeted them with a smile and a hello.

Usually the holidays brought more winter visitors from up north, but Kim supposed it was still too early. She was sure she would have more company the closer it got to Christmas. She flipped opened the book she bought for the trip and turned to the first chapter. She sat staring at the page, not reading a single word. The thought of Mark popped into her mind again. And this time, the passion came flooding back.

For an instant, she felt as if the affair had happened only yesterday. She could feel herself getting warm, the youthful intrigue of an eighteen-year-old rushing back, and before she knew it, she was in the arms of her long-ago lover, Mark. Each sip of her wine drew her deeper and deeper into the past.

CHAPTER SIX

Kim went right back to where her thoughts had taken her on the plane ride down to visit her family. It was twenty-five years earlier, and she was in a car, seated behind Mark, headed for Harlingen, Texas. Maite was less than thrilled with her presence, giving her occasional glares from the front seat. The threesome entered the city, making their way to what was going to be Kim's new home. The trip had taken them two and a half days, driving non-stop, except for bathroom breaks and to eat. They drove through the night, each taking their turn at the wheel, while the others slept.

"We live in an association type of a neighborhood," Mark told Kim. "All the houses look very similar." Mark pulled into the complex and Kim quickly found he was talking about a trailer park, where all the homes were lined up side by side, with very little room between them. It appeared as if someone could reach out the window of one trailer and touch the person in the next. *Oh well,* Kim thought, *it's an adventure.*

Kim's new home was a modest, three-bedroom, double-wide modular home. The kitchen and living room were in the middle, with the bedrooms and baths on either side. Her living space was located on one end, while Mark and Maite's was on the other.

As she settled into her new surroundings, she was very pleased with her decision to venture to the south and leave her small northern community. Yes, she was a very long way from home and her parents, but she felt her wings expanding and was experiencing a newfound freedom. The hot, sticky, and windy weather in south Texas was much different from what she had left behind, but she didn't mind. The sultry air made her feel alive and sexy.

Almost immediately, Kim started to search for a job. Mark wanted to help her, but she assured him she could do it herself. After several weeks of job hunting with no luck, she reluctantly agreed to let Mark help.

"What would be the most logical place for you to work?" he asked.

Kim wasn't sure what he was referring to. She thought a moment and then replied, "Well, I have worked most of my life in a restaurant," then she paused, "but I also could put cleaning cabins on my resume." Kim narrowed her eyes and shook her head and continued. "No, I'm going to stay away from cleaning cabins or anything remotely close."

"Exactly," he replied. "I mean the restaurant experience. I have a friend who owns a restaurant, actually a pizza bistro. You can get a job there."

"Shouldn't you talk to him first?"

"You have the job," he assured her.

And Mark was right. Kim quickly became accustomed to her new position as a waitress and soon settled into a routine of work life, home life, and soon after, a social life.

Most of the people she worked with were her age, so she fit right in and made friends with just about everyone. A group of fellow employees socialized regularly at a nearby bar after their shifts ended. Even though Kim and some of her new friends were not of drinking age yet, the bartenders didn't ask for identification or question anyone.

Mark and Maite still owned the candle business that he and Alison had started. He had a small manufacturing building in town and employed five immigrant workers. Adjacent to the manufacturing area was a small outlet store, selling directly to consumers. That was where Maite spent most of her time, while Mark traveled all over south Texas, selling his products to small and midsize gift shops.

Kim lived with Mark and Maite in modest surroundings; however, Kim found that Mark's lifestyle was far from modest. His wallet always had a wad of bills and he would often pay for things with hundred dollar bills. She could not imagine that the candle-making business was that lucrative.

When Kim was searching for a job, Mark had offered her a position working for him but she declined, knowing the position was with M&A Chandler Company. If she took the job, most of her time would be spent with Maite and it was apparent Maite didn't like Kim very much. Maite hardly ever spoke to Kim, and when she did, it was when all three of them were together. And anyway, her questions for Kim were really directed to Mark. Kim got used to this very early on and avoided her when she could, but was respectful when around her. After all, Kim was a guest in Maite's home and her life.

One day when Kim stopped at the warehouse, she

caught Mark alone and out of earshot from Maite, so she took the opportunity to ask him what had happened to Alison. "She got tired of the south, I guess," was his answer. He explained that she longed for her family up north and just decided to up and leave one day. He said that she told him she didn't love him anymore.

"How can someone love someone one day and not the next? You can turn love on and off just like that?" she questioned. Mark rolled his eyes at her and smiled. He went on writing in the notebook he was holding, ignoring her with silence as he jotted down numbers. Kim got the message and walked away, but his flippant attitude about his former wife left her uneasy.

At first, Mark never brought up the desires he had expressed in his letter to Kim on his visit in Maine, so she thought he had changed his mind and was not interested in her anymore. It was just fine with her. But then about a month after they arrived in Texas, Mark once again began to show his desire for her. At first she learned to avoid his advances, not knowing how to handle the situation. But her desires for him were soon intensifying, and she had a hard time not giving into his advances, even the little playful innuendos. Kim knew if she said yes, they would immediately fall into bed.

One night the three of them were sitting in the living room, watching television. Maite was on a chair, Mark and Kim on the floor, their backs against the couch. At one point, Mark slid his hand along the carpet, resting it on top of Kim's hand. She knew Maite could not see from where she was sitting, so she did not pull away; she just sat there, staring at the television. But internally, her heart raced and her breath became rapid.

"I have to go down to Brownsville this weekend, Kim. Do you want to go with me? Maite has to work at the store," Mark asked during the next commercial break.

Kim looked away from the TV and fixed her gaze on Maite, who showed no expression. Kim then looked at Mark, who was smiling at her as he squeezed her hand.

"I have to check my schedule for Saturday," she said. Mark squeezed her hand one more time before he got up to go into the kitchen to get another beer.

"Do you want anything, Kim?" he asked.

"No," she replied.

"Maite?"

"No thanks," she said. "I'm going to bed." Maite got up from her chair and headed down the hall to their bedroom. Mark looked after her and when he heard the door slam, he came back into the living room and sat down next to Kim again. This time his hand did not stop; it lingered at her wrist for a while. Then his finger traced a line up her arm to her shoulder, and slid under the spaghetti strap of her tank top. He continued to slide his hand gently beneath her shirt before she jerked away. She was having feelings that she had never experienced before. They were wonderfully different, but also shamefully so.

—▶ •••◀—

Kim could hear a ring in the distance, realized it was her phone, and was suddenly brought back to reality.

"Kim." Connie's voice was on the other end. "How are you?" she asked.

"Oh, hi," Kim stammered. "I'm good, soaking up some sunshine, enjoying a glass of wine; life is good."

"You sound a bit out of breath, honey."

"I was just deep in thought. I seem to be scrounging up all kinds of old memories, some real doozies."

"Do tell."

Kim hesitated. "I don't know if I can. I'm still sorting things out for myself. I haven't thought about this old boyfriend of mine in years, and suddenly on the plane, the memories of my affair with him came rushing back."

"Affair?"

"It was a long time ago, a schoolgirl crush, really." Kim suddenly felt she had revealed more than she wanted to. "I'll tell you about it someday. No big thing. Now how are you doing? How's San Diego? Are you staying out of trouble?" Kim interrogated her friend.

"I just got here! How could I possibly get into any kind of trouble already?"

"Hmm," Kim answered back.

"I landed a few hours ago and just got to the beach house. It is absolutely gorgeous, Kim. I wish you were here with me. We could have so much fun."

"I know it would have been fun to spend our vacation together, but I'm really glad I decided to spend some time with my parents. It feels good to be here."

They chatted for a few minutes more about how nice it was to feel warmth and how the sunshine did wonders as a mood enhancer. As Kim was about to hang up, she made Connie agree they should talk every couple of days so they could each catch up on the other's vacation. "And I have to make sure you stay out of trouble," Kim warned.

"Wow!" Connie said, slightly offended by the tone in Kim's voice.

"I'm just kidding," Kim said, her voice softening.

— •●• —

Connie pressed the END button on her phone when they finished their conversation. She stood looking at it for a few minutes, thinking how much she wished Kim was with her. She wanted everyone to believe she was brave and independent about taking off on her own, but in reality, she was scared to death to be alone. Back in Raleigh, she kept herself busy with her job and social life, making sure she always had something planned to keep her occupied most evenings.

Connie walked over to the window and peered out the glass door toward the ocean. She opened the door and stepped on the deck; the ocean breeze swirled around her. She closed her eyes, lifted up her head, and took a long, deep breath in, filling her nostrils with the salty air. She continued standing there with her eyes closed, trying to ward off an impending feeling of panic and loneliness. *What if this was a bad idea? I can't be alone for the next month.* She opened her eyes and stared straight ahead; her gaze fixed on the ocean and she promised herself that she would give this an honest try. She would make sure to venture out each night to one of the many restaurants and bars located along the boardwalk.

Connie walked back into the house and started to unpack, preparing to settle in for the next month, still trying to convince herself that she was going to be fine and that she was going to have fun.

———•●•——

That night, Kim snuggled into her makeshift bed on the couch. Her thoughts darted back and forth in her mind, flitting from what had happened so long ago to how her life had fallen apart so recently. These two parts of her life should not have intertwined, but they did. Kim could not help thinking of her affair with Mark some twenty-five years ago, and how that affair so suddenly made what had happened between her and Alex that much worse.

Over the last several years, Kim learned to squelch feelings that she did not want to think about. She was sure it was not a healthy tactic, but it was something she had become accustomed to, so she used it. She needed to stop thinking, so she used her sure bet—yoga breathing techniques—to fall asleep. Her breath came in long, deep inhales and then long exhales, soothing her into unconsciousness.

CHAPTER SEVEN

The sunshine was beaming through the window when Kim woke up, cascading its light over her face. The amazingly warm sunlight gave her a new outlook on the day and let her forget about the tossing and turning of the night before. What seemed so bad last night faded away. She stretched her arms over her head and let out a long, slow sigh.

There was something to be said about warm weather and sunshine to brighten up a mood. She understood why some people suffered from the "winter blues." Connie told her once it is called the SAD syndrome, something about a lack of vitamin D, she explained to Kim.

Kim couldn't hear her mom or dad yet, so she assumed they were either sleeping or had already left for whatever was happening at the recreation hall. She immediately assumed her daily routine, donning her running clothes and heading out the door. Kim took a right and started past the many rows of cookie-cutter houses, each with just a bit of its own personality.

Most had a hint of Mexico displayed somewhere: hanging ceramic chili peppers, clay sun dials, and small chimeras, all precious treasures bought in the neighboring Mexican border towns. This time of the year, the permanent fixtures were intertwined with Christmas lights, giving most of the small homes the appearance of a Mexican brothel. How she thought she knew what a Mexican brothel looked like, she didn't know, but it was the first thing that came to her mind.

As Kim ran though the rows and rows of park models, turning down street after street, she thought of how she would want to spend her retirement. Not like this, she knew that for sure. This was great for her parents, but it was not the lifestyle she would look for. She wanted a little more pizzazz and excitement. The country club lifestyle would be more to her liking, assuming, of course, she had the funds at that time to support a lavish retirement.

After Kim ran what she thought was three miles, she headed back toward her parents' home, thinking she was taking the right way back. But it wasn't. She took two more wrong turns before she spotted Longhorn Lane, and then saw the painted sign in front of the house. The sweat poured into her eyes as she climbed the stairs to the deck. The aroma of coffee greeted her as she slid the glass door open. Nita was sitting in her favorite chair, sipping a cup of coffee.

"Good morning," she said, greeting her mom.

"Good morning," Nita replied. "Your dad is already up and down at the hall, having coffee. He wants you to go down there and have breakfast with him. It's Pancake Day."

That was just what Kim needed to undo the efforts she just accomplished with her run, but she would indulge her dad. "Sounds good; I'll get dressed and go find him. Is the coffee ready?"

"Dad told me all about what happened to you and Alex. I am so sorry, Kim. We didn't know all the trouble you were having." Nita turned toward her daughter. Kim searched for some sort of judgment or concern in her eyes. She saw neither.

"I know, Mom. I didn't want to worry you guys." Kim walked over and sat in the chair next to her mom. She continued looking straight ahead at the television. "I'm going to put all that behind me and start a new life. I'm glad I'm here and I think this month is going to do me good. I've set my mind on relaxing, enjoying the weather, and spending time with you and Dad."

Nita gave her daughter a quick smile then turned back toward the television. "The coffee is ready. Get yourself a cup." She motioned toward the kitchen without looking at Kim.

After searching the cupboard, Kim found a mug, poured coffee into it, then went outside to sit on the porch before she took a shower and headed over to the hall to find her dad. She looked up and down the street and saw a number of men working in the yards. Some of them were picking up garbage, while others were trimming the bushes. Kim watched as they worked, noticing that they were all of Hispanic descent. *Perhaps migrant workers*, she thought.

"That's Julio," Nita said, coming out of the house and pointing to the worker closest to them. "I want you to meet him. He's such a nice man, always helping us with work we need around the yard. He and his company are employed by the park and do all the maintenance, from landscaping to building repairs. I think they also take care of other parks throughout the valley. It's a nice business the owner has set up," she explained. "Julio, I want you to meet my daughter, Kim." Nita motioned him over. "Kim, this is Julio. Kim is my daughter, she is visiting us for a month," she said with a smile.

"Nice to meet you," Julio said as he tipped his hat toward Kim. His accent was thick.

"Nice to meet you as well," Kim replied.

Julio turned to Nita. "Going to be a hot one today, Mrs. Whitman."

"Yes, I know; a little too hot for me, but Kim loves this weather."

"Si," Julio said and smiled at Kim. "I had better get back to work. Nice to meet you, Kim. I am sure we will see you again, no?" He smiled and went back to cutting the shrub next door.

"Is he the owner?" Kim asked Nita when Julio was out of earshot.

"No, but I think he is the head maintenance man. Julio is one of the few who speaks English, so he does all the communicating. The owner comes around once in a while to check on things and make sure the park owners are happy with their work. He is a nice young man, very handsome and very kind. The ladies love him in the office, always giggling when he comes around. It's so funny to see old ladies act that way," she said and laughed.

"How about you, Mom? Do you get all goofy when you see him?"

"Not me. Your Dad is enough for me to handle," she

said as she flashed a quick smile at Kim and turned toward the door. "Well, I had better get going. I have to get to the office by nine o'clock."

Even in her retirement, Nita couldn't fully give up work. They didn't need the money, but Nita needed to keep busy. Even though she had her hobbies, they were not quite enough to use up her endless energy. So when a position came open in the office, she applied for it. Her duties included doing the cash receipts and bookkeeping, which was the same type of work she did when she and Jack owned the restaurant.

"Okay, I'll be right over after I take a shower."

Kim knew Jack was anxious to show off his daughter to all his friends, that all of the old folks loved when their children came to visit. It gave them a chance to brag and show them off like they were trophies. Kim was not sure why, exactly, but figured that if she had kids, she'd understand.

It didn't take Kim long to shower and find her dad among the other retirees gathering for breakfast. "Hi, Dad," Kim said and slipped into the chair next to Jack. The recreation hall was a big, open room with parquet floors and long banquet tables lined up in rows. All the tables had white plastic tablecloths and were set up for the morning breakfast crowd. People mingled and chatted in the area closest to the kitchen, ordering coffee and pancakes at the big window that separated the kitchen area from the hall.

"Well, it's about time," Jack said and smiled at his daughter. "Want some pancakes?"

"Sure, but coffee first would be great."

Jack turned to the two men sitting across from him. They were both grinning ear to ear, smiling at Kim.

"This is my daughter, Kim. Kim, this is Bob Reardon and Sam Corley. They're a couple of my golfing and bowling buddies."

"Hi," Bob said and smiled.

"Hello," Sam said and also smiled, but a little too much for Kim's comfort.

"I'll go get you some coffee," Jack said. He got up and walked over to the line at the counter, smiling and talking with people all the way there.

"So what brings you down to God's country?" Sam asked Kim. She hoped her parents hadn't revealed too much information about her life to their friends.

"I'm lucky; I get a month off from my job this time of the year," she explained. "I work for a manufacturing company in North Carolina. The tradition for many years has been to shut down the whole company around the holidays. They found there isn't a whole lot of business this time of year, and it's a nice perk for their employees. Ones with little children absolutely love it."

"And you, do you have a family?" Bob asked.

"No, just me," she said, quickly turning away to search for her dad. "Boy, could I use some coffee. I hope he doesn't get lost," she said and nervously let out a laugh.

"He could be gone all day. He has to talk to everyone. Some days I think he is running for mayor," Bob said and smirked.

Sam joined in. "He and your mom are sure well liked around here. They're very nice people. You're lucky."

Kim was still looking around the room searching for

her dad. "I know. Thanks." She smiled when she saw him heading their way with a cup of coffee, a spoon, and a handful of cream containers. *How sweet,* she thought, surprised that he remembered that she couldn't drink coffee without cream. She definitely was daddy's little girl. She always told people she was the youngest child and only girl, but quickly added that she was not spoiled—she really did not believe that. She especially knew her dad spoiled her.

"Here's your coffee. When you're ready, you can go and get as many pancakes as you'd like. The syrup is over there," he said and pointed to a small table draped in white plastic. "Don't pay, though," he said. "I've already taken care of you."

Throughout the course of Kim's breakfast, she met no less than twenty people. She knew some of them from previous visits, but most she had never met before. Kim was sure that some people she had met in the past were no longer with them. That's the nature of the life at the retirement community: You're not sure what friends will come back the following season and which ones you will say your final goodbyes to before heading north.

Jack and Nita were busy, so Kim spent most of the day again at the pool. She didn't mind being by herself, enjoying the sun; however, she promised herself she would not let her mind drift back to the past. She was afraid that if she did, she would find that her life was even more screwed up than she thought it was. So instead she read the stack of magazines she bought at the airport for the plane but never got a chance to read. The magazines were ones that Kim regularly read to keep her informed on the latest trends—*Cosmo*, *Vogue*, and *Mademoiselle*. She thumbed through, checking out the hottest styles, reading up on beauty tips, and getting caught up on the latest celebrity gossip.

When lunchtime came around, she decided to head back to the house to make a salad and find a glass of wine. Anyway, the sun was getting hot so she thought she'd better get out of it for a while. She didn't need any premature wrinkles, especially since she had managed to avoid them so far.

Kim took the back way to her parents' home, cutting through people's yards even though she felt uncomfortable doing so. She laughed the first time she followed Nita this way, telling her that they were doing exactly the same thing she and her brothers were forbidden to do when they were kids. Jack scolded them for trampling on his lawn, but mostly for running across the neighbors' yards.

Kim went around the side of the house, and just as she was about to step up on the deck, she looked up and stopped. There, standing in the middle of the street, was one of the most beautiful men she had ever seen. And although she didn't usually use the word "beautiful" to describe men, this man, at this moment, was certainly beautiful to her. He stood sideways, looking up at a palm tree that was dangerously close to a power line.

His jet black, wavy hair was cut short and styled away from his face. His tall, slender body was clothed in a white T-shirt and blue jeans. He wore brown cowboy boots and was obviously either a construction worker or a regular at the gym. When he noticed Kim was staring at him, he smiled, revealing brilliant white teeth against his dark skin.

Wow, Kim thought and ran up the stairs into the house. *What a stupid, girlish way to act.* She laughed to herself. Then she did another stupid, juvenile thing: She went into the living room and opened the corner of the curtain to get another look at him. "Wow," she said out loud. "That's one fine man."

Just as she went into the kitchen to start making lunch, she heard a knock on the door. It didn't come from the back door, the one the Whitmans usually used. It came from the front door, but because Kim's suitcase and belongings were blocking it, she went out the other door and came around to the front of the house.

"Hi," Kim said as she looked into the most stunning pair of eyes she had ever seen. They were mostly choco-late brown, but when the sunlight hit just right, she could see hints of sparkling sea green.

"I'm looking for Mr. and Mrs. Whitman," the gor-geous man asked as he smiled back at her.

"Hi, I'm Kim, their daughter. I'm visiting from North Carolina. I needed a little R & R, if you know what I mean. Warm weather and all that, you know?" She was rambling and he was smiling at her.

"I noticed that the palm tree over there is very close to the power line. If even a small wind comes up, the branches might hit the line. That could affect the service for the peo-ple on the block." His low, husky accent mesmerized her. She only heard about half the words he was saying.

"I want to trim off some of the branches, but I wanted to alert people." He pointed at Jack and Nita's house and at the neighbor's house. "As I trim, some of the branches may fall on the roofs and I don't want the owners to become alarmed."

"Um, do you work with the maintenance people? I think I met Julio this morning."

"Sorry. I am very rude. My name is Camilo," he said as he extended his hand. She took it, savoring his strong grasp.

"Hi, Camilo," she said, butchering the pronunciation of his name. "My name is Kim Thompson. This is my parents' home."

"Yes, you told me that." He smiled and she blushed. "My name is pronounced Kah-mee-loh." He said it slowly.

"Oh, I'm so sorry," she said, sure that she was crimson at this point.

"No need to be sorry, señorita," he smiled. "Try again, Kah-mee-loh."

"Kah-mee-loh," she repeated after him. The sounds came out slowly.

"Perfect," he said and winked at her. "It means 'free-born child' in Spanish. And yes, I am with the maintenance people," he continued. "Julio is one of my men on the crew doing work around the park. You meet him this morning?" She noted the hint of broken English.

"Yes, my mom introduced me to him. He is a very polite man."

"Good. I need them to be friendly to the winter Texans. That way, I can assure them they will have jobs. If they are respectful, the office managers will call us back to work. Everyone is happy." He smiled again.

"I'll be sure to let my parents know. Do you know

when you or your workers will do the trimming?" she asked.

"I will tell Julio to talk to your mom or dad before he climbs up. He is like an acrobat, hanging on by a single rope. He is amusing to watch. I hope you will be here to see him?" It was half a question, half a statement.

"I'll be here for about a month, so if he does it before that, I'll be able to watch the show."

"Good," he said and smiled down at her. "I better get going. Nice to meet you, Kim. It was my pleasure. Ciao."

"Isn't that Italian?"

"It also means goodbye in Spanish: both beautiful languages. Adios then. Is that better?" He winked as he walked past her to the white Chevy truck that was parked on the street a few yards behind her. She turned around when he got into the truck and stood there, watching as he drove away.

"Mom, I met Camilo today," Kim announced when Nita came in from work a few minutes later. "You just missed him."

"Who?" Nita asked. She walked back to the bedroom to put her shoes and keys away. "Who?" she said again when she came into the kitchen and walked to the refrigerator to get a glass of water.

"Camilo; he's the guy you were telling me about who owns the company Julio works for."

"Oh, yes. Camilo. He is cute, isn't he? And he's such a nice young man, very respectful to us old folks."

"Cute!" she exclaimed. "Mom, he is much more than cute. He's gorgeous."

"Maybe we can get you two together," she said as she opened the refrigerator door to grab the pitcher of water.

"No thanks, Mom. I'm done with men for a while. Besides, he has to be twenty years younger than I am."

CHAPTER EIGHT

The next few days went by quickly, even though there was not much for Kim to do. Her parents were busy with their activities, so she spent her days running, reading by the pool, and socializing with the retirees. She was able to squelch old thoughts and replace them with new ones, more specifically thoughts of a young Hispanic man named Camilo. Nothing else entered her mind and it was wonderful.

As late afternoon approached on one such afternoon, Kim walked onto the porch and sat down on the swing. Pushing herself back and forth with her feet, she laid her head back, closed her eyes, and smiled at the thought of Camilo.

"Hi, Kim," Nita said as she came around the corner.

Kim jerked her head up. "Mom, you scared me."

"Sorry, dear; I thought you heard me. How was your day? Did you get in your run?"

"Yes; I went over to the other side of the park. I didn't realize there was another recreation hall and pool over there. Is that something new?"

"It's been there for a while. We go over there to line dance sometimes."

"Hello," Jack yelled from down the street. He was driving a golf cart filled with brown paper-wrapped packages.

"Hey, what kind of job do you have now? Postman?" Kim yelled back as she stood and walked down to the curb.

"I'm delivering Christmas presents. We get a lot of packages this time of year from families sending presents to their grandmas and grandpas."

"I'm surprised you get it all done in one day, the way you have to stop and talk with everyone."

"I get my job done, thank you very much." Jack pulled the golf cart alongside the curb.

"By the way you two, we're going to go over to Violet Carson's house for dinner tomorrow night," Nita told the two of them.

"Violet. Wow, I haven't thought about her in a while," Kim said and then winced, hoping her parents couldn't read into her lie. "I didn't even know she was still alive."

"She still lives in the valley with her daughter, Beth. They want us to come over for dinner. You know, Beth and your dad have always tried to celebrate their birthdays together since we've been down here. Tomorrow was the only night they were free, so we'll celebrate early, even though the birthdays aren't until next month. I told them you were in town, so they're very excited to see you."

Beth and Violet stayed in Texas after Art died. Kim wasn't sure where the eldest child was living, somewhere in the Midwest—Wisconsin, Kim thought. She was looking forward to seeing the two women; it would be fun to catch up on old times.

Kim settled back on the swing as Jack drove off to continue his deliveries and Nita turned back into the house. Alone once again on the porch, she picked up her cell phone from the small side table and dialed a number.

"Hi there," Kim said. She had decided to call Connie to fill her in about Camilo. She wanted to bring her into her fantasy. Since she couldn't stop thinking about him, she needed to share, and besides, she knew Connie would be proud of her for becoming interested in men again. Kim knew that her attraction was just lustful playfulness, but she didn't care. After all, it allowed her morning workouts to pass like a breeze, and when she was done, she didn't know if she was sweating from the workout or from shameful, erotic feelings.

"Hi." Connie breathed the word heavily.

"Okay, what are you doing? Why the heavy breathing?"

"Well, if you need to know, I just came back from the beach with my yoga mat in tow. Yes, girl, I am finding my inner Zen and I'm loving it."

"I'm so proud of you. The gym was not your friend, even though you look amazing, but maybe Zen is."

"I love it out here. It's so hip and crazy and spiritual. I think I've found my advent."

"Your what?"

"My advent, my beginning. It's the dawn of the new horizon, and the dawn of the new Don."

"What are you talking about?"

"Don, my new yoga instructor. He is my dawn, my day, my twilight, and beyond."

"Alrighty then, and what did you do with my friend Connie?" Kim asked and laughed. "Hey, can I tell you about my sexual encounters?"

"What? You! Hey, do tell."

"I guess it's not quite an encounter and not quite sexual, but boy did I meet the most gorgeous man the other day. I can't stop thinking about him."

"Is he seventy years old? Because aren't those the only men you hang around with down there?"

"This guy is the owner of the maintenance company that the retirement park employs. He is gorgeous. You know the tall, dark, and handsome fantasy? Well, he is ten times better than that. He is Latino at its finest. He's got jet black hair; deep, intriguing brown eyes; and a sexy white smile that shines against a deep, dark complexion."

"And his name?"

"Camilo."

"Oh, my God; he sounds like a god. Have you had sex with him yet?"

"No!" Kim let out a laugh. "I just met him and that is all. It's fun to fantasize, but that's all it's going to be and that's okay."

—•••—

Connie met Don while she was taking a morning stroll along the boardwalk. Even though she was always very conscious of her weight, exercise was not in her normal routine; instead, she kept the pounds off by watching what she ate. Her walks were usually leisurely and involved very little effort—something she knew she was going to have to change as she got older. She didn't want to go back to being overweight. The attention she got from men made her feel good—making up for all the years she was teased in high school. *If they could only see me now,* she would often think.

When she walked past the small yoga studio, she was intrigued with the musky aroma of incense mixing with the warm ocean breezes. When she stopped to take in the smell, she noticed a very tanned and lean man sitting behind a small counter just inside the door of the tiny space. He wore his hair long and in a ponytail—the effects of the sun had left it streaked and golden. Almost immediately she was drawn to this man and had a yoga appointment the next day. She decided this would be the start of her exercise routine, and hopefully something more.

CHAPTER NINE

The next morning began just as the previous days had for Kim. The radiant sunshine quickly warmed up the morning air, while a warm wind blew through the trees, shaking the palm branches, blowing some of them onto the street. Kim clicked on the television to the morning news to catch the weather forecast, which seemed to be more important to her these days than what was happening in the world.

"Seventy-eight and sunny with a wind advisory," the weatherman told his audience.

"Julio is going to have to come and clean up the palms again," Kim said and got up to look out the window. Nita was in an unusually quiet mood. She didn't answer her as she poured a cup of coffee in the tiny kitchen. Jack was already up and gone to the hall. She walked over to her usual spot and sat down, still not saying a word to Kim.

"Mom, is everything okay?" Kim asked after a few minutes of silence.

"I'm fine," Nita answered back, still looking at the television. Then she softened her tone. "Maybe his boss will have to check up on him to make sure he gets it right." Nita grinned, then turned toward Kim.

"Whatever," Kim responded as she flipped through the channels.

Suddenly there was a loud bang on the side of the house. Kim stood up to look outside and saw a palm branch lying on the ground next to the window. She looked up to see where it had come from and noticed a white Chevy truck coming down the street. It stopped two houses away, and when the door opened, out stepped Camilo. Mr. Brower came out of his house and she watched as his hands wildly motioned toward the sky.

An enormous branch barely hung on right above Mr. Brower's carport. From what Kim could tell, he probably wanted Camilo and his crew to cut it down before it fell and damaged something. But who cared about that? She was more interested in why Camilo was here again; Nita had said that he didn't come around too often. "Looks like Julio is going to have to come sooner than later to do his circus stunt."

"His what?"

"When I met Camilo the other day, he said that Julio was going to have to trim the branches off the palm tree on the side of the house. He was going to let you know when he would do it. He says Julio is like an acrobat." Kim kept looking out the window. "Mr. Brower looks like he wants it done now, so I guess we'll be seeing a show soon. I thought that Camilo doesn't come around much."

"Usually not. Why?"

"He's the one talking to Mr. Brower."

"Do you see Julio? I hope everything is okay."

She looked up and down the street, but didn't see Julio or the crew. Mr. Bower seemed to have calmed down—his arms weren't flying anymore. Instead, he had them on his hips, but also had a smile on his face. Camilo got back into his truck, and Kim continued to watch as the truck came closer to the house. She thought he was going to drive right by, but the truck pulled into the driveway behind Jack's minivan.

"Hi. What are you doing in our neck of the woods?" she asked as she walked onto the porch. Camilo opened the truck door and came around the front.

"Hi," he said and smiled up at her. "Quite a wind we are having *hoy*."

"Ah, today; *si*," she replied back

"Señorita speaks Español?"

"No, not very much. I only know enough to be dangerous." Kim looked across the street. "Mr. Brower seems a little agitated today. Are you going to cut down that palm tree?"

"No, not the whole tree. We'll trim the top and get it cleaned up so no damage to his carport." Camilo set his foot on the bottom step. He was wearing the same brown cowboy boots he had on the other day, but instead of a white tee, Camilo wore a long-sleeved red cowboy shirt. *How can it be seventy-eight degrees and the locals still dress as if it were winter?* Kim thought. *But of course, it is winter to them.*

"I came by to see if you want to go for a drink with me tonight," Camilo said.

Kim was taken aback that he would ask her out. He didn't even know her, or if she was even available. And most astonishing of all, she had to be at least twenty years older than he. "I'm not sure," she replied. *Okay, that was a dumb answer.*

"Don't be afraid," he said and laughed. "I am a good person. I am a responsible businessman, I don't smoke, I don't drink—I take this back, I do like a beer once in a while and I especially like wine."

Kim looked at him sideways. "For some reason, you don't look like a wine drinker."

"What does a wine drinker look like?"

"Well, I mean, most men don't come out of the chute saying they like wine. It doesn't seem very manly, that's all. Okay, I didn't mean anything by that," she quickly added.

"No offense taken. Well? Would you like to go have a drink with me this evening?"

"Camilo, you don't even know who I am. I might be married for all you know, and besides, I'm probably old enough to be your mother."

"I know you are not married and as for your age, who cares? I don't. Do you?"

She was not sure how he knew she was not married, but was intrigued that he had an interest in her. She was tempted to say yes. But she said, "Besides, I can't tonight. I have dinner plans with my parents. We're going to visit some relatives. . . . And how do you know I'm not married?"

"I ask around. Everyone knows *tus padres*, your parents, and they know your story, too."

Kim's heart started to race and she could feel sweat bead up on her neck. "My story?" she asked.

"I heard you just got a divorce. I am sorry, Kim. I have never gone through divorce, but I am sure it must be a hard thing to handle."

"It's okay," Kim muttered as she looked down at her feet. She paused before she answered, "It's a tough thing to go through, but I'm going to be okay." She looked back up at Camilo. "I should've known about the gossip chain around here," she said and laughed.

"They were not really gossiping, Kim. I asked them, so that's not gossip. I liked you right away when I met you the other day, and I wanted to know more about you. How about tomorrow night? I won't take no for an answer."

"Well, there is still that age thing, you know. I'm sure that I'm at least twenty years older than you," Kim repeated.

"Again, Kim, who cares? I don't. I bet you would like to get away from the old people for a while." He grinned. "I could take you to a nice little wine bar on the other side of town. . . . I forgot to ask, do you drink wine?"

"There's a wine bar here? Harlingen doesn't seem a likely town to have an establishment such as a wine bar. And yes, I guess I'm known to have a glass now and then . . . but a wine bar, here?"

"Don't seem so surprised. The locals have some culture, too. Tomorrow then?"

"Wow, you don't give up, do you? Okay, yes; I would like to meet you for a glass of wine. That sounds nice."

"Great. I will pick you up about six o'clock tomorrow night, then."

That sounded too much like a date to Kim. "No, no, you don't have to pick me up. I'll meet you there; just give me the name of the place and I'll ask my parents for directions. I am sure Jack will let me borrow his mini-van," she said and smiled.

"I don't mind picking you up, really." Camilo walked

toward the front of his truck and opened the door. "Six o'clock then?"

"Really, I'll meet you there. I will feel better if I do," Kim pleaded.

Camilo laughed. "Okay, the name of the place is Corks. It's over by the mall. I am not sure of the exact address, but it's on Forty-sixth Street."

"No problem. I'll look it up. See you at six o'clock then?"

"*Si*; I am looking forward to it." Camilo got into his truck and backed out of the driveway.

Kim opened the sliding glass door and went into the house. Nita had not moved from her chair, her eyes glued to the TV, drinking her coffee. "What did Camilo want?" she asked.

"I'm going to meet him for a glass of wine tomorrow night, some place called Corks. Do you know where it is?"

"Are you going on a date with Camilo?" She shot a puzzling look toward Kim as she took a sip of coffee.

"Not a date, Mom. I'm meeting him there. He seems like a nice person. It's just something to do, that's all."

Kim poured a cup of coffee and smiled to herself. She couldn't wait to call Connie. Kim's head swirled at the thought of the next evening. *It is just a glass of wine and nothing else*, she convinced herself. But the age difference had her on edge, even though it didn't seem to bother Camilo. He had never revealed his age, but she was guessing he was only in his twenties. *So what?* she thought. *He is right; age does not really matter*. Besides, she was only having a glass of wine with him. She wasn't going to date him or start a relationship.

Her finger pressed three on her cell phone and she got Connie's voice mail. "Call me when you get this," Kim said, slipped her phone into her pocket, and went outside to go on her morning run. The wind was still whipping and the resistance gave her quite a workout. She turned down street after street, thinking only of the tall, handsome Mexican boy. And she couldn't stop smiling.

CHAPTER TEN

Violet and Beth Carson lived in a small southern Texas town about forty-five minutes from Jack and Nita's winter home. Beth had never married, according to Nita, and lived with her mother. "She told us last time we visited them that it was cheaper that way," Nita said on the ride over. "She said she was saving her money for something but she didn't say what."

Beth worked full time as a nursing assistant and helped her mother on her days off in the small fabric store that Violet owned. It seemed to Kim a rather mundane life, but if they both were content, what did her opinion matter?

An hour after they left Sunbeam RV Park, Kim and her parents pulled up to the Carson's modest rambler for the birthday celebration. The lawn in front of the house was not a lawn at all, but instead resembled a junkyard. There wasn't a single blade of grass. The yard was filled with old tires, cracked flowerpots, and pieces of bent wrought iron fences. Kim supposed Violet thought it was some sort of art, but to Kim, it just looked like junk.

The threesome stepped onto the half-crumbling

cement porch and knocked on the door. A very large Violet greeted them, smiling, showing a mouthful of cracked teeth. She had pulled her thinning gray hair back in a tight ponytail and it looked as if it had not seen soap in a week.

"Come in," she said and motioned them through the door. "So glad you could make it, and it is so nice to see you, Kim," she added. "How long has it been? You were nineteen or twenty when you left Texas." She yelled down the small hallway. "They're here!"

When Violet finished yelling, Kim answered, "I was nineteen when I lived here, but we've seen each other since then," she said, feeling embarrassed at correcting Violet.

"Oh, yes," Violet answered, seemingly unaffected by her absentmindedness.

The inside of the house was in just as much disarray as the outside was. Dishes were stacked all over the countertop and more were piled in the sink. Kim couldn't imagine that there was a dish left for them to eat dinner on. *Maybe Violet is having pizza delivered*, Kim thought hopefully. She glanced over to the dining room table, adjacent to the kitchen, and noticed the table was set, confirming they were not having pizza.

Beth came in and greeted them. "Hello. Happy birthday, Jack." Beth flung her short, mousy brown hair behind her ear before she slapped him on the back, making him stumble forward. Beth was a rather large woman, like her mom; each was close to two hundred pounds, Kim suspected. Beth handled herself in a manly fashion and spoke in a deep voice.

Beth was Violet and Art Carson's third child and only girl. Beth had been born thirteen years after Mark, and her birth was a jubilant time for the family, especially for Violet, who wanted a daughter more than anything. And if Violet was happy, the whole family was happy. So Beth's place in the family was number one, revered by her mother, father, and two older brothers. She could do no wrong and, God forbid, her brothers could do no wrong to her.

Kim was seven when Beth was born. She remembered her first visit to the resort after Beth's arrival and noticing the great amount of attention focused on this little baby girl. Up to that point, Kim had been the youngest female child at the resort and usually received the attention that was now being bestowed upon someone else. So for Kim, this baby was only an inconvenience and competition.

As Beth grew, Kim became accustomed to having her around. In fact, Beth became the little sister Kim never had. As the years went by, Kim found herself spending more time with Beth, becoming friends with Beth's friends. Living on a resort defined friendships in a different way. Friends were friends for a short period of time during the summer months, and then the next summer, the friendships started again.

Kim and Beth's friends were the children of families who spent the same two weeks each summer at the resort. As soon as two weeks were over, one family left and the next moved in and those friendships were renewed again. Kim always knew, year after year, who she could look forward to seeing, based on which week of which month it was.

Kim and Beth had not been the only ones who made friends with the visitors at the resort. The boys also had their own recurring set of friends; most of them, however, where the opposite sex. This made for some very interesting situations and challenges. Kim remembered one time overhearing her grandmother telling Jack that the Snellings would not be returning the next year—something about their daughter getting into trouble with one of the dock boys.

The boys had no ties to these girls, whom they only saw two weeks out of the year. So they took risks they shouldn't have, and occasionally, the playfulness went too far. They had no commitments. After all, the girls were at the resort for only two weeks and when they were gone, more girls would arrive.

"Do you want a drink, Jack?" Beth asked as she showed him to a chair. "You still like your brandy, don't you?"

"I do. I'll have just a little glass." He held his fingers up an inch apart to show her.

"Go ahead and celebrate, Dad. I can drive home if you have more than just a little bit," Kim said as she sat down next to him on the couch and squeezed his arm.

"Nita, what can I get you?" Violet came around the corner from the kitchen with a plate of cheese and something else that looked like salami, but was darker and denser.

"Oh, nothing for me, thanks," she said.

"Kim, how about you? Dinner will be ready in fifteen minutes. What would you like, a beer?"

"I'm not much of a beer drinker; wine is more to my liking—"

Beth interrupted. "Mom, I told you we should've picked up a bottle of Lambrusco, just in case."

"It's okay," Kim said. "I can have something else. Actually, I'll have some brandy with my dad. Only do you have some Diet Coke to mix with it? I can't do straight up like he does." She glanced over at her dad and smiled.

"But you know I just have a little bit." Jack held up his two fingers again.

The dinner that night consisted of baked pork roast and boiled potatoes with carrots, apparently from Violet's garden. Kim ate very little, still apprehensive about the state of the house. And along with the few brandies she had, her appetite was squelched and she forgot about food.

The night focused on talk of the old days in northern Maine, what life consisted of for Beth and Violet, and how Jack and Nita were enjoying their retirement. Violet and Beth asked Kim only about her work and not about her life, which was just fine with her.

Violet talked about the fabric shop she owned and the challenges of ordering cloth these days. Kim just couldn't imagine the lady sitting across from her as being a fabric sort of person. Beth did not have a job at the moment. She was laid off from the nursing home she worked at for the past year.

"I like working with old people. I hope to find something at another nursing home," she told them. "But for now, I'm helping my mom at the store." Then Beth abruptly changed the subject. "Kim, remember the time we went across the border to get that watch you couldn't live without?" She was sitting across from Kim, slouched back in her chair.

"Yes, I remember," Kim answered.

Kim had been in her late twenties at the time. She was visiting her parents for a long weekend break and they were spending the afternoon with Violet and Beth. Kim talked about a watch she had seen the day before when she visited Progresso, one of the border towns in Mexico.

As the conversation shifted away from Kim and her parents relayed the day's news from the retirement community, Kim let her mind drift back to that day.

—•••—

"I don't know why I didn't get it," Kim told Beth. "I always do that—procrastinate—and then I lose out."

"You don't have to lose out, Kim. I can take you across to Reynosa. I'm sure they have the same watches there. All the Mexicans seem to have the same knockoffs. We can leave now and be back before dark."

"I'm not going to drive across the border!" Kim adamantly shook her head.

"Don't worry. We don't have to drive over there. We can park on the American side and walk across," Beth told her. "It'll be fine, as long as we don't stay over there after dark."

Jack and Nita were all in favor. "I know how much you want that watch, Kim," Nita said. "Go with her. The two of you will have fun." So Kim borrowed Jack and Nita's car and the two women headed for Mexico.

The parking lot adjacent to the border crossing was almost full when they arrived at three thirty that afternoon. Kim parked the car and the two got out and headed for the gate. "We're going to have to walk a ways into town to where the market is," Beth said. "I hope you wore good shoes." She looked down at Kim's feet and smiled.

They walked across the fence-lined bridge that joined the United States with Mexico. Underneath them ran the dirty water of the Rio Grande River. On the mucky banks of the river below, they saw children playing, while others lined the sidewalks of the bridge overhead, begging, with their hands stretched out, almost touching the people as they passed by. "Pesos, please, pesos," they cried in unison.

Beth and Kim crossed the border after paying their twenty-five cents to the guard at the gate and headed into town. It was a hot afternoon and Kim wished she had grabbed a bottle of water before they left. She followed Beth down the cracked cobblestone streets, worn from years of weather and neglect. Fearful she was going to trip and break an ankle, Kim kept her eyes focused on her feet as she followed Beth, who kept five steps ahead of her. They turned down street after street until Beth suddenly stopped.

"I thought it was this way," she said as she squinted down one of the narrow streets.

"You mean you don't know where we are going? I thought you knew this place?"

"I've not been here for quite a while, haven't been over the border since . . ."

"Since when?" Kim questioned.

"Oh, never mind," Beth answered. "It's nothing. Okay, I think it's this way," she said and headed to the right. Kim followed.

The number of tourists thinned as they approached the open-air market. They heard shouts from the vendors standing in their doorways, prompting people to come into their shops. "Good price for you today," they yelled out, hoping to get in a few last-minute sales.

They found a small shop that displayed watches in the

window. Everything from Rolex to Timex lay on black velvet cloths behind dirty, dusty windows.

"You know they aren't real, don't you, Kim?" Beth asked.

"Of course I do, but I don't care. I just thought it would be fun to have one. Who would know the difference anyway?" Kim found the one she had been looking at the day before and they walked inside the tiny shop. A man came out from behind a small curtain in the back of the store and greeted them with a toothless smile. Kim picked up one of the watches on the shelf in the window and handed it to the man. "How much?" she asked.

"For you, señorita, twenty American dollars," he said.

"You can do better than that; fifteen American dollars," Beth told him.

"Beth!" Kim whispered. "What are you doing?"

"Shh," she hissed and elbowed Kim. "Fifteen American dollars and you got a sale," she said as she turned back to the vendor.

"Señorita, I have more cost than that in the watch. I make no money if I sell for fifteen American dollars." He shook his head.

"Okay, then we don't want it," Beth said and started to walk toward the door.

"Wait, señorita. Let me see what I can do. I be right back and ask the boss."

"They always do that," Beth whispered to Kim when the man went back behind the curtain. "You never pay what they say at first; you always have to bargain with them."

"I hate that," Kim said as she looked around the shop. "Let's just get out of here."

"Nonsense. I bet you he comes back and takes fifteen

dollars for the watch." As soon as she said that, the vendor came around the curtain and showed his toothless grin again.

"It's your lucky day, señoritas; my boss sell to you for fifteen American dollars!"

Kim smiled at Beth as she handed the money over to the vendor. The two walked out of the store. Kim waited until they were a safe distance before she started laughing. "That was quite a scene."

"That was not a scene, Kim. *That* is called shopping Mexican style. It's done all the time. If you think that was a scene, you must live a very sheltered life." Beth looked around. "We'd better head back. It's getting late. I think it's this way," she said, motioning to Kim.

The two headed down the narrow streets again, Kim following Beth and once again watching her step. They turned down street after street, and the farther they went, the streets became less and less crowded. From what Kim could tell, they were not even close to the bridge and the gate that would let them cross over to the American side.

She looked toward the sky and looked at the setting sun. She was getting nervous, thinking about what Beth said when they left the parking lot: "We better be back before dark."

"Are you sure you know how to get back?" Kim asked.

"I thought I did, but I guess I forgot the way," Beth said, looking up and down the side streets as she hurried along, Kim now right beside her. Pretty soon, the two picked up their pace to a slow jog. Storefronts emptied out and there were no tourists in sight.

As they turned a corner and headed down a street, a

Mexican teenager stuck his head out of a storefront doorway, looking in the direction of the two women. When he
saw them, a smile came across his face. "Hey, señoritas,"
he yelled out.

"Don't look at him," Beth whispered to Kim. "Just
keep on walking and don't look up." When they got to the
doorway, Kim obeyed. She was next to the street and Beth
was on the inner side, closest to the boy.

"Señorita, don't ignore me," he said as he grabbed
Beth's arm and jerked her closer to the door.

"Run!" she shouted and pulled away from his grip.
Kim ran after her as fast as she could. *What in the heck am
I doing here?* she thought. *All for a stupid watch.* They could
hear shouts behind them as two other boys joined the
first one. They were laughing and talking in Spanish as
they chased the two women down the vacant streets. Beth
turned down one street and could see the border crossing
ahead of her. "I see it!" she panted.

They could hear the boys' voices getting louder
behind them; one boy reached out to try to grab Kim by
the arm, but he missed when she jerked forward. Then all
of a sudden, a loud shout came from a doorway across the
street, just ahead of them. The voice was deep and gruff
and yelled something at the three boys in Spanish. A huge
man came out of the doorway. He looked past Kim and
Beth as he drew a gun from his side and pointed it straight
in the air. He yelled something else at the boys and then
fired a shot. The sound made Kim scream as she put her
hands to her ears, and her throat tightened with fear.

"You're okay, señoritas; no need to worry," the man
told the women as he approached them. When he got

closer, he suddenly stopped and stared at Beth. She quickly turned and started to walk in the direction of the border gate. The man stepped up behind her and whispered something in her ear. Kim followed, but couldn't hear what he said. She looked in the direction of the boys, who were still shouting something at them in Spanish.

She turned back and the man moved in between Kim and Beth and spoke louder. "You better get across the border right now. This not a good time for young girls to be in the streets."

"Yes, we are going," Beth told him.

"I've never been so scared," Kim said to Beth when the man left. She looked back and saw he was still arguing with the boys. Then she looked back at Beth, who looked as if she were going to pass out. Her face was bright red and her breath came fast and heavy. "Are you okay?" Kim asked her. She put her hand on Beth's back; it was wet with sweat. "And what did he say to you?" Kim asked.

"Nothing," said Beth, her response firm.

Kim and Beth made their way to the gate, where they showed the customs officer their identification, gave him two pesos each, and quickly crossed back over to the United States, feeling very lucky to be on American soil again. They were silent as they walked back toward the parking lot. When they reached the car, Beth spoke. "I'm so glad we got out of there," she said. When they got into the car she continued. "If I get caught, they know who I am. I've not been over there since it happened."

"What happened? And what do you mean they know who you are?" Kim's voice got louder with each word. "Is that what was going on back there?" She motioned back in the direction where they had just been. "Did that man recognize you?"

She turned on the car and rolled down the window, but before pulling out of the parking lot turned to look at Beth. "What happened?" she repeated.

"It all happened when Mark was murdered. It was drugs we suspected," she explained.

"What are you talking about? I thought Mark had an accident." Kim was shaken; this was the first time she had heard anything about this. Her parents had told her years earlier that Mark had been killed in an accident. She remembered how devastated she felt over the loss of her long-ago lover and friend.

"That's what we told everyone. However, that wasn't really the truth," she explained. "Mark was involved with some illegal stuff." Beth didn't elaborate any further and they drove back to the house in silence.

CHAPTER ELEVEN

The birthday celebration ended early. After saying their goodbyes, Kim, Nita, and Jack headed back to Harlingen, with Kim in the driver's seat. It didn't take long before Nita and Jack dozed off. So Kim had forty minutes of silence to think about the past. She thought back to that day when she found out that Mark had been murdered.

It had been a long time since she thought about his murder, and now she couldn't get it out of her mind. She looked over at Jack, with his eyes closed, dozing next to her and she could hear Nita in the back seat, softly snoring. She looked back through the windshield and her thoughts drifted back in time.

—•●•—

She stood in one of the large hallways of the candle company, with all its activity, the coming and going of all kinds of people who helped in the shipping department. Men who wore heavy stocking caps, despite the Texas heat, quietly walked into the warehouse, not speaking to anyone, and headed straight for Mark's office, shutting the door behind them. A few minutes later, they would come back out and head straight for the door, all the while looking directly ahead with expressionless faces.

Toward the end of her stay with Mark and Maite, she suspected there was trouble between them; she would often hear them yelling at each other from the other end of the house. Kim usually could not make out what exactly the conversation was about, but many times it ended with Maite saying she was leaving if it didn't stop.

Kim and Mark's love affair had blossomed and by that time was flourishing. Kim became more comfortable with their relationship the more time they spent together, and she was convinced that Maite was not aware of the affair; she felt they were being discrete enough to avoid getting caught. But then she wondered if Maite was referring to her and the affair in her arguments with Mark.

The first time they made love started out as an innocent drive to Brownsville. Kim accompanied Mark on one of his business trips, leaving Maite behind at the candle shop. Mark told Kim they were going to be gone only a few hours; they would leave at ten o'clock in the morning and he would have her back by early afternoon.

They drove the forty-five minutes in silence. Mark appeared to be agitated about something and Kim was concerned it had something to do with her. She wished she had not agreed to join him on this trip.

When they arrived in Brownsville, they drove to a warehouse on the edge of town. Kim waited in the car for Mark for thirty minutes. When he returned, he was much more relaxed and calm. He kissed Kim on the cheek when he slid behind the wheel.

"What was that for?" she asked.

"I'm in such a good mood, and when I noticed a beautiful girl sitting in my car, I had to kiss her."

"You sure are in a different mood than when I saw you half an hour ago," she said, squinting her eyes in disbelief.

He started the car and headed down the vacant street toward the city. "Let's go to the beach," he said, ignoring her skepticism.

"Don't we have to get back?" Kim asked.

"Not really. It's a sunny day and the weather is great, so let's go spend some time relaxing." Mark looked over at her, a devilish smile on his face.

Just before they got to the beach, Mark pulled up to a small neighborhood grocery store. "I'll be right back," he said. A few minutes later, he returned with a brown bag and set it in the back seat.

"What's that?" Kim inquired.

"That, Kim . . . is a picnic. I feel like celebrating."

"What are we celebrating?"

"Business. Business is good, life is good, and I feel great." Keeping his eyes on the road, he reached for her, grabbed her chin, turned her head toward his mouth, and kissed her on the lips, lingering before he let her go.

They headed over the causeway to the island. Kim rolled down the window to feel the warm breeze of the gulf. The smell surrounded her and made her giddy with happiness, high on life at the moment. She didn't have to work at all that day, so there was nothing to go back for. And it was a perfect beach day. So why not spend it with Mark?

They drove down the main thoroughfare, past the hotels and restaurants, until they reached a secluded area of the beach. Mark pulled off the road into a small clearing and stopped the car. They got out, Mark grabbed the bag from the backseat and then opened the trunk and pulled out a blanket. "Come on, Kim. Let's have a picnic."

Kim followed Mark as he headed over the sand dunes to where the beach flattened out. He seemed to know just the spot he was looking for, and when he found it, he laid the blanket down on the sand. The water was in front of them, the weeds and sand dunes behind. Kim looked up and down the beach and found it totally vacant, except for the seagulls flying overhead.

Mark opened the bag and pulled out a bottle of wine, followed by a corkscrew and two glasses. "Looks like you've thought of everything," Kim said as she laughed, pulling her sweatshirt over her head and revealing slender bare shoulders. Mark poured them each a glass of wine and Kim took a sip as she watched the waves roll in. "I love the sound of water," she said. "It calms me down, no matter what mood I'm in."

"And what kind of mood are you in now?" Mark asked.

"I wasn't in a bad mood before, but now I'm in a great mood. This was a good idea. Thanks, Mark. What else is in that bag? I hope it's something to eat. I'm starving."

"Your wish is my command," he said as he flashed her a smile. "How about a sandwich? I have one turkey and one roast beef. Which one do you want?"

"I'll take the turkey, please," she said, and she batted her eyes at him and then laughed. They sat quietly for a few minutes while they ate their lunches. Mark was the first to talk.

"Kim, you know how I feel about you, don't you?" He set his sandwich down, picked up the glass of wine, and lifted it to make a toast. Kim followed his cue and lifted hers as well. She didn't respond, but sat in silence as she sipped her wine. After a few minutes she turned and looked at him.

"I think I do," she said, "and the feelings are mutual." She smiled. Mark slid closer and lightly touched her arm with his finger. Kim noticed his wedding ring was missing, but thought little of it. He traced his finger up her arm to her cheek and turned her head so he could look straight into her eyes. He then leaned toward her and drew her nearer to him for a long, slow kiss. "Kim, do you know how desirable you are?" he whispered.

She pulled away for a second, hesitating before sinking completely into his arms, returning the kiss as feverishly as he was kissing her. Mark's arm came around her back and he untied the strap of her halter. The front draped forward and she jerked her hand up to cover herself while nervously looking around to see who might be watching.

"It's okay," Mark said, his voice husky with anticipation. "Come over here." He pulled her closer to the weeds where they were more sheltered. She fell back against the soft sand, yielding to Mark's caresses. Soon the two were lying naked in the weeds, intertwined as one, tuned out to the rest of the world around them. Mark rolled on top of her and Kim surrendered to his love-making.

When they were done, Kim felt exhilarated. She was in love with Mark, and she was quite sure he was in love with her.

CHAPTER TWELVE

Kim opened her eyes and listened for Jack and Nita, but heard nothing. She lay back on her pillow and closed her eyes, still exhausted from the night before. Even though she had gone to bed shortly after they got home, thoughts of Mark kept her from falling asleep. She couldn't stop thinking about him, the affair, and the deceit, all so long ago. How did she do that to another woman? She didn't realize at the time what a horrible thing she had done. And now, she knew how it felt to be the person who was cheated on.

The thoughts didn't stop as she put on her running clothes and tied her shoes. She couldn't get Mark or his murder out of her head. Until last night, she hadn't thought about his death in many years, and now it haunted her. She remembered when Beth told her it wasn't an accident and that actually it was a homicide, but couldn't remember if she ever told her if they solved the case.

Kim realized that Mark's drug dealing was probably going on while she was living with him, the illegal activity happening right under her nose. She thought about Alison and Maite and their involvement in the whole thing, and then came to the conclusion that that probably was the reason they left him, fearing for their own safety.

Kim went out to the porch and sat on the step, foregoing her usual need for a cup of coffee. She laid her head in her hands and sat in silence. After a few moments, she looked up and stared out onto the street. She wanted to know more about Mark's life and death. She decided right then to search for any information she could find about the murder and the investigation.

Her first thought was the library. *They must have some sort of record.* She needed to know how close to danger she had been in and what might have been going on while she was living here. It may have been the smartest decision she had ever made when she decided to leave and go back home. She needed to confirm that.

Kim stood and headed away from the house, but not in the direction of her usual run. Quickly arriving at the park office, Kim opened the door. "Mom, can I borrow the car?" she said as she walked toward the desk were Nita was sitting.

"Of course you can," Nita replied. "The keys are on my dresser in the bedroom."

"I also need directions to the library."

"The library?" Nita inquired. "If you want to find a book to read, there are many here in our library," she said and pointed to a small room adjacent to the office.

"No, not a book," Kim said. "I'm just looking for some information about something that I have been thinking about lately. Now that I have some time, I thought I'd do some research," she said.

"Okay, but don't be too long. Remember, you have to get ready for your date." Nita held up her hand to shield her mouth as she spoke in a hushed tone.

My date? What was she talking about? Camilo! She had forgotten all about meeting him that evening. "It's not a date, Mom, but thanks for reminding me." Kim walked out of the office.

The directions Nita gave Kim were sketchy, and she took a few wrong turns before she spotted the sign: Harlingen Public Library. Kim parked the minivan in the parking lot across the street and walked through the library's front door. It was a dilapidated, two-story brick building; she could see where chunks of the walls had fallen off.

Considering the condition of the structure, Kim wasn't sure if this library would have the resources she was looking for, but when she got inside, she was surprised at how modern it was. *They must have done some major remodeling,* she thought as she searched for the reference area.

"Up the stairs and to the right," the librarian told her. Kim followed her directions to the second floor, and when she got to the top of the stairs, she looked around until she found a sign that read REFERENCE above a group of computers. The computers were sitting side by side on a high counter, with a stool tucked underneath each one. She searched until she found an unoccupied one, sat in front of it, and followed the instructions listed on the screen to access the Internet.

She typed in "Mark Carson," and after a few seconds, several hundred matches appeared. She then typed in "Mark Carson, Harlingen, Texas" and a page full of entries came up. The top three were state and federal public records, then a police record, followed by an article from the *Valley Daily News*. She clicked on the public records link for the county, looking for death notices to determine the year he died. Kim typed in Mark's full name and hit the enter button, but the results came back, "no matches."

She then searched the neighboring counties, but still did not find the death record. Then she did a search for the entire state of Texas, but still found nothing. Kim was puzzled as to why she couldn't find any record of Mark's death, but quickly brushed it off, assuming she was doing something incorrectly.

She clicked on the entry for the article in the newspaper and read about a young reporter who wrote a series of articles about the life and death of Mark Carson. When she clicked on the entry, however, the archived articles did not appear in full, but only showed their first few lines. Kim walked over to the reference desk and inquired about how she might find old articles from the *Valley Daily News*. Barely glancing up, the person behind the desk asked, "What are you looking for?"

"I'm looking for an article that was written about a murder that took place in the valley, many years ago."

The girl behind the desk still didn't look up from her computer as she spoke. "You will need a time frame, subject, or author," she stated.

"Well, I have the name of the journalist who wrote the article and who the article was about."

"That'll do," the girl replied. Then she abruptly got up and walked toward a young man carrying a white bag that appeared to be from some sort of fast food place.

What? I guess it must be lunch time. Kim watched as the girl took the bag, eyed the contents, then returned to where Kim was standing. "It's my lunch break," she told Kim. "You can go to the next desk over there," she said as she motioned to her left. Kim shook her head and walked in the direction the girl was pointing.

When she approached the desk, the woman smiled at Kim.

"How can I help you, ma'am?" The woman's Texas drawl was thick.

"I'd like to find some old newspaper articles from the *Valley Daily News.*"

"I can help you with that," the lady said. "We have all the old articles archived on microfilm. What time frame are y'all looking for?"

"I don't know when the article was written, only who wrote it and who the article was about."

"That won't be a problem. Just give me one or the other and I will search it for you."

Kim hesitated before she answered, "Can you search by the name Mark Carson?" she asked.

There was silence as the librarian focused on the screen in front of her, clicking the mouse several times. "Here's something," she said after a few minutes. "You're looking for an article written by Jake Michaels?"

"Yes," Kim responded.

"Okay," she said as she picked up a piece of scrap

paper and wrote down some numbers. Kim stepped back as the lady heaved her massive body up, showing off a brightly colored, flowered smock. "Follow me just over here, and I'll get you set up."

Kim followed her down narrow rows, stopping occasionally so the librarian could turn herself sideways in order to fit. When they got to a back corner, the librarian continued, "We have papers dating all the way back to the eighteen hundreds. Okay, here we are," she said as they came to a desk with a black machine sitting on it. "The films are located in this room," she said and turned around, motioning toward a door with a window on the top half that was covered by a blind.

"We have to have a special room so they stay preserved," she told Kim. "You want to look in the cabinets in that room. They are sorted by numbers." She handed Kim the piece of paper she had written on just a few minutes earlier. "Then you can sit and thread the films through here," she said, pointing to the side of the monitor. "All you have to do is search by this number." She smiled at Kim. "Good luck, and let me know if you need help." Kim watched as the woman slowly made her way back between the rows of books.

She turned to the desk. Of course she needed help. How did the machine even turn on? Sitting down, Kim ran her fingers on both sides of the black box, but found nothing that resembled a switch. After a few minutes, she found a button on the bottom left of the screen and pushed it on; a loud hum sounded and a light came on. Kim turned toward the door behind her. *I guess I need the film first,* she thought.

She got up, slowly opened the door, and found four file cabinets lined against the far wall. They were six feet in height—taller than Kim—so if she needed to see what was in the top drawer, she was going to have to get help. Each drawer was only about six inches in width and was marked by a series of numbers indicating which drawer held what. She was relieved to find that the drawer she needed was in the middle. She opened it and saw the rolls of films, categorized by numbers. She thumbed through until she found a roll with the same numbers as what was on the piece of paper.

Kim sat back down at the table and pulled the films, which resembled old filmstrips from her past school days, out of the envelope. *This will be interesting.* She ran her finger over the opening the librarian had indicated and proceeded to feed the start of the film through the hole. She turned the knob clockwise and the screens advanced, showing different dates. Soon the first article appeared on the screen in front of her. She turned another knob to adjust the focus. It revealed a picture of a young man with a full head of hair and horn-rimmed glasses; "Jake Michaels" was typed underneath.

Kim turned the scroll button past the biography of Michaels until she came to the first article. "How It Began" was the title. She started reading about Mark and Alison's business, M&A Chandler Company. She remembered the company's logo, and how when she first saw it, it reminded her of a seagull in flight. When she mentioned this to Mark, he confirmed she was right. "This is Jonathan Livingston Seagull," he told her.

She recalled the movie by the same name. It was

about a seagull, Jonathan, who was bored with his life and looking for something better than what he had. In his search, he became an outcast. But the search led him to find strength within himself, strength that brought him back to the flock, and strength that led him to teach and enlighten his fellow seagulls.

She thought about the movie, and how odd and strange it seemed now, but back then it was one of the most popular movies on the big screen. She remembered Mark playing the soundtrack in his car and how he would rewind it repeatedly to the "The Flight of the Gull."

The article talked about the candle company, the author describing how peace and harmony emanated throughout the building. "It almost felt like a hippy commune," he wrote. Mark's laid-back manner unnerved those around him. "He did not have a sense of urgency in the least," the writer stated. The article ended by describing a peaceful picture of a perfect world for the young couple who were just beginning their lives and their dreams. Kim sat back in her chair and smiled. She remembered how Mark had the ability to command respect and at the same time relax those around him.

She pushed the forward button until she reached the second article, "Trouble in Paradise." It described Mark's newly formed friendship with Carlos Martinez, a struggling contractor in the valley. Carlos was looking for a bidder for his projects and was confident the first time he met Mark that he had the right personality for the job. Carlos needed additional cash flow for his company, and he knew that if he were successful in winning a few bids with some of the local city projects, he could turn a very nice profit and make himself—and a partner—very rich.

Mark took the entire proceeds he had gotten from a line of credit he set up for M&A Chandler Company and used it to start the partnership with Carlos. The newly formed company was called Carlos and Associates Construction Company. Mark wasn't pleased that his name wasn't mentioned, but he reluctantly agreed to it after many arguments with Carlos.

Mark began to bid projects under Carlos's guidance, and with his charm and drive, became successful in winning bids and gaining the respect of the project leaders. Carlos nicknamed him "Golden Boy," not only because of his golden sun-streaked locks, but also because any project he bid on, he won. Carlos provided Mark with the technical language he needed in order to appear to be an expert.

According to the article, Mark had little to no knowledge of the construction business, but "he could talk a mean streak," as Carlos often said. The company's project list began to grow, and the two of them were set up to make a hefty profit. But as Jake Michaels explained, while Carlos knew the right lingo for the construction business, his knowledge beyond that was limited. Mark was setting up projects and signing contracts that neither of them had the ability to deliver on.

Kim looked at her watch and realized it was getting late. She had spent the last two hours at the library, and now she needed to head back to her parents' to get ready to meet Camilo later that evening. Kim pushed the button, turned off the machine, and while she was listening to the hum, she closed her eyes. Mark's image popped into her head. She could see his broad, toothy smile and the twinkling of his eyes. What course had his life taken and how close to danger had she been? She had only scratched the surface in the last couple of hours, and she wanted to know more, so she made a commitment to herself to come back and pick up where she left off.

CHAPTER THIRTEEN

Kim stood in front of the mirror, analyzing her reflection, turning her head from side to side. She placed her pointer finger on the side of her eye, lifting the skin up, then moved closer to examine her crow's feet. She was surprised to find very few lines, and smiled at the image in the mirror. *Good thing I've taken good care of my skin.* Kim had always made sure she paid attention to a healthy routine and now it seemed to be more important than ever. "Maybe it's because you are going on a date with a child," she said out loud.

Not a date. Just a nice glass of wine and something to do. She took one last look at her reflection, pleased with what she had chosen to wear. She picked a short black halter dress that showed just enough cleavage—but not too much—to still look respectable. The dress flared out slightly around her hips and stopped an inch above her knee, showing off her tanned legs.

"Add a little color, honey," Connie always told her. Kim liked black, and it was the staple color in her wardrobe. She could mix and match many of the pieces of clothes she owned, and always felt put together and stylish. She got many compliments on her clothes, so she thought her color choice was just fine.

Kim wrote down the directions to Corks wine bar as her mom recited them to her.

"It's over by the mall," she told Kim. "It shouldn't take you more than fifteen minutes to get there."

"Just in case I get lost, have your phone with you," she said and smiled at Nita.

"Have a nice date, Kim."

"Mom, it's not a date. I keep telling you that. He likes wine, I like wine, and besides, it would be nice to have a conversation with someone who is less than sixty-two years old." She stepped in front of her mom, reached over to grab the keys for the minivan from the table, and stuck the directions in her purse.

On her way over to the wine bar, the Jake Michaels articles occupied her mind. She was uneasy about how close she had been to drug trafficking and that she probably had been just a step away from disaster. Kim thought that she must have met many of the people the story highlighted, but couldn't remember the names the author wrote about.

As Kim thought about the past, she failed to pay attention to the directions and missed her turn. She really didn't want to call Nita and admit that she was lost, so she turned at the next right and then went right again to get back on the road she had just been on. But when she wanted to go right again, she couldn't; it was a one-way street.

She kept going until she found a turn she could take. She went a few blocks until she came to a stoplight, and as she waited, she checked the directions again, realizing that she was still not on the right road. Kim glanced at her watch; it was six fifteen. She was already fifteen minutes late and hoped Camilo didn't think she was standing him up.

At the next stoplight, Kim turned left, went down a few blocks, and saw the mall in front of her, so she knew she was in the right area. She made a few more turns until she saw a sign that read CORKS WINE BAR JUST AHEAD. *Finally*, she thought and parked the van in a spot close to the bar. She headed for the door and looked around, noticing there weren't very many cars in the parking lot.

She stopped and searched for Camilo's truck, and when she didn't see it, her stomach did a flip. At first she assumed that he hadn't waited for her, but when she turned the corner of the building, she spotted it. Kim glanced at her watch, which read six twenty-two, and hurried into the building.

"Sorry; I got lost," she said when she found Camilo sitting at a high table near the back of the bar.

"It's okay, Kim. I am glad you are here. I was worried that you were not going to come and now that I see you, I am happy." He smiled as he stood up to pull a stool out for her.

Kim glanced around at the tiny wine bar. It bore a remarkable resemblance to Buglios back home. She had expected the décor to have the usual flavor of the local Mexican heritage, but that wasn't the case. The walls were painted a deep henna, and the woodwork was a dark, rich mahogany that matched the tables in the middle of the room. The perimeter consisted of large mahogany booths with rich, plush brown cushions. The artwork on the wall was an eclectic assortment of watercolors and oil paintings, some of them landscapes, some abstract.

"Nice place," she said and looked at Camilo as she struggled to lift herself onto the chair. "Short legs," she said with a laugh. "I got lost," she said again.

"Yes, you said that already," he said and smiled.

"I missed my turn, and no, I was not going to stand you up."

"You look nice," he said and winked at her.

"Thank you." Kim felt her face warm. "You look nice as well." The waitress came over and Kim hesitated before ordering. "I think I'll have a glass of the house chardonnay," she said without looking at her.

Camilo looked strikingly handsome in a black rather tight short-sleeved golf shirt. The shirt conformed around his broad shoulders and enhanced his muscular arms. "We match," she continued, as she pointed to her dress and then to his shirt. "I like black." She smiled.

Camilo stopped the waitress before she left the table. "We can order a bottle, Kim. I like chardonnay also. Let's take a look at the wine list. My treat. Is that how you say it?"

Kim smiled at him. "Yes, that is how you say it, but you don't have to buy. We can go dutch."

"Dutch?" Camilo cocked his head to the side and narrowed his eyes.

The waitress was getting impatient, so Kim told her to give them a few minutes. "Dutch is slang; it means we each will pay for our own," she explained.

"Oh, no!" Camilo exclaimed. "I asked you, so I pay. That is the way I do things. Let's order a nice bottle of char-

donnay. I will show you some of my favorites. We don't
have to settle on the house wine," he said and smiled.

Kim started laughing. "You sound like my friend Connie. She gives me a hard time when I order house wine,
but I don't have the budget that she does. Besides, we
don't have to order white. You're already drinking red,"
she said and pointed to his glass.

"That is okay. I can switch. I will cleanse my palate."

"Wow, listen to you, the wine connoisseur!"

Camilo picked up the wine list and turned to the
whites. "This one is one of my favorites," he said as he
pointed to the fourth selection on the list.

"If you buy, you are not spending that much on me!
Forty-eight dollars?"

"Kim, don't worry. Yes, we are ordering this one. You
will like it." He motioned to the waitress and ordered the
wine when she came to the table.

Kim was anxious to get to know Camilo. She was
intrigued about where he came from, his family life, and
how he could afford to order a forty-eight-dollar bottle
of wine.

"By the way, I usually don't wear black," he explained.
"It's not a good color in the heat. But I guess it must be
fate that I wear black tonight with you." He smiled at Kim
and gave her a wink.

Kim looked down at her hands for a minute and then
back at Camilo. "Well, I'm not sure that fate has anything
to do with it. I think black must be the second most common color of attire worn by Americans. I'm sure that it
comes in at a close second, right behind white." Kim was

not sure what the wink meant, but she wanted to make sure that he knew that it wasn't fate. It was nothing more than a coincidence.

The waitress brought over the bottle of wine and opened it as the two watched. She poured a small sample into Camilo's glass and waited for him to taste it. He picked the glass up and started to swirl it. "I am just looking for the legs," he said to Kim.

"I'm not sure if you should be looking for legs in a white wine," she answered back.

"Ah, just testing your wine knowledge," he said with a smile. He lifted the glass to his lips and took a sip. "Very good," he told the waitress. She filled his glass, then Kim's, and set the bottle in the ice-filled bucket stand she had brought to the table.

"A toast," Camilo said and lifted his glass. "A toast to new friends."

"To new friends," Kim responded. She lifted her glass to his and the sound of the clank rang out in the quiet bar. "So, Camilo," she continued, "tell me about yourself. Where are you from? Where is your family? And why are you wasting your night on an old broad who's probably twice your age?" Kim took a sip of her wine. "Boy is this good!" she continued before Camilo could answer. "I've become so accustomed to house wine and haven't tasted anything this good in a long, long time."

"I am glad to please you. I knew you would like it."

"Well, enough about the wine. I want to know more about you. And why do you know so much about wine? It's not a typical thing a man of your heritage and occupation would know about, is it?" As soon as the words came out of her mouth, she regretted them. It sounded so prejudiced. Camilo's response confirmed her fear.

"A man of my heritage? Kim, you don't know anything about me."

"I'm so sorry, Camilo. That sounded bad, I know. That's not really what I meant to say. I'm sorry. I didn't mean to offend you."

"No offense taken," he said with a slow smile. "I am teasing you. I am not the stereotypical Mexican migrant worker," he said and smiled again at her uneasiness. "Really, it's okay, Kim. Don't worry; you did not offend me. My taste comes from my *madre*. She acquired expensive taste after she experienced the money that my father made."

"And what was that from?" Kim asked, intrigued.

"Oh, a family business, but that is long ago, so no more I think about it."

"So where was this family business?" Kim leaned closer to Camilo, catching a hint of musk. She stared at him as he spoke, thinking how handsome he was.

"I am from an area west of Matamoros, if that is what you are asking me," he answered. "It's across the border from Brownsville. That is where I was born, grew up, and still go home to. Right now I live in America, but I still have a small *casa*—excuse me," he clarified, "my home on the beach."

"*Casa*; I know what that means. I know *pequeño* Spanish." She put her forefinger and thumb together to show a small amount. "But I recognize some words." She smiled.

"So tell me about your house on the beach; it sounds lovely."

"It was my family home for many years. After my *madre* died, I wanted to keep it and I go there whenever I can. What do you Americans call it—escape?"

"Yes, escape. That's sort of what I am doing in Texas: escaping."

"Yes, about you, Kim, as I told you, I heard about you at the park. I know you are not married anymore. Is this a sudden thing?"

"Not so fast Camilo; we were talking about you, remember?" Kim smiled at him, feeling herself becoming more relaxed. She listened to Camilo's deep, soft voice, which was both soothing and mesmerizing, lulling her into a state of calmness.

"Not that there is much to tell," he said. "You see what you get." His hands framed his face and he smiled.

"What kind of business was your family in?" Kim asked.

"Not necessarily one business. My father had all kinds of business deals going everywhere. Now tell me, are you doing okay, Kim?" She could tell Camilo wanted to change the subject and divert attention away from his family.

"Yes, I'm doing okay, if you are asking me about my divorce. It was a long time coming; we didn't have much of a marriage, anyway. So it probably wasn't as painful as I suppose it could have been. It just was finalized before I came down here, so that is why I decided to take a hiatus from life."

"And I am glad you did." He smiled back at her.

Finishing off the bottle of wine, they chatted about the senior communities in Texas and how the presence of the winter Texans boosted the economy in south Texas. In the past, many retirees made Florida or Arizona their winter home. But in recent years, Texas had become a popular choice. Kim thought it was because the weather was relatively mild, but Camilo said he thought it was because it was more affordable than other areas.

Kim told him that her grandmother moved to Texas, which is how her mom and dad fell in love with the idea of retiring here. But when her grandmother lived here, south Texas looked a lot different.

"When we would visit during our spring break," she explained, "Padre Island had only one restaurant on it; the rest was undeveloped beach. When I first came back here as an adult, I was amazed at how much it had grown. I was surprised to see all the spring breakers descending on the place."

She purposely left out telling Camilo about the time she lived in Texas when she was eighteen. Kim looked down at her watch and realized how late it was. "I have to go. My parents will be worried."

"Oh, please; do you have to leave so soon?" Camilo coaxed. "I am just getting to know you."

"Sorry. I really must go. Two glasses of wine is all I need when trying to maneuver these crazy streets." Kim got up from her seat and waived to the waitress for the check.

"No. My treat, remember?" Camilo caught her arm and pulled it down. She turned to him and smiled.

"No Camilo, it's my treat. You have saved me from the retirement folks for a few hours and I owe you for the serious adult conversation. Thank you."

"Serious, huh?" Camilo showed his brilliant white teeth. A flashback came to Kim for a split second.

"I still don't know much about you and I want to know more. Perhaps I can buy next time, then?" he asked and smiled again at her.

"Maybe." Kim caught the waitress's eye and motioned for her to bring over the bill. When she did, Kim pulled out her credit card and handed it to her. "You are a very nice man, Camilo, but really, don't you want to spend time with young women your own age? I must be at least thirteen years older than you."

"Kim, you are a beautiful woman. You must forget about age. You are stunning, intriguing, and funny, and I like you." He touched her arm when she reached for her card. She stopped a moment and looked into his eyes. A flutter came over her as she peered into the deep chocolate pools. Without knowing it, she moved toward him, then caught herself, but not before he reached for a strand of her hair and brushed his finger against the side of her cheek. Kim blushed as she looked down at the table and signed the bill.

"Again?" Camilo whispered.

"Again," Kim replied over her shoulder as she walked to the front of the bar.

"Wait, Kim!" Camilo shouted. "Can I have your phone number?"

Kim walked back toward Camilo. "I don't know," she said smiling. "That's kind of forward of you, isn't it?" Then she took a piece of paper and pen from her purse, wrote down her number, and handed it to him. "I don't give that out to just anyone," she told him and gave him another smile then headed back toward the door. When she got to the van, she unlocked the door and slipped into the driver's seat. As soon as she did, she let out a sigh and gripped the wheel.

CHAPTER FOURTEEN

Kim decided to forego her usual morning workout to call Connie and fill her in on the events of the night before. And since she hadn't talked to Connie for a few days, she needed to find out what she was up to and make sure she was not in any kind of trouble. Most of all, she wanted to know more about her Don and how Zen was working in her life.

The phone rang once, then twice. Kim waited through two more rings and was just about to hang up when a groggy voice answered.

"What?"

"Hello?" Kim said. *Wow, Connie must have had on hell of a night,* Kim thought. Then she heard the voice respond.

"Hello," it said. It was not Connie at all. Kim glanced at the clock and suddenly realized it was six o'clock in the morning in San Diego.

"Oh, my God; I'm sorry. I must have dialed the wrong number." *Wait a minute, I have Connie on speed dial,* she thought. *How could I have gotten the wrong number?*

"Who are you looking for?" the voice interrupted.

"I was actually calling my friend. Again, I am sorry," Kim said.

"Is her name Connie?"

"Yes . . . is this her phone?" Kim asked, confused.

"Just a minute," the voice said.

A few seconds later, Kim heard Connie's husky voice. "Hello? Who is this?" Connie asked.

"Sorry, honey. I didn't realize it was so early out in California. I forgot about the time difference. Who answered your phone?" Kim could hear heavy breathing coming from Connie's end of the line, and then she heard a chuckle and Connie's giggle. "I must be interrupting something. I'll just hang up," Kim said.

"Wait, it's okay; just a minute," Connie responded. There was a muffled conversation between her and her male companion as Kim waited.

"Yes; honey." Connie was back on the line.

"Well then, was that Don?"

"No, that was Juan."

"Who is Juan and what happened to Don? Connie, what trouble have you gotten yourself into? Are you being safe?"

"I'm fine. Quit worrying about me."

"And Don, what happened to him?"

"Oh, he was good for a few lessons, yoga and otherwise," Connie said as she chuckled. "Now I have Juan. I am having so much fun. California men are gorgeous."

"It sounds like you are. Are the condoms all gone?"

"You know what? They supply their own out here, so I'm good," Connie said, with a slight sneer in her voice.

"Really, I *am* fine. Stop worrying so much, Kim. Now, tell me; how is that hunk of a Mexican man you are seeing?"

Kim walked out onto the porch to scan the street, subconsciously looking for Camilo before she answered. "Well, I would not call it seeing him, but I did have a great time last night with a gorgeous Hispanic fellow." Not spotting anyone, Kim stepped back into the house and continued telling Connie about her evening the night before.

Jack and Nita were out, so she was free to talk. She didn't need her parents hearing her fantasies about their Mexican groundskeeper. "He asked me if I wanted to go out again, and I think I answered yes."

"What do you mean you think? Yes or no? Are you going to see him again?"

"Yes, I am but I'm going to be cautious. He's a youngster, Connie. I'm old enough to be his mother. Even though he doesn't seem to mind, I think it's kind of weird."

"Oh, who cares? Live a little before you head back to your humdrum life in North Carolina. I know you. You'll just settle into your own little routine once you go back to the real world. And who knows if you will ever find another man to have fun with—no strings attached?"

"Remember, I'm not like you, Connie. I will have fun, but I'm not going to jump into bed with just any man I lay my sights on."

"Ouch, that hurts," Connie quickly said. "I live my life the way I want to, and you live yours the way you want. That's why we love each other so much. We give each other the extensions in our lives that we both need."

"Wow, is that the Zen talking? Because that is so profound of you. I'm sorry. I didn't mean to offend you. I do love you, you know. You're a dear friend, and a part of me admires you for your unconventional behavior. It's just not me." Suddenly, Kim's thoughts shot back to years before and her affair with Mark. Maybe she was more like Connie than she thought, or maybe her indiscretions when she was a young girl made her so ashamed that she not only squelched the memories but also allowed herself only to live a subdued and quiet love life.

"Kim!"

Kim heard a shrill scream from behind the house. She stepped outside to see her mom running through the yards.

"Kimberly!" Nita screamed again.

Kim stepped off the porch and ran toward her, her phone still in her hand and Connie still on the line. "Mom, what is it?" Kim put her hands on her mom's shoulders when she reached her.

"It's your dad. They have taken him to the hospital . . . by ambulance," Nita said, gasping for air.

"Connie, I'll have to call you back. Something's wrong with my dad."

—•••—

Connie wrapped the sheet tighter around her body and clicked her phone shut. She stood looking at it for a moment, worrying about her friend.

"What's wrong?" Juan asked, stepping up behind her and kissed her on the neck. He slipped his hand under the sheet and caressed her lower back. When she turned around to face him, the sheet fell to the floor and he picked her up and carried her back to the bedroom.

"Wait," Connie said with a laugh. "I need to get some water." Juan frowned and set her back down on the floor and kissed her neck again. She picked up the sheet and headed for the kitchen, twisting the ends of the sheet over her chest, a long train following her.

"Don't be too long," Juan called to her.

As Connie walked past the patio door, she spotted the shirt she had worn the night before lying on the floor next to the one Juan must have worn. She bent down to pick it up, and when she did, she could hear the sound of the waves crashing against the shore. She turned to look out the window. *What a great view. I wonder where I am?* She dropped the sheet as she turned away from the window, revealing her fully naked body. Juan came around the corner and whistled as she pulled his white cotton shirt over her head. She laughed at him, then walked to the kitchen.

Connie nearly knocked over one of the empty wine bottles sitting on the counter as she searched the cupboards for a glass. *Three bottles of wine between us?* Connie winced at the thought. She poured herself some water from the pitcher in the refrigerator and scanned the small kitchen. It was small, but had an amazingly exquisite California-style motif, just like the rest of the condos and was right on the beach, which made it that much more wonderful.

She walked over to the window, saw the ocean straight ahead, and then looked down at the boardwalk, which was empty this time of the morning. She took another gulp of water, ran her tongue across her teeth, and cringed at what felt like sandpaper.

CHAPTER FIFTEEN

The thought of anything happening to her dad was more than Kim could bear. She usually allowed herself only the briefest thoughts about the possibility that one day he would be gone. Jack Whitman had not been sick a day in his life, or so he loved to say. But she always knew health issues would be inevitable.

"I don't need a doctor," he would tell her when she inquired about his health. So often co-workers would talk about their elderly parents' medical conditions, and sometimes the office would grieve over the loss of an employee's parent. The customary flowers were sent and sometimes Kim would attend the funeral. When she did, she would think about her own parents and their mortality. She spent so little time with them, but to have them gone would be unbearable.

Purely by accident, Kim had discovered that Jack was dealing with some health issues and visited the doctor more times than he cared to admit. Eight months prior, Jack's eyesight began to deteriorate, and the doctor's diagnosis revealed that he had diabetes. Jack kept it under control with diet and exercise, so Kim was surprised that somehow he was experiencing complications and needed an ambulance.

Kim sat in the waiting room of the Harlingen General Hospital, sipping the latest of the four coffees she had purchased at the vending machine just down the hall. An hour earlier, she had driven the minivan, Nita in the passenger seat, following the ambulance that carried Jack. Kim wanted her mom to ride with him in the ambulance, but Nita insisted she drive Kim to the hospital. "No, Mom," she had told Nita. "If you won't ride with him, at least let me drive. You shouldn't be driving right now."

Kim remembered back to a few days earlier. Her mom had been unusually quiet. Maybe she had been worried about Jack's health. Jack could hide his discomfort from Kim and the rest of the world, but not from Nita. She would surely pick up on any problems he was having.

"Kim."

A voice came from the distance. Kim looked up to find an attractive young doctor walking toward her. *Boy, do they make them handsome here,* she thought to herself. *Kim, shame on you. Your dad is sick and this is what you're thinking about?*

"Are you Kim?" the doctor continued.

"Yes, I am. Are you Jack Whitman's doctor?" Kim stood up as the doctor approached, looking up to meet his eyes.

"I'm Dr. Lopez," he said as he extended his hand toward her. "Your mom wanted me to come out and talk to you. She is in with your dad while he is resting. Do you want to sit down?" He motioned toward the chair.

"Do I need to?" Kim hesitated before she cleared her

throat. "He's okay, right?" She sat back down while Dr. Lopez continued to stand in front of her.

"We'll have to do some more tests to come to a final conclusion, but for now, I'm afraid we think it's cancer."

Way to sock it right to me, she thought. Her hands started to shake. *The C word. It can't be,* she reasoned. Kim's throat began to tighten and tears welled in her eyes. *I am not going to cry in front of this doctor.*

"Your dad is a tough man. His pain threshold must be very high." Dr. Lopez sat down next to her on the baby blue seventies-looking couch she had made her home for the last hour. "Given the MRI we just completed, it looks like the cancer is in his back. He said he had been having back problems over the past several weeks, but didn't want to worry anyone. Today the pain reached a point where it was excruciating, which is why he collapsed and needed an ambulance."

"In his back? That doesn't sound too good." Kim could feel the tears in her eyes again as the reality of it all began to set in.

"We aren't going to jump to conclusions until we get all the results back from the blood and other tests," he said, patting her hand, reaching over to the side table and pulling a tissue from a box. "Here," he said, handing it to her and standing up. "You can come and see him now if you'd like. I'll show you the way."

Kim stood up, not sure if she was ready to see her dad and face the fact that her future might not include him. She poured out the half-empty cup of coffee in a water fountain as she made her way down the white sterile hallway, her flip-flops slapping on the shiny linoleum floor.

She cautiously followed ten steps behind Dr. Lopez as they entered room 212. Her dad was lying in the bed, her mom sitting at his side giving him something to drink. Kim's heart sank at the sight of her once vibrant dad brought now to this state.

"Hi, Dad," she said softly. "How are you feeling?" She went over to the bed and leaned down to give him a hug.

"I'm just fine," he said. "Don't worry about me. I'll be all right," he said as he smiled up at her, reaching for her hand and squeezing it.

"The doctor talked to me . . . they think . . . you have cancer," she said, struggling with the words as she sat down next to Nita. She noticed her mom softly crying as she gave Jack sips of water. The calmness she saw in her earlier had disappeared.

She put her arm around her and hugged her shoulders. When she did, she felt her mom sink forward. "I am here. I'll take care of you guys," she assured them. Her earlier tears were gone. She needed to be strong now for her parents. *It's funny how life takes you down certain paths.* If it wasn't for her newly finalized divorce, she would not have been there—when the two of them needed her most.

CHAPTER SIXTEEN

Jack spent the day getting pricked and prodded by one nurse after another and never once did he complain. He laughed and joked with each of them, telling each that the one before had done a better job than the last. "I'm going to rate how well you can find my vein and then I'm going to determine which of you gave me the biggest bruises," he'd say. The laughter in his voice told the nurses he was only teasing, so they smiled and joked with him right back.

Kim stayed at the hospital until after five that evening. She tried to convince Nita to come home with her, but she would have none of it. She told Kim she wanted to stay with Jack until he fell asleep.

"Are you sure you won't come home with me, Mom?" Kim asked one more time before she left the room. "They're not going to know anything until morning, anyway."

"No, I'm going to stay here. I asked the nurses and they said they would bring in a cot for me so I can spend the night."

What a true, old-fashioned love they shared, Kim

thought. *You don't see that kind of devotion these days.* And then she thought of her own ruined marriage.

Kim left her parents behind in the hospital, headed for the parking lot, got into the minivan, and let out a sigh as she buckled up her seat belt. The thought of what was to come in the months ahead hit her. She folded her arms over the steering wheel, put her head down, and started to cry.

The events of the past several months, including what occurred that day, seemed to well up inside of her and all of a sudden, she couldn't keep it in any longer. She sobbed uncontrollably. After a few minutes she lifted her head up. "Enough of that," she said out loud. She looked in the rearview mirror and wiped away the mascara from under her eyes. "It's going to be fine," she assured herself.

As she drove back to the retirement park, Kim pulled out her cell phone and saw she had missed nine calls, all of them from Connie.

"They think my dad has cancer," she blurted out when Connie answered the phone.

"What?" Connie exclaimed on the other end.

"He collapsed today at the recreation hall from the excruciating pain in his back," Kim explained. "They think that's where the cancer is. They've been running tests all day and tomorrow they're going to do another MRI to confirm their diagnosis."

"Oh, honey! How are you doing?" Connie's voice was soft.

"I'm just glad I was here when they got the news," Kim said. She sniffed and wiped her finger across the bottom of her nose. "Enough talk about that. What were we talking about when I had to leave? Oh yes, my meeting with Camilo."

"We don't have to talk about that now; it can wait."

"No, that's okay. I need a diversion. I want to think about something else." The memory of the night before made Kim smile, and she filled Connie in on everything, from her late arrival, to their matching outfits, to the bottle of chardonnay.

"I can't believe I'm feeling this way about a man—a boy, really," Kim said and laughed.

"Don't think of his age or yours," Connie once again advised her.

"I know I shouldn't, but really . . ."

"Really what?" Connie interrupted.

Kim knew she would not win this argument, so she didn't try. "Okay; I should enjoy it, right? Enjoy the attention he is giving me?" Kim said and laughed again. "You know what?" She paused. "I really am having fun, and he is so gorgeous and so nice. There has to be something wrong with him, right?"

"Quit analyzing it all," Connie scolded.

"I know, I know you're right," Kim said, and spotted the exit sign for the park. "Connie, I have to go now. I'm almost to my parents' home and I'm so tired. Sorry, but I really don't want to talk anymore."

"You go get some rest, honey." Connie's voice was soft. "I'll talk to you tomorrow."

Kim hung up the phone and noticed she had a missed call and a voice message. She held down the key on her phone until she connected to her voice mail. "One new message and five old messages," the voice said back to her. Then she hit two and soon heard Camilo's voice.

"Thank you for a very lovely evening." His voice was gentle and quiet. "Please, I hope we can see each other again, Kim."

Kim smiled to herself and clicked the phone shut. She neared the Sunbeam RV Park sign and turned into the driveway. "Please, God. Let my dad be okay," she suddenly said out loud. "Please . . ."

CHAPTER SEVENTEEN

Jack was discharged from the hospital two days later. The doctors and nurses marveled at his good spirits and humor. "With that state of mind, I'm sure you will pull through this with flying colors," one of the nurses told him. Kim laughed when she heard this from Nita. Her fear about losing her dad had subsided a bit over those two days. The doctors had determined the cancer hadn't spread yet and they explained that there were some new aggressive treatments available. She was optimistic and decided to remain hopeful, both for her own sake and to support her parents. She needed to remain strong for them, so she was going to at least project a positive attitude.

"Kim, do you want to go over to the hall with me?" Jack said, coming out of the back bedroom and buttoning his shirt. He had slept later than usual, so he was running behind his usual morning schedule. Nita had left earlier to go to the office. She needed to keep her mind on something, she told Kim after Kim had raised an eyebrow, questioning her when she announced where she was going. Nita told her there was no use sitting around worrying and work was the best thing she could think of.

Kim had waited in the kitchen all morning for Jack to wake up. She had poured a cup of coffee, sat in his chair, drank the coffee, poured another cup, and then tiptoed to the bedroom door to listen to make sure he was still breathing. When she heard his deep, low breaths, she sat back down, had another cup of coffee, and waited for what seemed like an eternity until she finally heard him fumbling around in the next room.

"I need to go and see if the shuffleboard is going okay," Jack continued.

"Dad, don't you think you should rest more? You don't need to be gallivanting all over the place."

"Nonsense," he quipped. "I'm not an invalid, Kim."

She realized she had upset him, so she didn't push it.

"Okay, Dad," she said and quickly got up to join him. "Yes, I'd love to go with you. Let me grab my jacket." The weather that day had turned unseasonably chilly, even though it was still about fifty degrees warmer than back home in North Carolina.

"You're always cold," Jack said as he put his arm around her. The feel of his fingers on her shoulders brought her back to when she was a little girl, and she felt like she was twelve again. *I can't lose him,* she thought and then turned and smiled as she lightly punched his arm and headed toward the door.

When they arrived at the hall, Kim stepped inside ahead of Jack. The room was buzzing with laughter and talking. There was a swarm of activity throughout the entire space. Jack immediately headed to the far end of the hall where a group of men were carrying on what looked like a heated discussion.

She watched as he slowly made his way over to them. He took a step, then shuffled his feet, stopped, and took another step, which he followed with another shuffle. She wanted to go to his aid and hold his arm to make sure he didn't fall, but she forced herself to hold back. *It would only embarrass him,* she thought. *What did he tell me earlier? He is not an invalid.*

When Jack reached his destination, Kim looked around the room, scanning to see who she was going to talk to now that her dad was occupied with what she imagined was a very important shuffleboard meeting. She decided that she needed another cup of coffee, so she headed for the counter where the pot sat. As she held the white Styrofoam cup under the silver coffee cylinder's spout, she glanced over to the kitchen. Suddenly, she lost her concentration and let the coffee flow over the cup. She jumped when the hot liquid spilled on her hand. She instinctively licked her fingers and grabbed for a napkin.

Her distraction was the handsome young man she had enjoyed a glass of wine with the night before. Camilo was talking with the cook, intently giving him instructions, gesturing with his hands as he spoke. She was embarrassed at spilling the coffee, and her face flushed. *I'm probably as red as the apple sitting on the counter next to the cups,* she thought.

She poured some of her coffee out, put cream in it, stirred it, and started to walk toward Camilo. When she got closer, she could hear his words spoken in a soft, low voice. He smiled at the cook in between sentences. "*Si usted podría embalarlos todos en las cajas para su almuerzo,*" she heard him say. Camilo turned his head toward her when he saw her coming, stopped mid-sentence, and then smiled. He wore a white, crisp, long-sleeved shirt and was a stark contradiction to the man he was talking to, with his greased-splattered apron and toothless smile. She wondered what he was doing in the kitchen, since he oversaw the crew that took care of the grounds.

"Hi," he said. He came through the kitchen door and walked up to her, and put his hand on her shoulder. "How is your *padre*?" he inquired.

"He's better. He's right over there." Kim pointed in Jack's direction. She noticed he was sitting on a chair in the middle of the group. The rest of the men were standing around him and it appeared as if he were holding court; their complete attention was on him.

"He just couldn't stay away," she continued. "He needed to make sure his shuffleboard league didn't fall apart without him." She laughed. "With his state of mind, I have no doubt he'll be just fine. And you, what are you doing in the kitchen? Aren't you supposed to be outside with your men? You shouldn't be bothering the cooks, you know," she said with a smile. Camilo put his hands on his hips and smiled down at her.

"What are you smiling at?" she said, beginning to flush again.

"You are very beautiful, you know that?" Kim could feel a wave of crimson come across her face. "I am here to get my men some lunch," Camilo continued. "I told them I would buy today so they should not pack their noon meals. I arranged to have the cook make them a special lunch. Tamales." He took one hand off his hip and caught a strand of her hair between his fingers.

It was the same intimate gesture from the night before and his boldness made Kim suddenly back away. She looked around the room nervously, thinking that everyone's eyes had to be on them. "Sorry, Kim. I did not mean to offend you," Camilo said. His smile vanished as he looked down at her with a puzzled look.

"Oh, no; it's okay," she said, managing a quick smile then turning her gaze away from him. She glanced over in Jack's direction.

"Kim," Camilo said and put his hand on her shoulder. "Can I take you out to dinner?" She turned back and looked up at him. Camilo raised his eyebrows, a broad smile again on his face.

"Um, well . . . I'm not sure. I'll have to check on my dad, see what they are doing . . . I want to make sure he and my mom will be okay," she stammered.

"I will call you later after you talk to them."

"Okay," she said.

"I will call you," he said again. "Now I must get the lunch for my workers. I will talk to you later." He smiled and winked at her before he went back into the kitchen. She watched him and then, looking around, noticed several glances following him, mostly from the ladies. *He is a strikingly handsome man. No wonder he draws the attention he does*, Kim mused. She poured herself another cup of coffee and walked over to where her dad was sitting.

"He gave us quite a scare," Sam Corley said as she walked to the middle of the group and stood behind Jack.

Bob Reardon chimed in. "We don't like to hear ambulances in the park. They scare us old folks. We wonder which friend is in trouble and we all start to worry, but when we heard it was Jack, we were surprised. What could possibly happen to this old coot? He's too ornery to be sick." He laughed and turned toward Jack, who was also laughing.

"Watch who you're calling an old coot," he said.

"Is the shuffleboard league okay?" She looked down at Jack.

"Yes," he said. "They got along just fine without me."

"But we need you, Jack, so don't go getting sick on us again," Sam said. The rest of the group nodded in agreement.

"You can't get rid of me that easy," Jack told them. "I'll be around to boss you old coots for a long time." He laughed.

Later that day, Kim decided to go back to the library to finish her research on Mark. She waited for her mom to get back before she left. Jack was taking a nap and she didn't want to leave him alone. "Mom, can I use the car again this afternoon?" she asked Nita when she walked in the door. "I'd like to do some Christmas shopping," she half lied. She did want to stop by the mall, but she didn't want to tell her mom that she was going to the library again. She wanted to avoid any questions about what she was doing there.

"Don't buy us anything. Just you being here is enough of a gift," Nita said as she walked to the back room to check on Jack. She opened the door enough to see that he was still sleeping.

Kim stood watching her, stunned by the words that had just come out of her mom's mouth.

"I don't know if we'll do much for Christmas," she

said as she came back into the room and sat down in her chair. She sighed and closed her eyes. Kim sat at the table just a few feet from her. They sat in silence for a minute before Kim spoke. "Dad's going to be fine, Mom," she reassured Nita. Then she saw the tears in Nita's eyes. Kim got up and walked to her mom and leaned down to give her a hug. "Mom, they caught it in time. The doctors said with this treatment, he should get through this," she assured her again.

"I don't know what I'm going to be able to do without him," she said so softly that Kim could hardly hear her. "We have been married for almost fifty years. I don't want to be on this earth without him." She lifted her hand to her mouth and sobbed into the tissue she held.

"Mom," Kim said as she stood up. "You'll be able to enjoy the next fifty with him."

"Well, I'm not sure about another fifty. We will surely be tired and gone by then," Nita said. She sniffled, then looked up at Kim. "Thanks, Kimberly, for being here. I appreciate the support and comfort you've given me the last couple of days. I am just sorry you have to spend your vacation caring for us. You make sure you do something for yourself." Nita grabbed a fresh tissue from a box on the table next to her.

"Don't worry, Mom. Just relaxing in the sun is enough for me." Kim returned to the chair by the table. "Besides, I *am* doing something fun. I'm going to have dinner with Camilo."

"Is this going to be a date this time?" Nita asked.

"Maybe so. He said he was going to call me, but I wanted to make sure that everything was okay with you and Dad, so I didn't give him a definite answer." Now it was Nita who comforted her daughter. She got up from the chair and walked around the table. Kim stood up to accept the hug. Kim felt strange at the unfamiliar exchange between mother and daughter.

"Kim, go enjoy yourself and have fun. Alex is a thing of the past now." Nita put her hands on Kim's shoulders. "You said yourself that your marriage was done a long time ago. It's not too soon to move on with your life."

"Thanks, Mom. It does feel nice to have someone pay attention to me. But he's so young!" Kim moved away from her mom and sat down. She picked up a piece of paper that lay on the table and started tearing it into small pieces.

"I know I'm making you uncomfortable. We don't usually have these conversations, but I need to let you know that I'm proud of you and I want you to be happy. I may not always show it, but I do love you. I hope you know that." Kim nodded, but did not look up from the piece of paper she had in her hand. "And don't worry about his age," Nita continued. "Age is only a number. Isn't that what they say?" Nita smiled at her daughter.

"Will the two of you be okay?" Kim asked, putting the paper down.

"We'll be just fine. Go and have fun."

It had been just a week since she had arrived in Texas, and a lot had happened. She had experienced a newfound crush, her dad's health worried her, and her mom's affection surprised her. Life for Kim had been undeniably and unexpectedly altered.

CHAPTER EIGHTEEN

Kim spent that afternoon in the library again. She stopped by the mall on her way to pick up a few things for her parents. Despite what her mom had said, she still wanted to buy presents. After all, what would Christmas be without exchanging a few gifts?

She headed up the stairs and past the resource desk to the microfiche machine she had used the other day. This time, she did not fumble around; she started the machine up right away and when she heard the humming sound, she reached into her purse for the piece of paper with the document number. When she found it, she went into the file cabinet room to retrieve the same envelope she had had the previous day.

She inserted the film into the tray and searched for the spot where she had left off. "Trouble in Paradise" appeared on the screen. Once again, Kim started reading about Mark Carson's downward-spiraling life and the ever-increasing troubled state he was in. The article continued, detailing his business dealings, his broken marriage, his new marriage, and his womanizing tendencies.

Apparently, he was known to have had more than one

girl on the side while married first to Allison and then to Maite. Kim stopped scrolling and sat back, thinking about her affair with Mark. She realized she had not been the only mistress he had had, and how naïve and stupid she had been, not only because of the affair, but also because it appeared that she had been on the sidelines of some suspicious activity that Mark had been involved with.

Kim jumped when her phone started ringing and quickly dug in her purse to silence it before it disturbed the people around her. When she grabbed it, she saw an unfamiliar number come across the screen. She hesitated for a moment, realized it had to be Camilo, and shut it off anyway. *I would rather call him back later,* she thought.

She turned her attention back to the article and read further about Mark's construction activities and how he and Carlos's company never finished any project that he had bid on. The journalist's interviews uncovered the fact that Mark and his partner were too inexperienced to see an entire project through to completion. This meant that they accumulated a pile of unpaid bills, and Mark and Carlos's debt mounted. In short, they owed a huge amount of money to a lot of people who got increasingly impatient with Carlos and Associates Construction Company.

Kim came to a section of the article where Jake Michaels had interviewed Alison. She had become more and more frustrated with Mark's money problems and with his frequent absences. She thought he was having an affair and when she confronted him, he feverously denied it, promising her that he would change and would spend more time with her. Things got better, but only for a while. It wasn't long before Mark started staying out late again, frequently not coming home at all.

Jake Michaels described how Alison started to secretly follow Mark, wanting to find out for herself what he had been up to. What she discovered, she didn't want any part of, so she decided to leave. She had found out that Mark had used the candle company and his partnership in the construction company as a front for illegal drug trafficking from Mexico.

The ever-changing world of Mark Carson evolved into a life of drugs and deceit. Jake Michaels wrote about Mexican kingpins and the ever-increasing drug trafficking that had developed across the Mexican and Texas borders. Mark used the connections he had in Mexico through the candle factory to establish himself as a drug trafficker for the kingpins.

As his mounting money troubles grew, Mark was forced to turn to yet another scheme to generate income. Ironically, his partnership in Carlos and Associates began so he could fuel his diminishing candle company, which then led him to use M&A Chandler Company to meet the increasing debt that the construction company was taking on.

Kim immersed herself further into the story, scrolling from one page to the next. In the 1970s and '80s, the drug trafficking between Mexico and Texas had increased, due to the fact that the United States had shut down common drug corridors between the Caribbean and the United States. Drug traffickers in Mexico picked up the slack, crossing the border to get drugs into the United States.

The lax laws and growing corruption in Mexico allowed for easy transportation into the States. Smuggling in Mexico, according to the article, had a long history dating back to the 1800s. It started with alcohol and small contraband, moving to marijuana. Evidently, it became big business with the introduction of cocaine.

When Mark started the candle company in Texas, he found a paraffin wax supplier in Mexico that provided the essential material he needed to make candles at a much lower price than he could get anywhere in the United States. He used this supplier, based in Monterey, Mexico, on a regular basis for over two years. It wasn't long before Mark created a strong relationship with the owner of the company, Roberto Martinez. Roberto shipped a raw form of paraffin wax to the Mexican border town of Reynosa, where Mark would pick it up.

When he first started the company, Mark picked up shipments at least once every other week. As the candle business slowed down, Mark told Roberto he only needed supplies every other month and that he was concentrating more on his newly formed construction company. When the money problems started with Carlos and Associates, Mark contacted Roberto to have the wax shipped every other week again.

Kim's phone rang again and she scowled as she dug into her purse. She thought she had turned it off. She looked at the screen and saw Camilo's number again. *Boy, is he persistent,* she thought. Instead of hanging up, she whispered, "Hello?"

"Kim?"

"Yes," she whispered again. "Hold on a minute so I

can get to a place where I can talk." Kim turned off the machine, and hurried down the stairs and out the door to the sidewalk in front of the library, the sun blinding her as she walked outside. She quickly shaded her eyes and turned her back against the glare. "I'm here," she said.

Camilo started talking, but she wasn't listening; she was still thinking about Mark and his illegal activities. She wished she hadn't answered her phone, but since she had, she tried to focus her attention on what Camilo was saying.

"By the way, where are you?" he asked.

"Oh, just doing a little shopping," she said. Of course, it was a lie.

"Remember I call you for a dinner date?" There was that subtle broken English she found so attractive.

"Yes, I remember," Kim answered. "But I didn't think it was going to be so soon."

"How about tonight?" he asked.

"Wow, you are pushy, aren't you?" she teased.

"Not pushy. I just know what I want."

Kim paused a moment before answering. "Yes, I would love to have dinner with you tonight."

"Good, I will pick you up at six thirty and you are not going to drive. I will pick you up at your parents' house, *si*?"

"Yes, *si*, you have a deal. Six thirty it is." Kim flipped her phone shut and started to walk to the van but then stopped, turned toward the library, and went back inside. She looked at her watch; it was three thirty, so she had plenty of time to retrieve the article again and print it.

Kim walked back up the stairs and sat in the chair she had occupied a few minutes earlier. She turned the machine back on and soon the article was on the screen in front of her. She looked at the typed information on the table for instructions on how to print the article. She touched the screen, and a box came up that gave her directions to deposit money. She searched in her purse, but only came up with four quarters and several pennies. It wasn't enough.

Kim walked to the reference desk to search for the woman with the thick Texas drawl. She wasn't at the desk. In her place sat a petite Hispanic girl who looked no more than sixteen years old. "Can you help me with the micro-fiche machine?" Kim asked. "I need to print out some articles, but I don't have enough change with me. Can I use a charge card?"

"Oh, yes. No one ever uses cash," she said and smiled. "There is an attachment on the back that allows you to use a credit card. Do you want me to show you?"

"No. I'll figure it out. Thank you." Kim walked back down the narrow aisles. Once at the machine, she found the credit card slot and pulled out her card. After inserting it, another screen popped up, prompting Kim to print the article. After following the instructions, Kim walked over to the printer and picked up four pages from the tray. Frustrated, she saw that it was only the first article, so she went back to the machine and printed out the rest. Fifteen dollars and forty-five minutes later, she was done. It was five o'clock when she got back to her car. She was going to be late again, but she didn't care. She had gotten what she wanted.

CHAPTER NINETEEN

That night, Kim found herself sitting across the table from Camilo in an elegant steakhouse that emanated intimacy and romance. There were even strolling violinists. The rich, dark wood of the walls, coupled with the candlelight glow and soft music wrapped Kim in warmth, putting her in a mellow, dreamy mood. The tapered candles sitting on the heavy red tablecloth flickered, cascading a dim light over Camilo's face, causing his eyes to sparkle.

Camilo had picked her up from her parents' home at six thirty sharp—not a minute late. She had chosen a black halter dress for the evening, showing just enough cleavage to be alluring, but not overly sexy. This was the dress Connie always approved of when they went out for an evening on the town. "You should show off those girls," she would say. Camilo wore a crisp burgundy dress shirt with a matching tie that had flecks of navy blue. Kim found the contrast of the colors against his dark skin striking.

When Camilo came to the door, Kim was still getting ready, so Jack and Nita entertained him while he waited. She could hear the three of them talking about work around the park and what needed to be done. Jack prompted him on certain projects he wanted to be sure were completed.

"Hey guys; he's off duty, not on working hours," Kim said as she entered the tiny living room.

She noticed the smiles on her parents' faces. She wasn't sure if they were happy because she was moving on with her life, or if they were thrilled that she was spending time with Camilo. She didn't care either way, because she planned on enjoying herself. After they said their goodbyes, they walked out the porch door and into the street. Kim looked for the white truck but instead sat a black Corvette convertible in the driveway.

"Wow, guess we're going in style," Kim said, laughing.

"This is my fun car," Camilo had said and opened the door for her. "The truck is for work." When they were both settled in, Camilo brought the Corvette's engine to life and drove them to the restaurant.

"Kim, you look beautiful tonight," Camilo said as he sat across from her at their table. He had complimented her at her parents, then again when he opened the restaurant door for her, and now as they sat at the table.

"Thank you, Camilo, but you are going to make me start to believe it."

"Kim, you don't think that you are beautiful? You are a very pretty lady. You had better believe that you are!"

"You know what I mean. It's just easier to be humble and not allow myself to be conceited."

"It is not . . . ah, how do you say . . . conceited? My mother always said that your first admirer should be yourself. Believe in who you are and let it shine to the whole world around you. If you are beautiful, let the world know."

"Okay, but in America, our parents taught us to be humble, not flaunt what you are or what you have. It's hard for me to accept compliments. It's just the way I grew up."

"Tell me where you grew up, Kim." Camilo reached across the table and took her hand. She paused for a minute, looking at their intertwined fingers.

"Um, well," she started, clearing her throat. "A long way from here." Kim looked up at Camilo.

"I make you nervous?"

"No, it's just been a long time. But enough of that . . . Where I grew up? Way up north. Have you ever heard of Augusta, Maine?"

Just then, the waiter came over to take their drink order. "I think you know what I would like," Kim said, looking up at Camilo again. "I have a passion for wine."

"Wine it will be. May I have the wine list?" Camilo saw the list under the waiter's arm and stretched out his hand.

"*Si*, señor, my pleasure. I will be back to fulfill your request." The waiter turned and walked to the next table.

"Fulfill your request!" Kim said and laughed. "I've not heard it said quite like that before. What fancy establishment have you brought me to?"

"Only the best for you, Kim."

"Okay, that's way too much flirting. You're again making me blush. So Augusta, Maine. Have you ever heard of it?"

"Maine, yes, but Augusta? I am not so familiar. It's cold up there, *si*?"

"Yes, very cold," Kim said. "You get used to it. Well, at least you do when you are young. That's why you see all the winter Texans flock to the south. They're escaping the cold. That's what my mom and dad did. They needed to be in the warmer climate. They love it down here, so much so that in the fall, they can't wait to pack up their northern home and venture south," Kim continued. "I don't know if you know, but my dad had a pizza restaurant when I was growing up. I spent my younger years working side by side with him. And when I say younger years, I mean I started when I was four years old."

"You are joking, right?" Camilo asked, cocking his head to the side.

"No, really. I mean it. I'm not kidding. My dad bought the pizza business when I was four years old. Part of his business plan was to make and sell pizzas to the local bars and grocery stores and he became very successful at it. That meant that the pizzas were made during the morning and delivered in the afternoon. Since I was not yet old enough to go to school, and since there were no daycare centers at that time, there was no place for me. My dad didn't think it was a problem. 'She can come and work with us,' he told my mom. So I was instructed in the art of pizza making. He taught me how to count out the pepperonis on each pizza," Kim said and laughed. "I got a penny a pizza!"

"Jack was a slave driver; I will give him a hard time."

"No, not a slave driver, but I used to tell him I could turn him into the child services people—not when I was four, of course. I learned this fact when I was older. He admired my spunk, so I didn't really get in trouble for disrespecting him."

The waiter came back to take their order. "Sorry, señor," Camilo said and looked at him. "We have been talking too much. Let's see; Kim, you like red or white?"

"I'll like whatever you pick."

"Then you will have to trust me," he said and winked at her. *This is just what I needed*, Kim thought. *It is a wonderful night.* "We will start with the Sterling Reserve cabernet. Okay with you?" he said and raised an eyebrow at Kim.

"Just fine with me. I see that you are knowledge-able in your wine selections. As you know, all I've been used to these days is the house wine vintage, so anything you order will be superb." She gave him a soft, seductive smile. She hadn't even had a sip of anything to drink, but she was already feeling giddy.

"I learned a lot from my dad," Kim continued after the waiter left with their order. "Most of who I am today, especially in my career, is what my dad taught me when I was a child. 'You can be anything you want to be,' he used to tell me, and I believed him. He also required us to finish anything we started. For example, I begged and begged him to let me take violin lessons when I was eleven years old."

"You are a violinist?" Camilo interrupted.

"Not anymore. Now listen," she kiddingly scolded him. "I'm telling you my story." Kim smiled at Camilo. "He finally said yes and I started the lessons, but I really wasn't very good, so I ended up hating it. Then I begged my dad to let me quit, but he said that I had started some-thing and that I needed to finish it. So I played until I was in eleventh grade and then I finally convinced him to let me give it up."

When the waiter came over with the wine, Kim stopped talking and they both watched as he opened their selec-tion and poured it into Camilo's glass. Camilo picked up the glass and swirled it around a few times. "Good legs," he said as he turned to the waiter and took a sip. "Very good," he said and set the glass down. The waiter finished pouring for Camilo and then poured a glass for Kim.

She took a sip. "Excellent," she said and toasted Camilo.

"So you are not a quitter?" Camilo asked after the waiter left the table.

"I try not to be," she answered. "Maybe that's why I stayed in my marriage so long. I felt like I'd be a failure if I let my marriage fall apart."

"But you said it was not much of a marriage anyway, and you shouldn't stay in a marriage like that. Don't consider yourself a quitter." He took another sip of wine.

Kim lifted her glass in a mock toasting gesture. "Actually, he cheated on me," she said.

Camilo scowled. "He what?"

"Yes. He was having an affair and I found out about it."

"How could anyone be unfaithful to you, Kim?"

She half smiled. "I guess Alex could. Anyway, the affair was the last straw and we ended it, so here I am. Now about you. You grew up in Mexico? What did your dad do? A family business, didn't you say?"

Kim noticed that her question seemed to make Camilo uncomfortable, just as it had the other night. "Well, hmm . . ." He paused. "My father, at least the only father I knew, was not such a good man. My mother, however, was a good woman. She had a hard life having to live the lifestyle she did."

"So they are not living anymore?" Kim asked, but before Camilo could answer, the waiter came back.

"Are you ready to order, señor?" he asked, looking toward Camilo.

"Kim, are you ready? I have barely looked at the menu."

Kim turned to the waiter. "Can you give us a few minutes?" She waited until he left their table. "Why did he ask *you* if we were ready to order?"

"You are not one of those feminists, are you Kim?" Camilo smiled at her.

"No, I'm not one of those feminists, but he didn't have to direct the decision making to you, did he?"

"This is an old family restaurant and they do things the old-fashioned way. It was always the man who did the ordering in the old days. Our waiter appears to be one of the original staff, from the looks of him," Camilo said and laughed. "Don't take offense, Kim."

"I'm not mad, but in this day and age it surprised me, that's all. But when you explain it like that, I guess I can understand."

"Okay, then may I order for you?" Camilo asked and laughed again. "Sorry, Kim, I could not resist."

"Very funny." She smiled at him. "No, thank you. I'll order for myself." She looked down at the menu in her lap, then picked it up to see it better. The lighting in the restaurant was dim and she couldn't see the type. Although she hated to do it, she opened her purse and took out her reading glasses. *How embarrassing,* she thought. *At least these glasses have a stylish, metro look.*

"Very sophisticated," Camilo said and winked.

"No comments, please. I hate having to wear these. I guess it's what happens when you get older."

"Not age again, Kim. I told you it does not matter."

"Camilo, how old are you anyway?"

"Does it really matter?"

"Yes, it does . . . to me, anyway."

"I am twenty-six years old. Does that make you feel better?"

"Not in the slightest, Camilo," she said, quickly doing the math. "Okay, I don't really want to reveal my age, but I think you'd better know I am seventeen years older than you!" Kim took a big gulp of her wine, then looked back at Camilo.

"Like I said, it's only a number. You are a very beautiful woman, Kim. The age does not matter to me. I am finding myself becoming more and more attracted to you. I find you very irresistible," he said, turning more serious. "I can't stop thinking about you."

"You don't care that I'm old enough to be your mother?"

"If you were a mother at seventeen, you could be my mother, but no, it does not matter to me. I can do the math. You are a very attractive forty-three-year-old woman, and I like you. I like you very much."

"So why are you not married? Why don't you even have a girlfriend? You're not so bad yourself. I mean, you are a very, very attractive young man. The girls must swarm all over you . . . or is there some deep, dark secret that you are not telling me that makes you a horrible person?"

The waiter came over again. Camilo quickly announced to him they still had not had a chance to look at the menu but that he shouldn't worry; they were not in any hurry anyway. Camilo picked up the bottle of wine, filled Kim's glass, and emptied the rest into his own. "I guess we will need another bottle."

"We can wait until dinner," Kim said. She was already feeling the effects of the wine.

When the waiter came back, they placed their orders. Kim couldn't decide between the shrimp scampi and the blackened petite filet. She had a feeling that Camilo was going to want to buy, so she didn't want to go too expensive. She ended up ordering the filet. *When in Rome,* she thought.

Camilo ordered the porterhouse. "We will have the Ravenswood cabernet with dinner," he told the waiter.

All through the evening, the conversation bounced between Kim's life and Camilo's. Kim found out that both of his parents were dead and he never said exactly what his father did. From what he implied, she guessed that he had been involved with something illegal. The conversation centered more on his mother; she could tell that he had been very fond of her.

Kim learned that his mother had passed away six years earlier, when he was twenty. She had lived near Matamoras most of her married life and that is where she died. Camilo said she had very rarely come into the United States and stayed pretty much close to home. As for him, he rarely crossed the border when he was younger; it was not until after his father died when he was fifteen that he started to frequent America.

"It was much easier to cross the borders then," he said. "I would often go to the beaches at Padre Island," he said and smiled, "to look at the pretty American girls." He explained to her that it was not because of poverty that his mother had stayed in Mexico; their family had been very wealthy. His mother was just more comfortable in her own surroundings. She had a full staff of servants, including maids who took care of household chores and nannies who cared for Camilo and his older brother and sister. She also learned that Camilo never went to a regular school because his mother hired a tutor for her children.

Interesting, Kim thought. *Illegal activities and wealth.*

"Where are your brother and sister now?" Kim asked.

"My sister lives in Mexico City with her husband and children. I don't get to see them often. My niece and nephew are very good little children. And my brother, I am not sure where he is. He took after my father—not such a good man he turned out."

Kim found herself very comfortable and at ease with Camilo. He was such a polite and respectful man; it was hard for her to imagine he had the father he described— or at least the father he grew up with. She was curious about the relationship, but she didn't want to pry. It was apparent that his mother must have been a strong woman who instilled goodness in Camilo.

"So . . . about your age," Kim said.

"What about my age, señorita?" Camilo said with a smirk.

"Well, I mean, how did you get to be such a successful businessman at such a young age? You own the company, right?"

"I guess I was at the right place at the right time." He paused. "And I guess a lot of hard work doesn't hurt either." He smiled.

Kim looked at her watch and was surprised to see it was already ten o'clock. "Yikes; it's getting late!" She looked at Camilo and said, "I had a great evening."

"Kim, we haven't had the final course yet—dessert. No meal is complete without dessert."

"I'm going to have to pass," she said and smiled. "The girlish figure, you know." She patted her stomach. She really didn't want the evening to end, but she didn't want her parents to worry. She hadn't told them when to expect her home and if she stayed out late, she knew they would stay up until she got there, and her dad needed his rest.

"How about if I take you to one more place where we can have a glass of port? That can be your dessert."

"Boy, you *are* the wine connoisseur, aren't you?" Kim hesitated before she answered. "I *would* love to see what port you'd suggest for dessert, but I have to check in with my parents first."

When they left the restaurant, Kim called her parents to let Nita know where she was. "Don't wait up for me," she told them.

"We know you are in safe hands, so take your time," her dad said. "We'll leave the light on for you." He loved to mimic that old commercial advertising a motel chain.

They approached the car and when Camilo opened the door for Kim, he reached for her arm and pulled her to him. "I hope I am not being too forward," he said, "but I have to ask you; is it okay if I kiss you?"

Kim laughed. "American men don't usually ask. They just assume a girl wants to be kissed. But yes, you can kiss me, and thank you for asking." She smiled up at him and leaned closer toward him. Camilo wrapped his hands around her face and drew it up to his lips. She closed her eyes and he kissed her gently and slowly. They lingered there until Kim pulled back slightly, looked up, and saw his deep chocolate brown eyes.

"Were you looking at me the whole time?" she asked and laughed.

"You are even more beautiful from this direction. You should see." He smiled down at her, pulled her in again, kissing her lightly, and then wrapped his arms around her, giving her a firm hug. Kim didn't want that wonderful feeling to end.

Camilo took Kim to a quaint jazz bar not far from the restaurant. It was a small, darkly lit venue, and when they entered through the front door, Kim was confronted with a sweet smell of cigar smoke, a smell she didn't mind at all. It brought back memories of her step-grandfather, Peter. He would often sport a cigar as he went around doing his daily chores. Mark's dad partook in the habit as well, she remembered.

Camilo put his hand on the small of her back and guided her to a table in the corner. The touch of his hand gave her a sensation she couldn't put her finger on. Did she have butterflies in her stomach, or was it the wine? She was becoming even more attracted to him and she didn't care. She wasn't going to try to fight it, at least not tonight.

When the waiter came over, Camilo ordered two glasses of port. "The best you have," he told him. He turned to Kim, "A nice port wine will warm your body, from the first sip all the way through."

I am already warm, she thought.

CHAPTER TWENTY

"Is everything all right with your dad?" Connie was on the other end. "I was getting worried about you, honey. I hadn't heard from you in a couple of days."

"Not to worry. I'm in good hands—oh-so-good hands," Kim said and laughed.

"Are they the hands of a strong Mexican boy?"

Kim was sitting on the porch swing, enjoying the morning sun. She took a sip of coffee before she answered. "Why of course they are. I had a very romantic evening last night. And I found out he was a good kisser—a really good kisser. Or perhaps it's just been so long that I've forgotten. Remember the couple I told you about when I met you for drinks the night before I left?"

"Yes, I remember. You felt jealous about a relationship you imagined they had."

"What I imagined she must have felt when he bent down to kiss her was what I felt last night. And I don't even care that he is seventeen years younger than I am. I found out how old he really is. Am I crazy or what?"

There was a pause on the other end. "He's twenty-six?"

"You got it; a twenty-six-year-old hunk."

"What do Mom and Dad think about this youngster you are dating?"

"They have known Camilo for some time and like him. They think he is, in my mom's words, a very nice young man, so they don't mind. I think they're just happy to see me happy. My attitude has changed a lot from when I arrived a week ago."

"So how are you doing?" Kim asked her friend. There was silence on the other end.

"Is everything okay?" she asked again.

"Yes. Why should anything be wrong?" Connie answered.

"I didn't say anything was wrong, but now that you said it . . . what's wrong?"

"I'm okay."

"You sound funny."

"You know Juan from the other day?"

"Yes, the one you were with when I interrupted you doing who knows what."

"Yes, that's Juan. He has become insanely infatuated with me. I had just met him that night at a bar just off the ocean walk. We had a good time, talked smart, and the next thing I knew, I was at his condo. We sat around until the wee hours in the morning talking more and I think we drank four bottles of wine. Now he is stalking me."

"What do you mean—stalking?"

"He keeps calling me. He wants to take me out for dinner."

"Honey, that's not stalking; he is trying to ask you on a date. Besides, it's been only two days. How much can he be calling?"

"I don't want to get attached, and if I say yes, he may ask me out again, and then again, and before you know it, my free, fun-loving month will be gone and I'll be headed back to North Carolina."

"I think you should surrender and break out of your ways. You don't have to stick to one-night stands. You could find love, you know." Kim got up from the swing and walked over to the side of the deck closer to the road. She leaned over the rail and looked down the street and continued trying to convince Connie that it was okay to date. When she thought she had made the best case she could, she said goodbye.

— •••• —

It was two hours earlier in California and Connie was still in bed, savoring a cup of coffee. The master bed-room of the beach house she rented was on the second floor. French doors opened to a porch, where two white Adirondack chairs sat. She got up, stepped outside into the cool breeze, and sat down, smelling the distinc-tive scent of the ocean. Connie took a sip of coffee and thought about Juan.

Her temporary home in San Diego was a Nantucket-style townhouse. It was located right off the boardwalk overlooking the beach and ocean. Droves of people, some very strange, ran, strolled, and skated past the house. The variety of characters in California amused her.

The house was decorated with a nautical theme. Finding the place online had not been easy. Every time she inquired about a potential place, she found out that it was already rented, and then, finally, she came across this particular house by chance. The owner indicated there had been a tragedy in her life that prevented her from getting the home listed sooner. Connie wondered what that tragedy could be; perhaps it was an ill parent, or worse, the death of a child. She hoped it was neither; she wouldn't want her good fortune to be because of someone else's sorrow.

Connie thought about what Kim had said to her. She knew she avoided relationships; in her experience, getting involved with a man only resulted in hurt. She had had too many disappointments in her younger years that led to her inability to let men—or anyone else, really—get close. When she was growing up, she had felt that the insulation of her weight was what protected her. Now it was her risky lifestyle that was her shelter. She knew that others thought that her lifestyle was precarious, but to her it was safe; no one could look inside to see who she really was. Kim was the only one who knew her, and even Kim didn't *really* know Connie.

Connie was afraid she liked this guy, Juan. Something attracted her to him. At first, Connie suspected from his dress and the fact that he had a multimillion-dollar condo on the beach that he was one of those playboy types. But after talking with him, even though her head was cloudy from the wine, his philosophy on life and love startled her. He talked a lot about how the breakdown in the family system had caused many of the world's problems.

"The old-fashioned family-value system is gone," he had said. "And people in general. They just are not nice. What's wrong with smiling and saying hi when you pass a stranger on the street?"

Connie remembered laughing and saying, "Because you probably would get mugged if you did that."

He had replied, "No, really. Why are people so inwardly focused? They don't care about anyone but themselves."

Connie had learned that Juan was an investment banker in San Diego. "Funny," she told him, "my friend's husband—or ex-husband—who is also a financial guy cheated on her."

"Not all men are alike, Connie," he had assured her.

She also learned that he came from a big family. He had spent most of his life in California. He had been born in Mexico and when he was just a year old, his parents immigrated to the United States. His dad was a migrant farm worker who took jobs at farms throughout California. He moved his family to where the work was. He taught his sons and daughters that if they were good, honest people and lived their lives right, then things would turn out all right. This was the philosophy Juan told Connie he lived by.

Connie pondered the idea of calling Juan back as she looked out over the ocean. *What do I have to lose?*

CHAPTER TWENTY-ONE

Kim went for her usual morning run after she finished her conversation with Connie. She decided to take a different route and headed to the gate that led out of the park. There were very few trails along the side of the highway, so she had to dodge between the grass and the pavement. As she ran, her thoughts went back to the articles about Mark. She was anxious to continue reading them so she could learn the details of the events that resulted in Mark's death.

When she headed back toward the entrance to the park, she ran across the grass to the frontage road that led to the entrance gate. She looked up and saw a white truck parked two blocks ahead of her. When she got within earshot, she shouted, "Hey, are you stalking me?"

Camilo got out of his truck and smiled at her. "No, not stalking. Am I being a nuisance to you?"

"No, I'm just kidding. How are you today?" She stopped when she got to the side of his truck. "Thank you again for a lovely evening."

"My pleasure. I would like to take you out again, maybe tonight?"

"Even though I'd love to, I don't think I can. Jack is going in for his first treatment tomorrow and I want to spend the evening with my parents."

"I have a good idea, Kim. Let's take them out for dinner. I bet your *padres* have not been out for a week and I know they are probably longing for a night out."

"You know, I think they might like that. What a great idea. Thank you for thinking of it." Kim leaned over and gave Camilo a kiss on the check. "You are a good man." They agreed that Camilo would come over at five o'clock and they would go out to dinner. "I think we should let them choose where they want to go. What do you think?" Kim asked.

"*Si*, let's let them decide."

Kim headed toward the front gate and back to her parents' home, all the while smiling about the man she just kissed on the cheek. *What*, she thought, *is happening to me?*

The morning passed quickly once she got home. She had lunch with Jack and Nita, and then excused herself to sit by the pool. Before she left, she grabbed her bag and stuffed it with a towel, a water bottle, and the printed pages from the library. She was going to read more about Mark Carson.

Kim laid her towel on the lawn chair and sat down. There was a flurry of activity at the pool. More guests had arrived to spend the holidays with their parents and grandparents. Kim was no longer the youngest person in sight. There were all kinds of children running around, splashing in the pool, making an abundance of noise.

She could hear Christmas music playing from the

outdoor speakers and was glad that she had found a chair away from all the chaos. She smiled at "Rudolph the Red-Nosed Reindeer" and thought how it didn't really feel like Christmas—not just because she was in a tropical setting, but also because of all the other things that occupied her mind. Before long she was deep into the world of murder and drugs, her thoughts of Christmas far away.

Kim thumbed through the pages until she found the place where she had left off. The author went on to describe in detail how Mark had smuggled drugs across the border. The journalist had gotten much of his information from records of the testimonies of informants when they were questioned for other drug arrests. When interviewed, they had described the details of Mark's drug operation. This information, together with interviews the journalist had gathered from other sources, tied the pieces together. Kim recognized some of the names of those interviewed.

Apparently, Roberto Martinez regularly shipped the paraffin wax to an address in Reynosa, just across the street from a small café. Mark would park his truck behind the café and use the rear entrance. He always chose a seat by the window, one that overlooked both the back of the restaurant and the small warehouse next door. He would order his usual, a taco and bean plate, and ate while two Reynosa natives loaded the shipment into his truck.

The men were nameless to Mark. In fact, he rarely spoke more than two words to them. Mark's business dealings were with their boss. The journalist discovered, through his investigation, that Mark had become good friends with a famous drug lord, Javier Perales. From accounts given by Mark's friends and colleagues, Mark spent a lot of time in Mexico, across the border from Brownsville, at one of the many homes that Perales owned.

The journalist described how the two Reynosa men transferred drugs into the bags holding the paraffin wax. It was a rather intricate operation. The fully refined paraffin was packaged in crystal form in five-pound bags. The two Mexican men would delicately slit open the ends of each bag and then pour a raw form of cocaine into the crystals and seal the ends of the bags with a hot sealer press. They concealed any marks so well that it appeared that the bags had never been opened.

After finishing the integration of the wax and cocaine, the men would pack the boxes back up and load them onto Mark's truck. When Mark saw that the truck was fully loaded, he would quickly finish his lunch and exit the café the way he came in.

At the border crossing, Mark had no trouble when the immigration officers inspected the load in the back of his truck. He had the paperwork from Martinez affirming that the contents was paraffin wax and that is exactly what it looked like when the officers slit open the boxes to examine the contents.

Back in the United States, Mark delivered the load to a small warehouse in McAllen, Texas. There, workers melted the paraffin wax completely away, leaving only the cocaine behind. From there, Mark shipped the drugs all over the United States, making a lot of money for a lot of people.

Kim looked up from the pages in her hands. *That was a pretty innovative method,* she thought. She easily imagined Mark coming up with this scheme; his mind never stopped working. He was always thinking of new ways to do things. He was such a talented man. *What a terrible tragedy*, she thought. *Not only about his death, but that he wasn't able to put his talents to good use.*

Kim sat staring across the pool area, thinking about the timeframe in which the drug trafficking took place. According to the article, it was going on the same time Kim lived with Mark and Maite. She thought back to the time they went to Padre Island and Mark's stop in Brownsville on the way.

She couldn't help but think how glad she was that she had left when she did. Jack and Nita had urged her to come home after six months, convincing her to do something more with her life than work in a restaurant. She remembered being angry with them, but she went home anyway, knowing deep down that they were right. She clearly remembered the day she got the plane ticket in the mail from her parents. She didn't tell Mark she was leaving until just before she was ready to leave. When she showed him the ticket he was disappointed.

"Kim, why do you have to leave?" he asked. "We have something here," he said and pulled her into his arms.

"What do we have here?" she whispered, her cheek against his chest. "You are married. This is just not right."

Just then, a ball came at her, landing on her lap, startling her back to the present. She picked it up and threw it back to the little boy standing in front of her. She smiled at him and instantly felt a pang in her heart.

—•••—

Later that evening, Camilo knocked on the door, right on time, as usual. Jack let him in and immediately offered him a beer, but Camilo declined.

"Well, I'm going to have a glass of wine," Kim said as she came around the corner and put her hand on Camilo's arm, giving it a light squeeze. "Mom, would you like one as well?" She turned to Nita and then to Jack. "Sorry, Dad. I'm sure a brandy wouldn't be what the doctor ordered." She grinned at Jack. He frowned at her, but with an expression of agreement.

"Yes," Nita interrupted. "I would like a glass."

"Camilo, would you like wine instead?" She walked into the tiny kitchen, opened the refrigerator, and pulled out the chardonnay sitting on the bottom shelf. "I have a great vintage here," she said and laughed.

"Sure, I will have a glass, "Camilo answered. He got up and stood by Kim's side, placing his hand on the small of her back.

Jack and Nita decided on a restaurant. They both were hungry for Chinese food, so they chose one of their favorite places. "This is so nice of you to take us along on your date," Nita told them. All Kim could do was smile.

CHAPTER TWENTY-TWO

The next morning, Jack was up early, shuffling around in the kitchen as he made coffee and did the dishes that had piled up in the sink. Kim woke up when she heard him and lay still for a while, listening. She was sure he must be nervous about the treatments and the long day ahead of him. The doctors had warned him that the treatment could be grueling and urged him to get plenty of rest. But she wasn't sure he had followed those orders, since she had heard him get up more than once during the night.

Before long, Nita came out of the bedroom and whispered something to Jack that Kim couldn't hear. She waited a few more minutes, then sat up. "Good morning," she said as she lifted herself off the bed. "Big day, huh Dad?" She was trying to be funny.

"Oh, just a walk in the park," he said and half smiled.

"You two!" Nita picked up the cup of coffee Jack had poured for her. "It's not funny."

Jack kissed her on the cheek. "Sorry, dear. It's going to be all right. I can feel it in my bones." He let out a snort, looked at Kim, and winked again.

"Now that's really not funny," Nita said and frowned at the two of them.

Dr. Lopez and a team of oncologists had told Jack and Nita about a new clinical study that might benefit him. Because of the type of cancer Jack had and the fact that it was still contained in his back, his participation in this trial could yield a better outcome than traditional treatment.

The doctors explained to Kim's parents that they would extract marrow from Jack's bones, combine the cancer cells with viruses, and let the combination marinate for a time. The idea was that the viruses would destroy the cancer cells only, leaving the good cells alone. When the procedure was done, the good cells would be reintroduced back into Jack's body. After that, Jack would undergo chemotherapy. The doctors told them the results from chemo have a better outcome when preceded by gene therapy.

At first Nita was nervous about doing such an unconventional treatment. She was worried it was too new of an approach to do any good, but after she got some of her questions answered and Jack convinced her it was what he wanted to do, they agreed to the procedure. The first step of the treatment was what was scheduled for that day. The rest would be performed in the following days. Jack would stay in the hospital until all the steps of the treatment were completed.

Kim insisted that she drive them both to the appointment, even though Nita thought she should stay back, go to the pool, and enjoy her day. Nita told her she didn't need spend her time waiting around the hospital. "Nonsense," Kim told her. "That's right where I need to be," she said, smiled, and gave her mom a hug.

Arriving at the hospital and making sure her parents were taken care of, Kim sat in the waiting room all morning during the initial tests. The doctors had to check Jack's white blood count and make an assessment before they proceeded. When lunchtime came around, Kim joined her parents. A young volunteer delivered a meal of all liquids to Jack, but Nita and Kim were served deli sandwiches and soup. *Not bad for hospital food,* Kim thought, feeling guilty as she and Nita sat at Jack's bedside eating their lunches. He scowled at his food and tried to convince Nita to give him a bite of her sandwich. Kim admired his outlook on things; nothing ever seemed to get him down.

After lunch, they took Jack to another room where they were going to draw his bone marrow. Nita went with him, but Kim decided to excuse herself to take a break and sit by herself for a while. When she settled into the waiting room, her thoughts went back to Mark and the drug scheme she had read about the day before. A chill went up her spine as she thought about the accounts of the article and how close to danger she had been. She had stuffed the remaining article in her bag before she left that morning, and she now pulled it out and began to read "Body Found in Trunk."

Mark's body had been found in a trunk in an airport parking lot about a hundred miles north of where he lived in McAllen. Violet had informed the police that Mark had been missing two days; he was supposed to have dinner with her, but never showed. The article stated that Mark, now divorced from Maite, lived off and on with his mom and sister, Beth.

On the last day that Violet saw Mark, he told her that he needed to borrow her car while he was getting his own fixed. He needed it, he said, to drive an hour west of McAllen to a business meeting. He was going to be gone for a few nights, but would be back in two days in time to have dinner with her. At first when he didn't show, Violet wasn't too concerned. It wasn't unlike Mark to get tied up with business and lose track of time. She figured he was working on a construction project that involved more work than he had expected. However, she thought it strange that he did not phone her; that was not like him. Mark's body wasn't found until six months after Violet filed the missing person report.

Kim stopped reading and looked up. The article gave such vague accounts of Mark's death. This wasn't good enough for her; she needed to know more. But how? Then she thought about Beth. Surely she could fill in some of the blanks. Kim recalled the trip she had taken with Beth across the border to Reynosa and Beth's connection with the older Mexican man and her fear about being there. Maybe Beth knew more than what the journalist had uncovered.

Kim decided to call Beth and invite her out to lunch. Then Kim remembered the evening she and her parents spent with Beth and Violet; Beth had enjoyed a beer or two. *Better yet*, Kim thought, *I'll invite her out for drinks. I bet she'll be more inclined to talk if she loosened up a little.*

"Miss Whitman?"

Startled, Beth dropped the paper she had in her hand.

"Sorry; I didn't mean to alarm you." It was Dr. Lopez. "It is Miss Whitman, isn't it?"

"Mrs. Thomp—, um, Kim Thompson." Kim hesitated as she picked the article up from the floor, put it back in her purse, and stood to greet the doctor. "How is my dad?"

Dr. Lopez smiled at her, his dark eyes beaming. Kim became embarrassed and quickly looked down at the floor. "He's doing well. We have just completed the first part of today's treatment. Now we have to remove his marrow and mix it with the vector, which is the virus." He laughed when he saw the shocked look on her face.

"That can't be good, can it?" she asked and grimaced.

"Don't worry; we'll leave plenty of marrow inside him. It does take a lot out of a person, though, and he's going to be very tired. We'll extract the marrow from his hip bones, but he shouldn't be in pain. We'll give him a local anesthetic, so he won't feel anything. It'll make him drowsy and sore, so he'll have to stay in bed for a few days. Come with me. You can say hi to him before we take him to start the harvest."

Dr. Lopez put his arm toward the small of her back and, without touching her, gave her an imaginary nudge toward the hall. Kim walked side by side with him down to her dad's room. When they got there, the doctor smiled at her again and left, walking down the hall in the same direction they had just come.

"He's cute, isn't he?" Nita asked. She was sitting next to Jack, who had his eyes closed.

"Is he okay?" Kim's voice revealed a hint of fear as she looked at her dad lying in the hospital bed.

"They gave him a sedative to relax him before they take him to the procedure room," Nita told her.

Just then, Jack opened his eyes and smiled faintly at Kim. His eyes lacked the usual sparkle and Kim's heart sank. "I hope they know what they're doing," she said with a sigh as she glanced toward Nita. She leaned over and kissed Jack's cheek. "How are you doing?"

"I'm ready for them to take the first batch out," he said. The doctors had warned him that they may have to do this more than once if they couldn't get enough marrow or if the marrow cells didn't react to the virus the way they needed it to. Jack put his hands alongside his hips and pushed himself up higher on the bed. Kim quickly pulled the pillows behind to prop him up. "Thank you, honey," he said and smiled. "I'm doing fine; don't worry." He looked at her with blank eyes.

"*Hola.*"

Camilo popped his head around the doorway's corner. Kim jerked her hand from the pillow she was situating behind Jack. "Camilo!" she exclaimed. "What are you doing here?"

"Kim, that's not nice," Nita interrupted. She went over to Camilo and laid her hand on his arm and gave him a soft pat. "Thank you for coming."

"Kim, I did not mean to startle you. I am very sorry."

"Don't worry, Camilo," Nita said, dropping her hand. "We're glad you are here." She frowned at Kim.

"I didn't mean that I wasn't happy to see you. I just didn't expect you," Kim hurriedly explained. "It's okay; I'm glad you're here." She turned to Jack. "He's getting ready to do the marrow extract. They gave him a sedative and he's very tired. We shouldn't stay too long."

"Nonsense!" Jack piped in. "I'm fine. She's worrying too much." He cocked his head toward Camilo. "You know women; they like to fret."

"Jack, maybe they are right," Camilo said. "You need your rest. How about if I take them off your hands for a while?" He nodded to Jack. "There is a quiet little place around the corner."

"I could go for a nice cold beer," Nita piped in.

"Mom!" Kim shot a surprised look in her direction.

"Kim, your mom needs to get away from this," Jack interrupted. "Camilo, take them for a beer. But that one won't drink a beer." He lifted his IV-draped hand and pointed to Kim. "You'll have to get her a glass of wine." He laughed, then closed his eyes just as two nurses wheeled a bed in. "Camilo, you take the girls. I'll be out for a while," Jack murmured.

"The procedure will take about an hour and then he'll be in the recovery room until he wakes up," one of the nurses told them. As they lifted Jack onto the bed to take him to do the procedure, Kim, Nita, and Camilo left.

Just over an hour later, Camilo brought the two women back from the bar just as Jack was wheeled back to his room. Nita went right to his side. "You look tired," she said and reached down to touch his hand. Jack gave her a weak smile.

"He'll be groggy for a while," the nurse said as she plugged all the machines back in and situated Jack in his bed.

"They said they would put all my marrow back tomorrow," he said, his voice faint. "I'm going to get a good night's sleep and you should do the same." He smiled again at Nita and then closed his eyes. Nita kissed his forehead, Kim took her arm, and the two women and Camilo left the hospital room.

CHAPTER TWENTY-THREE

"Mom, do you know what's coming up?" Kim was up early the next morning. She brushed past her mom as she reached for a mug hanging on the wall. She picked up the pot of coffee and poured the hot liquid into her cup. "We need to put some decorations up. It's only ten days until Christmas."

"We don't usually decorate; we haven't even had a tree for years," Nita said. She poured coffee into her cup and then went to sit in her chair. She searched for the remote to turn on the television. When Kim sat down in Jack's chair, she glanced over at her mom and couldn't help but notice how exhausted she looked. "I think we'll get you a tree," she said and smiled over at her mom. "A real one."

"Kim, real ones are very expensive here. They don't have many Christmas trees in south Texas, you know."

"Don't worry; I'll find one and I think it's the best thing for us to do. We'll really need to celebrate and celebrate big this year. Don't you think?" She sipped her coffee and raised her eyebrows as she looked over at her mom.

"Okay, but really, I don't know about a real Christmas tree, Kim," she said and laughed.

"You know what? I'll find one." She thought about asking Camilo to help her. She was sure he must have his resources, being in the landscaping business. She also had an ulterior motive. She wanted an excuse to get out of the house to see Beth. She decided she would call her when she finished her coffee to see if she would be free the next day. That would give Kim enough time to figure out where to get a tree, shop for decorations, and gather her thoughts about what she was actually going to ask Beth. First, she was going to call Camilo to ask for his help.

She picked up her phone and dialed his number. "Camilo, this is Kim. I'm sorry to bother you but . . ."

"No bother, Kim, I can assure you."

Kim walked out the door and sat on the steps, the morning sun beating down on her as she lifted her arm to shield her eyes. "Thank you, Camilo. I have a funny question to ask you. I'm looking for a Christmas tree. My mom says they're very hard to find here but I figured you would have an inside scoop."

"A what?"

"A scoop, the knowledge about where to find one."

"Yes, I know what 'scoop' means. It is a funny little word you use to find a tree," he said and laughed. "We live in a warm, tropical climate, so not many of these types of trees will you find here, and if you do, they cost a lot of pesos."

Kim felt like he was playing with her, and she became irritated. "If you don't have time, I understand."

Camilo sensed her frustration. "No, Kim; I have time for you. Sorry. I was teasing you. I know where to get a very nice tree for your Christmas."

"Not too big. You know Jack and Nita's house. They only have room for a small one. A tree and some decorations will cheer them up. Can you tell me where to find one? I'll go tomorrow."

"I will take you," Camilo answered.

"No, I don't want to bother you. Just give me directions and I can find my way."

"I will come and get you at lunchtime tomorrow. Will that be okay?"

"Camilo, I didn't call you to take you away from your work—"

"I know," he interrupted. "But I want to take you. I miss you."

Kim smiled. She had to admit it; she wouldn't mind seeing him again. *After all*, she thought, *it had been only . . . what? Less than twenty-four hours since she saw him last.* She smiled again. "Okay, at noon tomorrow. I'll be ready. Thanks." She clicked her phone shut and walked back into the house. "I'm going to get you a Christmas tree. Camilo is taking me," she told Nita.

Only one problem, Kim thought as she walked into the bathroom to change into her running clothes. Now she wouldn't have time to meet Beth tomorrow. Maybe she would try today. She could still use the excuse that she was going shopping.

"Mom, I'm going to go out today and pick up some Christmas decorations," Kim said when she had changed. "What time do you have to be at the hospital?" Kim zipped up her running jacket and grabbed a bottle of water from the refrigerator. Nita was still sitting in front of the television.

"I don't know. I thought I'd call over to his room this morning. I'd like to be there when the doctors come and talk to him."

"How about if we go when I get back from my run? It won't take me too long to get ready."

Nita agreed, got up, and went to her bedroom to dress. Kim paused before she went out the door. She wanted to see if she could get ahold of Beth before she left. She looked around the kitchen for a phone book and found one in Nita's desk, but it was only for Harlingen and the surrounding areas. The listings weren't for the rural area where Beth and Violet lived.

She looked up at Nita's computer and pressed the enter button, but Nita had it password protected. Kim laughed to herself. *Why does Mom need to protect the contents of her computer?* she thought. After all, Jack could barely turn the thing on.

Kim flipped her phone open and dialed 411; when she heard the operator's voice, she stated the state and city, then Violet's full name, and waited for the number. She couldn't remember the name of Violet's business, so she took a chance that her home number was listed. The operator came back with a listing for Violet Carson on Primrose Avenue. "I think that's the one. Thank you," Kim responded and wrote the number down when the operator recited it to her.

A few minutes later, Kim was on the phone with Beth. She had walked outside so her mom couldn't hear the conversation. "Um, Beth? This is Kim, Kim Thompson, Jack and Nita's daughter. How are you today?" Kim waited for a response. Beth greeted her and then began to tell Kim about her morning and how bad it was: Violet's car wouldn't start and she had demanded that Beth drive her to the store. But, Beth explained, she had been out the night before and wanted to sleep in. Kim immediately thought that getting together would be a bad idea.

"What's on your mind, Kim?" Beth finally replied.

"Well, um . . ." Kim hesitated. "I was wondering if you would like to go have a drink with me this afternoon, for happy hour? You like beer, right?"

"Yes; will your mom and dad be there?"

"No; Dad is in the hospital. He's having a procedure done." Kim didn't feel like telling her the whole story. "I thought just the two of us could talk. Is that okay?"

"Sure. What do you want to talk about?" Beth asked.

Kim was not going to reveal too much, just in case Beth would then refuse. "Just thought we could catch up on old times." She wasn't really lying.

"I guess so. Where do you want to meet?"

"I can come over your way at about four thirty. Name the place where you'd like to meet and I can find the directions." Beth gave her the name of a place and Kim wrote it down on a piece of paper lying next to the computer: the East Side Bar.

"It's right off the highway as you come into McAllen," Beth told her. "It'll be on your left-hand side."

"I'll be there at four thirty." She barely got the words out before Kim heard the dial tone on the other end of the phone. *This will be interesting,* she thought.

Nita and Kim arrived at the hospital just as Jack was finishing eating. "Some breakfast," he said and tipped the bowl full of yellow broth toward them. "At least I can get some pudding after I eat this." He pointed toward the small container on the edge of the tray. "I asked the nurse for some real food, but she said that I still need to be careful about eating solids—doctor's orders." Nita sat on the bed beside Jack.

"When can you go home?" she asked and kissed his cheek. She ran her hand down his arm and let it rest on his hand. Kim could see the relief on Nita's face.

Kim heard a voice outside the door; Dr. Lopez was talking to the nurse. When his conversation ended, he walked into the small room and pulled back the curtain back. "Good morning, everyone," he said and smiled. When he saw Kim, he stopped and smiled at her. "How are you today?"

"Good," Kim said and blushed. "I'll be better if you say that my dad can go home this morning."

Nita stood as Dr. Lopez walked over to the bed. "Well, Jack, shall we make your daughter happy? How are you feeling?" He looked at the chart in his hand as he spoke. "Your vital signs during the night were all good." He picked up Jack's wrist to check his pulse. After a quiet moment, he said, "I checked with the lab this morning and everything is going well there, too. But," he said and paused, "it looks like it may take a few days for the marrow to infuse with the viruses before we can inject it back in."

He laid Jack's hand back down and wrote a few things in the chart. He looked at Kim, shook his head, and turned back to Jack. "I'm going to have you stay here so we can keep an eye on you. I'll have the nurse come in to check your dressings." He walked past Kim and laid a hand on her shoulder. "I'm sorry," he whispered.

When the nurse came in, Kim stepped out of the room, searching the hallway for Dr. Lopez. She heard his voice next door and waited until he came back out to the hall. When he did, she walked over to him. "Hello, Kim," he said with a smile.

"Sorry to bother you again. I . . . uh . . . I just wanted to ask how you think this treatment is working?" Kim stumbled over her words. "I was surprised that you'll not let him go home today."

"It's a trial treatment, Kim, and from clinical studies we have seen, the results are promising. I know you are worried, but he's in good hands. We'll take care of him."

"I didn't mean to imply that you were not good doctors," she said as she winced.

"Don't worry. You didn't insult me," he said and laughed. He placed his hand on her shoulder and gave her a gentle squeeze. "I can only recommend treatments to my patients. But I can tell you, if he were my dad, I would feel very comfortable with this procedure."

"Thank you, Doctor Lopez." Kim felt relieved. He squeezed her shoulder again and told her he had to finish his rounds, but that if she had any more questions, she should call him. He handed her a card with his contact information on it, said goodbye, and walked to the next room.

Kim turned in the opposite direction and went down the hall to get a cup of coffee. She thought about what Dr. Lopez had said: The results were promising. She had to believe the treatment would work and that her dad would come out of this just fine. When she pulled the cup away from the spout, she smiled. For some reason, a vision of Camilo had popped into her mind.

When she walked back into Jack's room, the nurse was just finishing changing his dressings and putting another IV in his arm. "She did a good job; didn't hurt a bit," he said. He smiled at Kim as the nurse hooked a bag on the metal bracket beside the bed. Kim noticed that she was smiling, too, and imagined that Jack had been talking nonstop the whole time, making her laugh.

When the nurse left, Nita, Jack, and Kim sat awhile, chatting about Christmas and what they were going to do for their celebration, including dinner.

"Would you like to invite Camilo over?" Nita asked.

"I'm sure he has plans with his family, but . . ." She paused. "I'll ask. I'm going to see him tomorrow. He's going to help me find a tree."

"A tree?" Jack sat up in bed. "We don't need a tree—haven't had one for years."

Kim laughed. "That's exactly what mom said, but I'll tell you what I told her. I think this year we all need some Christmas cheer."

"It's going to cost a lot," he said as he sank back against his pillow.

"I don't care. We're getting a tree." Kim stood up. "I'm going to leave you two for a few hours. Mom, how long do you want to stay?"

"I'm going to sit right here. I brought a few magazines to read. I'll be okay. You run along," she said and flung her hand in Kim's direction.

Kim leaned over and kissed her dad on the forehead. "You be good. I'll be back after lunch."

When she stepped out of the hospital and into the warm air, she reached into her purse for her phone. She wanted to check in with Connie.

"Hey, girl," Connie said when she answered. She sounded winded.

"What are you up to?" Kim was almost afraid to ask.

"I'm out for my daily run."

"You're running?" Kim started laughing. "You don't run."

"I do now. I went with Juan yesterday, and I kind of liked it, so I thought I would try it again today."

"So you saw the stalker? What changed your mind?" Kim got to the van, clicked the lock on the key pad, opened the door, and got in. Connie was telling her that she had taken her advice and decided that dating might not be such a bad idea. "Good, I'm proud of you," Kim told her.

"I called him back after I finished talking to you the other day. He took me for dinner that night. Then yesterday, we went for a run after he was done with work, and then we went back to his condo and he made me dinner. Not only is he cute, he can cook too!" she said and laughed. "By the way, this is a gorgeous place to run. I'm looking over at the ocean and all the waves crashing into the beach right now."

"Not like the view I have when I run. I see rows and rows of little houses." Kim backed the van out of the parking spot. "I'm heading to the store to buy some Christmas decorations. Jack and Nita usually don't decorate, but this year I told them I was going to change that."

"That's nice—"

"What are you doing for Christmas?" Kim asked, interrupting her.

"Oh, I don't know. Maybe Juan and I'll do something . . . or maybe not." Connie remained silent for a moment. "He is probably doing something with his family. And I *will* definitely not be meeting the family. I draw the line there."

"It wouldn't be that bad. It's better than spending Christmas by yourself."

"What have you been up to?" Connie inquired.

"I can't stop thinking about the past. I keep getting drawn into it—"

"Hey, I'm going to stop into a shop for some coffee," Connie said. "What do you mean—the past?"

"I seem to be thinking a lot about the summers I spent at a northern Maine resort, about certain people there and then about the time I spent here in south Texas."

"Certain people? Hold on, honey; I'm ordering." Kim heard her set her phone on the counter and ordered a grande Americano. When she finished, she picked her phone up. "I'm back. What certain people are you talking about?"

"I'll tell you later. I'm at Walmart, so I have to go."

"Wait . . ." Connie yelled, but Kim had already hung up.

—•••—

All she heard was a dial tone. Connie stared at her phone. "Well alright, then," she said. She thought about what Kim had asked her, what she was doing for Christmas. She really hadn't asked Juan about his plans, but she thought that he was spending time with his family. He had talked about his sisters and brothers and their families; they lived in the area, so she assumed he would spend the holiday with them.

She drew in a deep breath of the crisp ocean air and let out a long sigh. She did it again, this time thinking of how good she was feeling. Somehow her life seemed changed, and she didn't know why. She hated to consider it was because of a man, but she couldn't help but think that Juan was making a difference in her life. This was the first time—well, the first time in a long time, anyway—that she had really gotten to know a man and let him get to know her. Over the past few days, she had discussed her innermost thoughts with Juan, and even though they had only known each other a short time, she felt very comfortable around him.

And she was working out. Even though she didn't see Don anymore, she was grateful she had met him. He not only taught her the art of yoga, but also how you can love your body—no matter what. She wasn't ready to give up on staying thin; she would just do it in a different way. She decided to try Kim's method of exercise—running—and found she liked it.

CHAPTER TWENTY-FOUR

Later that afternoon, Kim found herself in front of the East Side Bar in McAllen. The front of the building looked like it was once red, white, and blue, but Kim couldn't be certain, since the entire side of the wall was peeling. The only thing that looked as if it had recently received a fresh coat of paint was the bright red front door. She looked at her watch; it was only four fifteen. She was early and didn't want to sit in the bar by herself, so she sat in the van for a few minutes before going inside.

At four twenty-five, Beth still had not shown, so Kim got out of the van and headed for the bar. Just as she was about to open the door, a pickup truck pulled into the parking lot. She turned and saw it was Beth. Kim watched as she parked the rusted light green vehicle, amazed that the thing even ran. She wondered if Beth and Violet were having financial troubles. Given the shape of their home and this rundown truck, it appeared that they didn't have very much money at all.

Beth pulled herself out of the driver's seat and walked toward Kim. "Hi," she said without smiling. She was wearing a black sweatshirt and black jeans. When she got to Kim, she ran her hand across her forehead and then wiped it on her pants. Her hair was pulled back in a ponytail and she wore no makeup. Kim immediately noticed how much Beth resembled Violet.

"Hi," Kim replied. "Do you come to this place often?" She guessed this was probably one of Beth's regular hangouts. She started to walk to the entrance of the bar and Beth followed her.

"Yes. In fact, I was just here last night," Beth answered.

Then Kim remembered Beth telling her she had been out late the night before. "We could have gone to another place," Kim said as she let go of the door handle.

"No, this is good. Usually this is the only place I go. Besides, it's easy to get to from the direction you were coming. You couldn't miss it." Beth stepped in front of Kim, pulled the handle, and swung the door open. Kim followed her in, and as soon as she did, she let out a quick cough, overcome by the cigarette smoke. Three people sat at the bar. All were smoking, as was the bartender, who leaned on his elbows, talking with them. He looked up as Beth and Kim walked by. "Hi, Beth," he said as he nodded and smiled.

Beth waved her hand at him and kept walking to the back of the bar. She immediately went to one of the high tables close to the pool table, and Kim followed. She scanned the place and noticed they were the only others there besides the three at the bar. The space was long and narrow and appeared to not have been kept up any better than the outside had been.

"What do you want?" Beth asked as she took a seat.

"Do they have wine here?"

"I'm not sure. I only drink beer. What kind do you want?"

"White," Kim responded.

Beth sighed, heaved herself off the stool, and walked over to the end of the bar. The bartender stopped talking and moved toward her. Beth leaned over the bar toward him. Kim couldn't hear what they were saying, but she could see both Beth and the man behind the bar laughing. She supposed they were talking about last night, or maybe they were laughing at her choice of beverage. She figured that they didn't get orders for wine very often. Kim recognized the small bottle of wine Beth held up; it was one of those single-serve wines that have screw tops. She hesitated, then nodded. She was surprised they had even that.

"Did you start a tab?" Kim asked her when she came back to the table. "I'm going to buy."

"Yes," Beth replied, "but you don't have to." She took a drink from the tall mug of beer before she sat back down. Kim winced as she unscrewed the small bottle's cap and poured the wine into what looked like a juice glass. "Frank apologized he didn't have any wine glasses."

"That's okay," Kim said and took a sip.

"You said you wanted to catch up on old times?" Beth asked. She took another swing of her beer.

"Yes—and I needed to get away from the old people." She wanted to stall before she jumped in with the real reason she was there. She planned to wait until Beth's glass was almost empty; it didn't appear that was going to take very long, given the rate at which she downed her beer.

Kim asked about Violet and the store and how business was doing. Beth disclosed, without hesitation, that business was not very good at all. She told Kim that Violet's store used to be the only one in town, but over the past few years, two major fabric chains had come to McAllen. One of them opened right across the street from their store, the other across town. At first, Violet's regulars were loyal, but it was hard for Violet to compete with the prices of the big stores, and eventually her customers started coming in less and less.

Kim had a hard time believing that Violet even owned a fabric store, since it didn't fit with the way she kept herself or her home. Kim's perception of a fabric store was neat and orderly, a far cry from how Violet appeared to live. She took another sip of wine as Beth finished talking about the store. Then she took a deep breath and said, "One of the reasons I wanted to meet you was that I had a few questions about Mark, if you don't mind my asking."

Beth lifted her empty glass toward the bartender, seemingly unaffected by Kim's comment. "Frank!" she yelled. He nodded to her and then she turned back to Kim. "I don't mind. What questions do you have?"

"I have been reading a series of articles I found at the library, in the newspaper archives."

"Yes, I know what you're talking about." Beth looked intently in her direction, but didn't make eye contact. Kim couldn't tell if she was mad or just not interested in what she had to say.

The bartender came over with a fresh glass of beer and set it in front of Beth. "Do you want another one?" he asked Kim.

"No, I'm fine for now," she said. He left and she turned to Beth. "The articles were written a while ago.

Has there been anything done with the case since? Was anyone arrested for Mark's murder?" Kim went on to ask more about how Mark got involved with drugs in the first place and what had happened to Allison.

Beth kept looking past Kim at the wall behind her, keeping silent while Kim fired the barrage of questions at her. She picked up the mug of beer again and took a big gulp. When she set it down, she turned to Kim and gave her a half grin. "So many questions! Now I *am* curious. Why are you so interested in Mark's death and all of this?"

"When I was in the plane on the way down here, I started thinking about old times, the days at the resort, and the time I lived down here when I was nineteen. And then the other night when we talked about the time we went to Reynosa, I remembered that was when you told me about Mark's murder. I hadn't thought about Mark or his murder for a long time, and I was interested in finding out more, so I went to the library a few days ago to see what I could dig up."

Kim mentioned a few more facts she had learned from Jake Michaels's articles. Beth kept smiling as Kim talked, and when she finished her second beer, she gestured for another one. She turned to Kim and asked if she was ready. Kim looked at her glass, hesitated, and then nodded. When their drinks arrived, Beth proceeded to answer Kim's questions. "My mom never did get a death certificate, because they never did positively identify the body. Violet thinks he is still living and probably living in a foreign country or something like that."

"What?" Kim said in surprise, raising her eyebrows. *No wonder I couldn't find any of the records online.* "Why would she think that?" Kim asked. She never thought of the possibility that the body in the trunk was not Mark's. However, it wouldn't be that far-fetched for Mark to brilliantly stage his own death in order to avoid death at the hands of the drug lords he had been dealing with.

Beth said, "That last article doesn't tell the whole story, other than that the body was so badly decomposed that we couldn't make a positive identification. The investigators working on the case collected dental records not only from a dentist in Texas but also from a dentist back in Maine, the one we went to when we were kids. The results were inconclusive because the dentists had different opinions on the match between the teeth found in the trunk and Mark's records. Violet thinks he will come walking through our front door any day. I think she's crazy."

"Are you afraid of going to Mexico still?"

"I don't go over there. None of the men Mark knew know me personally, but they know my name, and that kind of freaks me out. You never know; one of those Mexican border guys could be secretly tied in with the drug lords. He could recognize my name from my ID and then tip off someone to follow me."

"But if that was really him in the trunk? Why would you still be afraid?" Kim took a sip of wine. Her plan had worked; she knew she could get Beth to open up with a few beers.

"That's just it. I don't know what I think. Maybe if Violet is right, we could be in danger if the bad guys thought he wasn't dead. They could try to use us to get to him. The drug lords don't usually give up when someone double crosses them."

"You mean that he was going to turn them in."

"Yes; that's what he told us he was going to do."

Kim remembered Beth telling her this when they went across the border to get the watch. "You do think Mark ever did drugs?" She hated to infer that he would, but she had to ask.

"No, I don't think he would. Mark was too smart for that. He wanted to always keep his mind clear, always thinking about the next scheme he was going to come up with."

Kim nodded in agreement. *Yes, that was Mark*, she thought. Then Beth brought up Alison. She said that Alison had become more and more frustrated with the failing candle company and Mark's ever-changing schemes to get rich.

"Yes, the journalist wrote that Alison thought that Mark was having an affair, but found out instead it was drugs." *But there were affairs*, she thought.

"An affair of sorts," Beth said and smiled. "Only it was with the drugs and money."

"Where is Alison now?" Kim asked.

"I don't know now, but when she left here, she went back to live with her family in northern Maine."

"What about Maite? Did she know about the drugs?"

"Yes, she did. At first she accepted that it was all part of the business, and besides, she liked the money. But then it got too much for her to handle. I think she felt it was getting too dangerous. So she left."

"Was this going on when I was living with them?"

"Yes."

Kim winced, mad at her naïveté as a teenager. Beth ordered another beer. Kim declined another wine, however. She knew her limit and she had to drive back to Harlingen. "I'm surprised I wasn't aware that anything was going on."

"Don't beat yourself up," Beth said, her tone suddenly sympathetic. "You couldn't have known. He was very careful. Maite only knew because he told her."

"Why did he tell her? Wouldn't that have put her in danger?"

"Sure, but I guess he didn't always care about that. He didn't tell us until the very end, and probably for that same reason, so we wouldn't be in danger. Why he didn't care about Maite, I don't know."

"Do you know where Maite is now?"

"No."

Kim could tell from Beth's firm response that she didn't care much for Maite, so she didn't press the issue. Kim continued. "Mark's construction company didn't do so well, either." It was more of a question rather than a statement.

"I guess that's what was going on, but we didn't know. We thought everything was just fine." Beth gulped the last of her beer.

Kim looked at her watch and noticed that it was already six thirty. "Beth, I'd better head back to Harlingen. Two glasses of wine are about all I can handle if I'm going to drive." She picked up her purse and went to the bar to get the tab from Frank. She paid for their drinks, then went back to where Beth was still sitting and said goodbye. Beth didn't say anything, but just smiled and nodded at her. Kim turned and walked toward the front door and when she opened it, she turned and noticed that Beth had moved to the bar, taking a stool next to the three people already sitting there.

On her drive back to her parents' house, Kim thought about her conversation with Beth and the idea that Mark could still be alive, that the body in the truck may not have been his.

CHAPTER TWENTY-FIVE

"Thanks, Mom," Kim said after picking up the piece of toast Nita had just buttered for her. It was not Nita's style to make breakfast, and Kim was grateful for her gesture. She figured Nita needed to be preoccupied with something to keep her mind off Jack and his health.

"I'm going to go over to the hospital this morning," she told Kim. "I told the ladies at the office that I wasn't going to go back to work until after Christmas."

"Really?" Kim asked. That was not like Nita either. "You really told them you were taking some time off? Wasn't it a few years back when you missed your grandson's basic training ceremony because you had to work?" There was a hint of sarcasm in Kim's voice.

"Kimberly!"

"Sorry, Mom. I didn't mean it like that, it's just not like you to give up work. I think it's a great idea to take a few days off. We'll get Dad home and have a nice holiday celebration. Remember, I'm going to get our tree today. Camilo is going to take me. I already have the decorations. I picked some up yesterday."

"Just don't go overboard. We don't need a huge tree."

Nita picked up her coffee and went to her usual morning seat. "I'll sit for a few minutes, then I'll get ready and head out. Do you need to drop me off?"

"No. Camilo is going to pick me up, so you can take the van."

After Nita finished her coffee, got dressed, and left for the hospital, Kim walked over to the pool. She didn't feel like running. Instead, she wanted to sit for a while and think about Mark and Camilo. *Strange,* she thought as they popped into her head at the same time. Her conversation with Beth from yesterday haunted her. What if Mark was not dead at all? What if he had staged his own death? It seemed absurd but she supposed it could be possible. And as far as Camilo, he occupied her thoughts more and more. The past was competing with the present. *Which will win?* she asked herself and laughed.

Kim sat by the pool for an hour, thumbing through Jake Michaels's articles. This time she had a highlighter, marking the areas of interest and the timelines that correlated with the time she spent with Mark. She read again about Javier Perales and Mark's growing friendship with him and his family. She wondered if this Mr. Perales was still living in Mexico, still trafficking drugs.

How many other people had died throughout the years at the hands of the drug lords? Or worse yet, how many of thousands of Americans had died as the result of drug overdoses from the drugs that were being brought illegally into the United States?

Mark had been a part of that and in some way, so had she, even though she had sat on the sidelines, not knowing about anything that what was going on. But just the fact that she loved him and was seduced by him while he was breaking the law made her feel like she had contributed to these criminal acts.

Kim sank back in the chair, closed her eyes, and thought about Mark's sea green eyes gazing into hers. It was so long ago, but she realized that she had never really felt that kind of passion for anyone since, not even with Alex. What was it about Mark that had such a strong hold on her? Then her thoughts suddenly went to Camilo. She could see the same intenseness in Camilo's eyes.

She let out a sigh. The same passion from long ago had taken her over again. *Nonsense,* she thought. She laughed and shook her head to clear the thought away. She quickly picked up the papers on her lap, gathered her towel and bag, and headed back to her parents' house.

At noon, Kim heard Camilo drive up, again, right on time. She grabbed her bag and headed outside. Camilo quickly got out of the truck and opened the door for her. "You are such a gentleman," she said and smiled at him, reaching up to kiss his cheek.

"I have a fabulous lunch planned for you."

"Camilo, the plan was to get a Christmas tree!" she said and gave him a soft punch on the arm before she slid into the passenger seat. "I need to get a Christmas tree." She could hear him whistle as he came around the front of the truck. "What do you have planned?" she asked as he got in, nudging him again.

Camilo started laughing.

"What . . . what are you thinking? You have some devilish scheme up your sleeve!" Kim said.

Camilo pulled her closer to him. "We will get your

tree; don't worry. I am not going to let you down. But first, I have a special day for you. I am not working anymore today, so I can spend the afternoon with you. We are going for a little drive."

Kim laid her head on his shoulder, surrendering to him, letting him take her to who knows where.

"Are we going to be gone for long? I feel like I should have written my mom a note."

"I will not dishonor your parents, Kim."

"Dishonor my parents? What are you planning?" she asked and sat up. Camilo, puzzled, looked at her, then pulled the truck out of the driveway, eventually taking them to the highway, heading west out of town.

"Where are we going? Shouldn't we be heading in that direction, toward the mall?" she asked and pointed over his shoulder.

"You didn't hear me. I take you to a special lunch," he said. He kept his eyes straight ahead and smiled. Kim put her head back on his shoulder. She was very comfortable, much more than she had been in a long time.

When they finally stopped, they were at a beach on Padre Island. Kim noticed familiar places within the populated city the island had become. Each year, a new multi-million-dollar hotel went up, one towering over the next. Camilo drove down the main street, past all the hotels and restaurants, until he finally pulled the truck into a parking lot on the other side of the island. Kim felt a familiar twinge as she opened the door. Camilo grabbed a basket and a blanket he had in the back of the pickup and then grabbed Kim's hand and pulled her toward the beach.

"A basket?" she asked. She pulled her hand away

from his and cocked her head sideways as she looked over at him. She grabbed the handle over his hand and smiled at him.

"It was my mother's," he said shyly. "I don't mean it to be an embarrassment."

"No, no Camilo; it's not that. It's just that . . . well, men . . . usually don't have picnic baskets. But I like it; it's very romantic. Let's see what's in there," Kim said and tried to lift the lid.

"Oh, no; you have to wait," Camilo said, pulling her through the tall weeds and over the sand dunes, which opened to the flat beach overlooking the Gulf of Mexico. The sun was high in the sky, and it heated the afternoon air, despite the periodic gusts of wind that blew in from the ocean.

Kim immediately was brought back to the time when she was here with Mark. She tried to shake the memory as she walked to the edge of the water while Camilo found a place on the beach to lay out the blanket. "Let's have a toast," he yelled. She laughed and then motioned for him to join her. When he reached Kim, he took her in his arms, and, before she could resist, he kissed her full on the lips. She leaned against his chest and they both lingered there.

"Here you go; a toast to us," he said as he handed her a glass of wine. He gazed intently into her eyes. "Kim," he said quietly, "I think I am falling in love with you." He raised his glass toward her.

Kim hesitated before she clicked the rim of her glass against his. "Camilo, you don't even know me. Yes, I *am* becoming very fond of you as well, but for all you know, I could be a lunatic." She took a sip of her wine and moved closer to him. She laid her head on his shoulder and kissed his neck.

Camilo backed away from her and tipped her chin up. He looked into her eyes. "Kim, I am not joking with you. I'm in love with you. I do know you. You are not what you say: a lunatic. You are a beautiful, smart, and passionate woman and that is why I am in love with you. Don't we have fun together?"

"Yes, but that doesn't mean necessarily that we love each other."

"I am not worried that you don't love me. I have love for both of us."

"Camilo, I don't know what I feel these days. I just got divorced and I ran away to escape from it and I found you. I'm going to just enjoy it for now."

"I can live with that, señorita," he said and kissed her again. "Let's have some lunch." He took her hand and led her back up the beach to the blanket. He sat down and pulled her toward him. Then he opened the basket and took out some brightly colored napkins. "From *mi madre*, too," he said and smiled. Camilo pulled out a loaf of French bread, three different kinds of cheeses, and an assortment of fresh berries.

"What a romantic lunch, Camilo." Kim took the bread and broke off a piece. "This is one of my favorite lunches. How did you know?"

He smiled. "Maybe I know you better than you think." He poured them each another glass of wine. They enjoyed the warm sunshine as they ate their lunch. The spot Camilo had picked had very few tourists, so they were virtually alone. Kim felt giddy. *Perhaps it is the wine, perhaps it is Camilo*, she thought. *I don't care. I just know that I like this eerily familiar feeling.*

When they were done, Camilo packed up the basket with the remaining food. He drank the last of his wine, reached over, pulled Kim down on the blanket, and then stretched out beside her. He folded his arms around her and she nuzzled her chin in his neck. He rolled her on her back and leaned over her, kissing her lips. His lips moved down to her neck and then to the top of her shirt. Before she knew it, she felt his hand on her skin; his touch sent shivers throughout her body.

She leaned her head farther back into the blanket and enjoyed the sensation. After a few moments, she sat up, pushed him back against the blanket, leaned down, and kissed his neck. She slid her hand under his shirt, his strong muscles pulsating against it, and kept it there for a minute, feeling the rapid beat of his heart.. When she looked up, Camilo's eyes were closed and he had a smile on his face. She leaned up and kissed him on the lips, then lay back down on the blanket, her head next to his, looking at the blue sky above where the seagulls were swirling, squawking as they searched for food.

"Camlio," she whispered, "you make me feel very alive, very beautiful, and very happy. I don't know if it's love. I'm not sure I really know what love is anymore, but whatever I am feeling, I like it. So thank you." She sat up and opened the picnic basket to find the rest of the bread. She took a piece and put it in her mouth. She took another piece and fed it to Camilo. "Now let's feed the seagulls."

She stood up and ran down the beach, laughing as she threw bread at the gulls. The number grew as she kept throwing bread, and the birds flocked around her. At times there were so many seagulls that they blocked her view so she could barely see Camilo.

They ended their lunch and then headed back toward Harlingen. "What time is it?" Kim asked as she leaned over and looked at the clock on the dashboard. It read three thirty. "You know, a ride in the Corvette would have been perfect today."

"But where would we put the tree?" Camilo said and grinned.

"Speaking of the tree, where are you taking me to get one? Can we go and cut one down ourselves? You must have a saw in this truck of yours."

"Kim, don't forget you are in south Texas. Christmas trees do not grow here; we have palm trees. But I know where we can go. There is a little place where I buy shrubs. They get Christmas trees from the north this time of year for those who want a real tree. That is where we are going."

An hour later, they were in the middle of nowhere, barren fields on either side of the road. There was virtually nothing in sight: no trees or homes, just flat, bare land where you could see for miles and miles. After driving for a while through the countryside, Camilo turned down a long gravel road surrounded by groves of orange, grapefruit, and lemon trees. He rounded a corner and the orchard opened up to a view of an enormous white mansion that looked as if it should be in southern Georgia.

"This is absolutely gorgeous!" Kim exclaimed.

When Camilo stopped the truck, he opened his door. "Come on. I will introduce you to the owner. But don't be alarmed, she is very, uh . . . what do you say? Eccentric!"

Kim soon found out what he was talking about. When they reached the front door, a fifty-something woman came out to greet them. She was wearing a long floral gown cut so low that it revealed most of the top of her breasts. She had a strong Southern accent and hugged Camilo tightly as he came near her. "Whatch y'all doing here, honey?" she kept her eyes fixed on Camilo.

"Belle, this is my . . . uh . . . *mi amiga*, Kim." He smiled at Kim and then turned back to Belle. "Kim, this is Belle. She owns one of the best nurseries in south Texas."

"One of the best? Camilo, I *am* the best!" Belle dug in the pocket of her dress and pulled out a tube of lipstick. She then covered her lips with a deep red hue and smiled at Camilo, all the while not taking her eyes off him. "Honey, you know I am the best—the best at a lot of things," she said and winked.

"Nice to meet you," Kim said as she extended her hand toward Belle.

Belle briefly looked at Kim, then turned back to Camilo without taking her hand away. "Is this your sweetheart, honey? She's pretty, but ain't she a little old for you?"

"Belle, that is not the southern hospitality you are known for!" Camilo winced as he looked over at Kim, who had narrowed her eyes, looking beyond Belle, in the direction of the orchards.

Camilo changed the subject. "We have come for a tree, a Christmas tree. You usually have a few, don't you?"

"Why yes, I do, darling. I didn't get very many this year. So I'm afraid they're a bit on the expensive side—"

"That's okay. The cost doesn't matter," Kim said, interrupting her.

Belle looked in her direction, her smile fading. "Y'all want to look at them?"

"Yes, please," Kim answered.

Camilo watched the two and smiled. Belle started to walk toward the white barn next to the house. "You know, I have always loved this child." This time she looked straight at Kim before turning back to Camilo, who was walking on the other side of her. She grabbed his cheek and gave him a kiss on the mouth. "This is the child I'm talking about," she said and laughed. "Not much of a child, though. He is one fine gentleman," she said and patted his butt. "I've been hoping to bed him, but so far, Camilo has not given me the pleasure."

Kim blushed while Belle spoke. *What brazen conversation for a southern lady,* she thought. She looked at Camilo, who was smiling. She could tell he was enjoying this and didn't seem at all alarmed about what Belle was saying. She imagined he was used to it.

"Not only does Belle have the best oranges and grape-fruits in the valley, she also grows some very beautiful plants. I come here sometimes if I need a bougainvillea for one of the parks."

"My dad loves that flower," Kim piped in. "He's so amazed at how they grow wild down here."

"Where y'all from, darling? I know you aren't from these parts, from the sounds of that accent of yours."

"I'm originally from Maine . . ."

"Oh, dear. We have a Yankee here, Camilo!" she exclaimed and whistled.

"But now I live in North Carolina"

"That is part of the South, isn't it?" Camilo asked rhetorically, smiling at Belle.

"Well, I guess so, but her heart is the heart of a Yankee." Belle looked at Camilo as she opened the two big barn doors and the light from outside flooded the room, showing off a large straw-covered floor. It smelled just like a horse barn, with hints of evergreen permeating the air. In the corner of the barn were two rows of cut evergreen trees stacked neatly against the wall.

"Blue firs from up near Houston way," Belle announced. "You can pick which one you like. I do prefer cash, though," she said and looked at Kim.

Why did she assume the tree is for me? Kim thought. Then she panicked. She didn't ever carry much cash.

"No problem," Camilo told Belle. "We have enough cash," he said and smiled at Kim. Kim scanned the trees and in a few minutes, picked out the one she wanted. She pointed it out to Belle and Camilo. A half hour later, they had it loaded and were heading back.

Kim looked at the clock in the truck. "It's almost five o'clock! My mom is probably back from the hospital by now, and I'm not even sure if my dad was able to come home with her." Kim paused and looked out the window. "I'm feeling kind of guilty," she said, glancing over at Camilo. She paused, then said, "But I did have a great time today. Thank you."

"I had a good time, too, Kim." He smiled at her and grabbed her hand.

"Now who is this Belle? And how do you know her? She's quite a character," Kim said with a grin.

"I told you who she is, señorita," he said and smiled. "I have known Belle for a few years now. She is really very nice and not as bad as she sounds."

"Well, she sure likes you. You'd better watch out."

"Are you jealous?"

"Well, no . . . I think I'm safe. I really don't think she's your type."

In another hour, Camilo pulled the truck into Jack and Nita's driveway. The lights were on, which told them that at least Nita was home. "Let's put up the tree tomorrow, if that's okay," she said and kissed Camilo on the cheek. "I'm kind of tired."

Nita came to the door when she heard them pull up. "Where have you been all day?" she asked. Kim could tell she was irritated. Both she and Camilo got out of the car.

"Sorry, Mom. I didn't mean to be gone so long. Camilo took me to lunch, and then we went to get a tree."

Nita came down the stairs and looked in the back of the truck. "Very nice . . . and it smells so much like Christmas." Nita hesitated for a minute before she spoke again, her voice soft. "Thank you, Kimberly." She gave Kim a hug, then walked over to Camilo and gave him a hug as well. Kim hoped the tears she could see in Nita's eyes were tears of joy and not sadness. It wasn't her intention to make her mom sad.

"Thank you," Nita said again as she wiped her eyes and walked back into the house.

CHAPTER TWENTY-SIX

Kim got up early the next morning so she could get started decorating the tree. Jack's doctors were pleased with his progress and the way his marrow was interacting with the virus. They were anticipating that they could start to put the marrow back in later that day, which meant he could be discharged either that day or the next morning. Kim wanted to make sure the tree was all done before he came home.

Camilo had brought the tree into the small house the night before, despite Kim's protest. "I will set it up for you so it's ready for when you want to decorate it," he had told her. Thank goodness the neighbors had a stand in their garage, as Kim had forgotten that she'd need a stand for a real Christmas tree. The fake ones she had had over the years had all came with their own stands.

She and Camilo had moved some furniture around and wedged the tree in between the living room and Nita's chair. It made the living space very crowded, but Kim didn't care, and she hoped her parents wouldn't either. By noon, Kim had the tree all decorated and ready for Christmas.

She stepped back to examine her creation, was pleased with what she saw, and smiled. She had picked out dark red and gold balls with gold beaded garland. It wasn't the old-fashioned ornaments from her childhood, but it was Christmassy, just the same. "Almost perfect," she said out loud.

"What did you say?" Nita asked after opening the sliding door and coming in. "Oh, my goodness; it's beautiful!"

"One more thing," Kim said. She picked up the gold star she had bought, climbed on the stool, and since the tree was only five feet tall, had no trouble putting the star into place on top. "There," she said and stepped down, turning to look at her mom.

Nita was looking at the tree intently, not saying a word, but just standing there. Kim started picking up the bags and wrappers that she had strewn all over the floor. From her mom's reaction, she was again afraid that her intention to cheer everyone up was failing. She had planned on putting a garland outside on the porch, but suddenly had second thoughts.

Finally, Nita spoke. "Thank you, dear," she said, and stood looking at the tree with her arms crossed in front of her. "This will make your dad happy. It's beautiful."

"It's okay, then, if I put some garland outside?"

"Of course; did you get lights, too?"

"Yes, I did!" Kim lifted up a bag filled with boxes of white lights and showed them to Nita. "Is Dad coming home today?" she asked and put her arm around her mom's shoulders.

"No. The doctors said not today, but they said for sure we can bring him home tomorrow. They want him to stay one more night so they can monitor him and they want to make sure he gets a good night's sleep. We'll pick him up in the morning."

Later that day, Kim ventured out to the mall again. Nita hadn't wanted to go with her. She had told Kim that she was tired and needed to rest before Jack came home. Kim wanted to get a few more things for Jack and Nita, and she also wanted to find a present for Camilo.

She hadn't asked him what he was doing for Christmas. She was sure he would be busy, but she still wanted to get him a gift. She just couldn't think of what that would be. She wandered around the mall for an hour looking for something that would be just right. She found Nita a necklace and earrings set, and was pleased with herself, because she knew Nita wouldn't buy anything like it for herself.

For Jack, she picked up a blanket that had a zipper and armholes. It looked rather funny, but warm, and she knew Jack would like it. He was always cold, especially when he watched television from his rocking chair.

After going into almost every store in the mall, Kim realized that she would not find the perfect gift for Camilo there. She needed to find a boutique, a shop that sold distinctive items. She wanted to find him something unique. She then remembered a little place off the highway that she had passed the other day on her way to the library. She noticed it because it struck her as oddly out of place; it didn't have the typical Mexican flare that so many of the other stores had. She was sure she could find something there, and an hour later, she did just that.

After looking through the Christmas ornaments and gifts, she spotted a wall adorned with painted artwork.

She stood looking at the watercolors and oil paintings. Some of them were abstract, some were landscapes, and some were still-lifes. When she had scanned almost the entire collection, she saw one on the end that caught her eye. It was a watercolor painting done of a sunny day at the beach. She was drawn to the serenity of the scene and then she read the title of the piece: "Padre Island, A Perfect Day." She felt goose bumps thinking about the afternoon they shared together the day before.

When Kim got home, Nita was taking a nap. She put her gifts away, grabbed her bag, and went out onto the porch. She sat down on the swing and took out the now-rumpled stack of papers she had been reading. She looked over the areas that she had highlighted until she found the name Javier Perales. She wanted to know more about him and where he was. *Another trip to the library,* she thought.

She then heard someone walking down the street, and Kim looked up from her reading. She smiled when she saw who it was. "Good afternoon," Camilo said, tipping his cowboy hat toward her. She had not seen him in a hat before; it gave him a whole new look.

"Hi, Camilo," she said with a smile. "I have the tree up; it looks great. Thank you again for helping me. Nita is taking a nap. Do you have time to sit and have a glass of wine with me?"

"No, Kim; not right now. I am still working. It is not too good to drink while working. It would not make a good impression for the men."

"Of course not. I'm sorry. You're right."

Camilo put his boot-clad foot on the bottom step. "I came over to ask you if I could see you tonight."

"Well . . ." Kim paused. "Yes, I guess that would be fine. Jack doesn't come home until tomorrow. I don't have anything planned. What do you have in mind?"

"Maybe you would like to come over to my home. I will cook for you."

Kim was surprised. He had mentioned he had a family home in Mexico, but he had never told her where in the area he lived. "You have a home here?" As soon as she said it, she wanted to take it back. "That sounded really dumb. Of course you have a place to live. Where is it?"

Camilo smiled at her. He took his hat off and ran his hand through his rumpled hair. "I am not sure if I should tell you where I live. No, I think I will surprise you," he said. His eyes twinkled as he teased her. "I will pick you up—"

"Oh, no. I'll drive myself," Kim interrupted.

"Kim, I think we are past worrying about whether we are or are not on a date, aren't we?"

"I didn't mean that. But if you are going to cook dinner for me, I can drive myself. Now where do you live?"

"Actually, we weren't far from it yesterday. I live on the river, about half an hour from here. Dinner will be at six o'clock," he said, grinning, then turning and heading back in the direction he had just come from.

"Hey, I don't know where I'm going," she yelled after him.

"Ah, *si*," he said. He walked back toward her, pulled a piece of paper and pen out of his pocket, wrote his address, and handed the paper to Kim. "Here's the address and the directions. You should have no problems." He turned and started to leave.

She looked at the address. "Hey," she yelled again. "I don't even know your last name."

"Perales," he responded.

"Perales," she repeated to herself. "I know that name," she said and ran after Camilo. "I know that name," she said again when she reached him.

"What?"

"Perales. I have heard that name before. I know that name."

"I am sure you have. It's one of the most popular names in Mexico, perhaps in the whole Hispanic culture," he said and laughed. "I should go," he said, and giving Kim a kiss on the cheek, he turned away while Kim turned to walk back to the house.

Kim opened her phone to check what time it was. She could still make it to the library and get back in time to get ready for dinner with Camilo. *They are going to get to know me well at the library,* she thought. It would be a lot easier to use the computer here but Kim still didn't find out what Nita's password was and Nita was bound to wake up from her nap at any time. It would be safer to search at the library.

Kim quickly gathered her things together, grabbed the van's keys, and set off for the library. Once there, she sat in front of a computer and typed in "Javier Perales," the name of the man from Mark's past who shared Camilo's last name. She thought it was ironic that Camilo and the drug lord had the same name, but like Camilo had said, it was probably one of the most popular Mexican names around. Several entries came up on the screen. *It must be a popular name,* she thought.

She needed to refine her search, but couldn't remember where in Mexico Javier had been from. She grabbed her bag, took out the article, and read that Javier was from Monterey, Mexico. She again typed, "Javier Perales" and "Monterey, Mexico." This time, Kim clicked on the first result that came up. It linked to an article titled, "Javier Perales—One of Mexico's Biggest Drug Bosses."

Kim scrolled through the article and found out what kind of a man this Señor Perales was. When Mexico's drug trafficking was on the rise, Perales had become mixed up with it all, becoming a very rich man along the way. He was involved with some of the most powerful Mexican law-enforcement officials who were corrupt, dangerous, and turned their heads at crime, allowing the export of drugs across the border.

Perales had paid these officials quite handsomely to ignore the illegal activity. He and his men even recruited American drug-enforcement agents to join the cartel, enticing them with cash that padded their small American salaries.

The Gulf Cartel had been one of the fastest growing cartels along the border. The headquarters were located in Matamoras, where Javier Perales owned a million-dollar complex. He lived there with his wife and three children. He also owned numerous other houses across that region of Mexico. The article stated his wife would often stay elsewhere with the children in order to get away from the life and business Javier had created. Kim clicked the browser button and went back to the search page, scrolling down until she clicked on another entry.

This account talked about the conviction of Perales. He had been tried in a United States court and found guilty of drug trafficking. The court documents stated that Perales had had a hand in smuggling over fifteen tons of cocaine and forty-six thousand pounds of marijuana across Mexican borders into the United States. He had laundered approximately ten million dollars as a result of his activities. She scanned the article further and read there had been pending murder allegations against Perales, but the defense attorneys hadn't had enough evidence to bring formal charges. Kim assumed the murder charges were still pending.

Kim sat back in her chair and thought about what she had just read. It was impossible to think that Mark had been a friend to this man. She wondered if the murder charges pending against Perales were for Mark's murder. She sat still and quiet for another minute, then looked around the library. She desperately needed a cup of coffee. She remembered seeing a coffee shop on the lower level. "Excuse me," Kim asked, turning to the young woman sitting at the computer next to her. "I have to run downstairs for a minute. Would you save this terminal for me?"

"Sure," the girl replied.

Kim was back in front of the computer in a few minutes. She set her coffee beside the computer monitor and typed in "Mark Carson" and "McAllen, Texas" and hit return. A reference about Jake Michaels's series of articles headed the list. She looked at the next entry. It looked as if it was about Mark and Carlos's and Associates Construction Company's dealings with housing authorities across Texas. Kim realized this was information she already knew, so she went back to the search page and typed in "Mark Carson," "Javier Perales," and "Texas." What she saw surprised her.

The search produced a link to transcriptions of the portion of the trial with Mark's testimony against his friend Javier Perales. Apparently, Mark had been instrumental in implicating Perales. He testified that Perales owned the warehouse in Brownsville, Texas, where Mark took his shipments after he picked them up in Reynosa. Kim thought back to the afternoon she spent with Mark. He had stopped by a warehouse while Kim waited in the car.

Mark's testimony also revealed how the two men had become business colleagues and friends. In fact, it gave a detailed account of the night they met. Mark had been at a bar in Matamoras, sitting alone on a barstool drinking tequila. He spoke to no one, only the bartender when he needed another drink. Perales walked into the bar just after Mark swallowed his fourth shot, and sat next to him. After the sixth shot, Mark began to tell him about his money troubles, both with the candle company and the construction company.

Perales questioned him about his candle business, and with all the tequila in him, Mark revealed everything about his manufacturing process and suppliers. Perales told him he might be able to help him, and handed Mark a napkin with a number scribbled on it. He told Mark to call him at that number the next day. But he warned Mark not to discuss their conversation with anyone.

Mark testified that he was desperate, so he called Perales per his instructions and they met a week later in Matamoras, at another dimly lit bar. The two men sat in a far back corner, with Javier facing the door. Perales asked more questions about Mark and his personal life; who his friends were, including his wife and any lovers. Then he wanted to know more about his two companies and his business partners.

Kim read in horror, shocked when she learned what Mark had said about Perales asking about his lovers. Mark's account in the transcript did not include the names of his friends and lovers; in their questioning, the attorneys only asked him about his business partners. But Kim knew one of those names was hers.

She could feel the hair rise on the back of her neck as she put her head in her hands. She felt sick to her stomach at the thought of what danger she had been so close to. After a few minutes, she looked back at the computer screen and touched the mouse again. She hesitated, not knowing if she wanted to go further. But she knew she needed to find out more.

Kim scrolled through the pages, feverishly reading each word. Mark said that Perales had his men thoroughly investigate him and everything about him before their next meeting. When Perales asked him questions a week later, he knew whether or not Mark was telling him the truth. Apparently, Mark passed the test, because they soon began to plan how to smuggle cocaine across the border.

At one meeting, Perales brought Mark a small bag containing a powdery substance. "That is some of the finest product in all the land," Perales told him. Mark tossed the bag back and forth from one hand to the other, staring intently at the contents. From there, Mark began to come up with the intricate plan of mixing the cocaine with the crystal form of paraffin wax.

Perales had his men investigate Mark's life; the words Kim read ran through her mind. *Investigate Mark's life,* she thought again. That meant investigate her. Kim wished she had had this information when she met Beth. She had many more questions, such as how long after Mark's testimony had his body been found. She tuned back to the computer screen and soon discovered the answer.

Mark's remaining testimony lasted only one day. The court accounts indicated that the judge declared a recess for the weekend. The prosecution would continue their questioning first thing Monday morning. When Kim scrolled through the documents, she saw no additional testimony from Mark. There was only an entry indicating that he had been found in contempt for not showing up as summoned.

Kim clicked off the computer and headed down the stairs and out the door. While she was walking to the van, she struggled to remember twenty-five-year-old details, details that would give her a sense of what she may or may not have known about the drugs or Perales. As she reached for the keys, Kim could feel the pit in her stomach swell.

CHAPTER TWENTY-SEVEN

At five thirty, Kim pulled the van out of the driveway. Before she left, she walked with Nita over to the hall where she was going to have dinner with some of her friends.

"I can get back by myself," she had assured Kim. "Now you go and have fun."

"Thanks, Mom," Kim responded, putting her hand on Nita's shoulder.

Kim followed the directions Camilo had given her and arrived at his home promptly at six o'clock. She turned down a narrow dirt road and proceeded down a steep hill. The yard had patches of sand and grass, with a few shade trees scattered around. When she came to the house, she pulled the van behind Camilo's white truck and got out. The door opened and Camilo stepped out wearing a red apron and holding a glass of wine.

Kim laughed. "Wow! You are the chef, aren't you?"

Camilo handed her the glass of wine and kissed her on the cheek. "Yes, señorita. I am. Please come into my home. I cook you a nice feast."

Camilo's home was a quaint little cottage overlooking the river. A porch wrapped around the entire house.

Camilo motioned Kim toward the steps that led to the porch. "Come, I want to show you something." Kim followed him as he walked to the side overlooking the river. He picked up a glass of wine he had setting on the railing and raised his glass toward Kim.

"What are we toasting to now?" Kim said and laughed.

"To us!" Camilo clinked the edge of Kim's glass and took a sip.

"To us . . . I guess," Kim said and took a sip of her wine. "What does 'us' mean, Camilo?"

"Too many questions. Let's just enjoy." He set down his glass and walked down the stairs toward the river. "Stay there," he called back to Kim. She stood and watched him as he stepped onto the small rectangle dock that jutted out about four feet from the shore. He got down on his knees, reached toward the water, and pulled up a wire-mesh box.

"What is that?" Kim yelled. She set her glass down and ran to where Camilo was standing, holding up the trap. "What are those?" Kim bent down to get a closer look.

"Blue crabs," he said and smiled. "Their brothers and sisters are going to be part of our dinner. I wanted to show you where I caught them."

"What? We're having fresh crab for dinner?" Kim clapped her hands together.

"*Si*, we are having fresh crab cakes for our first course," Camilo said.

Kim looked past Camilo at the water. "What's the name of this river?" she asked.

"Arroyo Colorado. It means red stream in Spanish.

Kneel down and put your hand in the water," he said. Kim leaned over and touched the water. "Now lick your fingers," he instructed.

"Wow, it's salty!"

"Yes; it always surprises my amigos when they see this river. They don't think of it as being salty like the ocean. The water here comes up from the Gulf, so that is why we get the marine life, such as these crabs."

The table inside was set with a red tablecloth and white napkins. Flickering red tapered candles gave the room a warm glow. Kim sat down at the table and looked out over the water. The sun was setting, and as it got darker, Kim could see the lights along the deck and the walkway down to the river start to come on. She noticed her reflection in the window and smiled. The candles flickered back at her as Camilo poured her another glass of wine.

Dinner started with the most wonderful crab cakes that Kim had ever tasted. For the entree, Camilo had made a blue cheese–crusted filet mignon, served with fresh asparagus and warm bread, right from the oven. Along with dinner, they enjoyed two different kinds of wine. The first was a white chardonnay that Camilo said was from a small vineyard in the south of France. "My amigo brought me a bottle the year he visited there and told me how beautiful it was," he explained. The wine was excellent with the crab cakes. The second was a full-bodied cabernet sauvignon that was paired with the filet.

By the time they were done with dinner, it was eight o'clock. They chatted the entire time, stopping only to fill their wine glasses or for Camilo to serve the next course.

Kim insisted they not talk about her divorce. So they talked mostly about Kim's childhood, the restaurant Jack owned, and the many summers she spent at the resort. Camilo listened closely while Kim described the resort life and how pretty northern Maine was in the summer.

After dinner, they moved to the living room. There was a chill in the air, so Camilo started a fire in the small fireplace that stood in the corner. Kim took her wine glass with her and curled up on the sofa, watching him. "Now I want to know more about you, what you like and dislike," she told him. "What is your favorite thing to do when you're not working?"

"That is easy," he began. "I like to spend my time here fishing, reading, and enjoying a nice glass of vino." He smiled, then hesitated. "No, here is my second-favorite place. The first is in Mexico, in the most beautiful casa on the beach."

"Is that your family home?" Kim asked.

"Yes, it is south of Padre Island." Camilo stopped what he was doing and looked up. "Kim, I have a great idea; why don't you come for a few days, spend some time on the beach with me?"

Kim took a sip of wine. "That sounds nice, but I really should spend the time with Jack and Nita."

"We could ring in the New Year together, another toast to us."

Kim thought for a minute. It would be a nice alternative to ringing in the New Year with the old folks at the recreation hall. "Speaking of Padre Island, I have a present for you." Kim took a package wrapped in brown paper out of her purse and handed it to Camilo. "I saw this and couldn't resist. Merry Christmas," she smiled.

"Señorita, you didn't have to buy me a present." He tore away the wrapping and took out the picture. "Ah," he said and smiled. "Thank you . . . It was a perfect day."

"Merry Christmas," she said again.

"Now, how about New Year's? We can make another perfect day."

"That sounds intriguing. I'll think about it," she said.

Camilo sat on the couch next to Kim and softly kissed her cheek. "Think hard," he whispered. He traced his finger down her cheek and kissed her lips gently. Kim closed her eyes and moved closer to him, kissing him back. Each time she did, their kisses became more passionate and intense. Camilo pushed her gently against the couch and put his hand at the back of her head, caressing her neck. Kim sighed at his touch and kisses. It had been a long time since she had felt this aroused. She let herself enjoy the sensation for a while, before she lightly pushed away from him. She knew she could easily fall into bed with him, but she wasn't ready.

"I'm sorry," she whispered.

"No need to be worried, señorita," Camilo said and smiled at her. "I don't want to do anything that will hurt you. Please, Kim, don't be sorry."

"You are amazing," she said, then looked at her watch. "I'd better get on the road," she said. "Nita will be worried."

"I will make you coffee and we can have our dessert. Coffee will keep you awake on your drive home. Of course, you could spend the night," he said and winked.

"Nice try," Kim said and smirked back at him. "I don't think Nita would like that, but yes, coffee will be good. My head's a little fuzzy from the wine." She picked up her clothes, put them back on, then got up from the couch and reached for her purse. *I should call Mom and tell her I'll be on my way soon,* Kim told herself.

CHAPTER TWENTY-EIGHT

Jack came home the next morning. Nita and Kim were at the hospital early to pick him up. Kim had not gotten back from Camilo's until almost midnight, and the lack of sleep left her exhausted. Nita had woken up at six o'clock and started to make coffee, which made Kim wake up sooner than she wanted to. She lifted her head off the pillow when she heard her mom in the kitchen, quickly laid it back down, and closed her eyes. She could feel a slight headache from the wine she had had the night before.

"Good morning," Nita said softly. She poured a cup of coffee and poked her head around the corner. "Late night at Camilo's?" she said and smiled.

"I hope I didn't wake you when I came home," Kim said as she sat up.

"No, I was awake anyway. I don't sleep much anymore."

Kim got up and poured herself a cup of coffee. She walked over to the Christmas tree, picked up the cord, and plugged it into the socket. She stepped back and looked at her creation. She was searching for some sort of Christmas cheer to well up inside of her, but it just wasn't happening. The sunshine coming in from the window drained the sparkle from the lights, so she unplugged them. *Maybe tonight,* she thought.

After more coffee and a shower each, Nita and Kim went to pick up Jack. When they arrived home, Nita got him settled in and went over to the office for a few hours while Jack took a nap. "I feel tired," he told Kim as Nita walked out the door. "Just the trip home took all I had out of me."

After he went back to the bedroom, Kim walked over to the pool area to get some sun. She brought a magazine and her phone. She wanted to forget about things for a while, so she left Jake Michaels's articles at home. She would read about the scandals of the stars instead.

After fifteen minutes, Kim's phone rang.

"Hello?"

"I miss you!" It was Camilo on the other line. "How are you today, señorita?"

"I'm good, thank you," Kim replied. She smiled at the thought of the night before. "Thank you for a wonderful evening and such a superb meal."

"You are very welcome, Kim. Have you thought about New Year's yet?"

"I haven't talked to Nita about what they are going to do. My dad just got home today, and I want to make sure everything is fine with him before I decide. We still have Christmas to celebrate." Without hesitating, she blurted out, "Do you want to come for Christmas?" After the words came out of her mouth, she wished she hadn't asked.

"That is very kind of you, Kim, but I must decline. You must spend the time alone with your *padres.* I will be going to Mexico City in a few days to see my sister and her family. I will spend Christmas there, and then I am going to go to my beach house in Fraccionamiento."

"Where?" Kim asked.

"Fraccionamiento. It's a small town just over the border from Brownsville and south Padre Island, the place I was telling you about. I will prepare and wait for you to come and see me."

Kim laughed, but it was sounding more and more intriguing. She was not going to say no, but she also was not going to agree, not just yet. "Just like I told you last night, I will think about it."

"Promise?"

"I promise," she replied.

When they were done talking, Kim leaned back and closed her eyes. It had been a very interesting ten days since she arrived in Texas. It certainly had not been what she had expected when she booked the flight here. She liked the feelings she was experiencing with Camilo, but not the contrasting feelings worrying about her dad. And then there was the discovery of Mark's past and the possibility of him being alive. *Wow,* she thought, *life will certainly be boring back in North Carolina.*

The thought of home prompted her to call Connie. She hadn't talked to her for a few days and wanted to tell her about her evening with Camilo, and to find out how she and Juan were doing.

—•••—

Connie searched her purse for her phone. She was sitting on a bench overlooking the ocean. The beach lay in front of her and the sunshine flooded over her, creating a warmth deep inside. She was not sure if it was the sun or the thought of Juan.

"Hello," she answered.

"Hi; it's me," Kim replied.

"Honey, how are you today?" Connie said and reached for the cup of coffee sitting next to her. "I'm sitting here waiting for the most gorgeous man in the world."

"Well, that can't be right," Kim chirped in a sing-song voice. "I spent last night with the most gorgeous man in the world."

"You slept with him?"

"No! Why must I keep reminding you that I am not like you? I approach my relationships much differently."

"I've changed, you know."

"You have? And how is that?"

Connie stood up and started walking toward the board-walk. "I've spent the last few days and evenings with Juan. We have been running, eating out, and having deep conversations; the sex thing seems to be on the back burner."

Kim laughed. "You really have changed!"

"Really," Connie repeated. Her tone of voice changed to a soft whisper. "I've not felt like this about someone for a long time . . . maybe never."

"I'm happy for you. What are we going to do when we both have to leave our men to go back to North Carolina?"

"Maybe we don't have to."

"All right, sister, you're sounding crazy. What have you done with my friend Connie?"

"I'm not crazy. I have just been listening to you. Relationships may not be so bad."

"I know I've been saying that, but really, why would you listen to a newly divorced woman who couldn't keep her marriage together? I hate to tell you, but I'm no expert on the subject." Kim laughed.

"By the way, when we last talked, you said you had been thinking about certain people from your past. What people were you talking about?" Connie asked.

"Something I'll tell you when I see you in person, not over the phone," Kim told her. "It's not bad, just some old memories I managed to scrounge up."

Connie reached the boardwalk and looked around. "What are you doing for New Year's?" she asked. She couldn't see Juan anywhere and she was getting a little nervous. He was supposed to meet her a half hour ago for a run and coffee. *No need to panic,* she thought.

"I have to get through Christmas first," Kim answered. "Camilo asked me to spend a few days with him over New Year's. He has a beach house in Mexico."

"Are you going?"

"I'm not sure yet, but guess what? I'm leaning toward yes! What are you going to do?'

"For New Year's?" Connie questioned.

"Well, yes for New Year's, but what about Christmas?"

"I'll hang low—not many plans. Juan will be spending it with his family. I only can imagine there will be lots of little nieces and nephews running around, making all kinds of noise. I shudder at the thought of all the little brats. I'll wait and spend an intimate New Year's Eve with Juan all by myself." Connie spotted Juan from the distance and waved in his direction to get his attention. "I have to go; Juan is here and we're supposed to go for a quick run. I'll call you later."

Connie hung up and started in Juan's direction. When she got closer, she saw that he was still wearing his business suit. "I thought we were going for a run?" Her words came out in the form of a whine and she winced.

"Sorry, honey," he said kissed her cheek. "Something came up and I won't be able to today. Can you forgive me?"

"Of course I can," she said and smiled. "We can at least go for coffee?"

"No, I can't even go for coffee. I only wanted to come and find you so I could tell you in person. I have to go." He smiled at her, kissed her cheek, and walked across the boardwalk to his parked black Mercedes. She watched as he opened the door, got in, and drove away. When he was completely out of sight, she turned back toward the ocean.

There was something odd about the tone of his voice. Perhaps she was just paranoid, paranoid because now she had let herself open up and become part of a relationship.

CHAPTER TWENTY-NINE

The next few days went by quickly. With each passing day, Jack showed signs of improvement and was feeling much better. Dr. Lopez said that he was confident that the treatment had worked, but cautioned Jack that he would not be able to fully tell for a few months. At that point, if the results were still promising, they would start chemotherapy.

"I trust you, doc," Jack joked with him during a follow-up visit.

Kim had gone along with Jack and Nita to the appointment, because when he was done, Jack wanted to go to his favorite Mexican restaurant for lunch. She waited outside the office while her parents talked with the doctor. When they came out, Dr. Lopez followed them into the waiting area.

"Kim!" he said. He looked surprised to see her. "How have you been?"

"I've been great, but more important, how is my dad?"

"It looks like he will be just fine. Now that we know he is out of danger, I'd like to ask you a question." Dr. Lopez gently laid his hand on her elbow and guided her out of earshot of Jack and Nita.

Kim was startled. *What could he possibly want?* she thought. "Sure; what is it?" she asked.

"I was wondering if you would like to have dinner with me sometime before you leave for home. Your parents said you were not going back until after the holidays."

"When did you talk to my parents about me?" Her words sounded harsh and she wished she could take them back.

"I know that it may seem like a bit of a professional conflict, but you're not really my patient, so I think it's okay."

Kim didn't know what to say. She didn't need one more thing to clutter her mind and add to the many thoughts swirling in her head. "Well . . . I, uh . . . ," she stammered. "I'm flattered, but you don't know me. I could be some sort of druggie, or worse—a serial killer." Her attempt at humor failed. *Didn't I just say this to Camilo a few weeks ago?* she remembered.

"Kim, I know you're not a serial killer. I also know that you just went through a very rough time and may need some companionship."

Way to go, Jack and Nita, she thought. Apparently, they had talked about her love life—or lack of it—to anyone who would listen. She would have to ask them to be more discreet. "Can . . . can I let you know?" she asked, stammering again. "It's just that, well . . . I'm really not looking to date." *That was a lie,* she thought. "Nothing against you. I'm flattered; it's just I need some time away from men for now." *Another lie.* Her face flushed and she turned toward her parents so he wouldn't see.

"How about if I call you after Christmas?" he asked.

"Well . . ." She turned to look at him again. "How about if I call you?" she replied. "I still have your card." She turned and looked in the direction of her parents again. "We should be going. We're going to Jack's favorite place to eat," she said and smiled.

"Are you going on a date with Dr. Lopez?" Nita asked when they got into the car. "What about Camilo?"

Kim shot a look at Nita. "Mom, you have to stop telling people about my divorce. I feel like my life is an open book. Camilo knew about my . . . situation, and now Dr. Lopez."

"It's not so bad that Camilo came around, right?" Nita asked and smiled.

Jack was sitting in the back seat, listening to the two of them talk. After a few minutes of silence he piped in. "Just so my little girl is happy." Kim smiled. She looked over at Nita, who was also smiling.

A few days before Christmas, Kim started to plan the dinner menu. Nita had said that she didn't care what they had to eat when Kim asked her if it was all right if she did the cooking. She felt like she needed to occupy her mind for a while. Camilo was in Mexico City for Christmas and thoughts of him invaded her mind constantly, so she needed a diversion.

In reality, she would soon be leaving to go back to North Carolina and was concerned about how far her relationship with Camilo had gone. She had decided that she would enjoy the time she'd spend with him while she was here, but after that, she would return to North Carolina and move on with her life.

The menu Kim chose consisted of pork medallions

with a cranberry and red wine sauce, accompanied with a side of wild rice pilaf and toasted almonds. She would serve it with a side salad with creamy Parmesan dressing, and for dessert, a golden-crusted crème brûlée. The dinner would be a far cry from what Nita and Jack were used to, but Kim wanted to indulge them a little and have some fun. When she was writing out the menu and searching for recipes on the Internet, Jack walked in from outside. He had been over at the hall visiting his friends and making sure shuffleboard and bowling were being handled correctly.

"Dad, did you get everyone straightened out over there?" Kim kept looking at the monitor as she spoke to him. "How are the boys doing?" she teased.

"Everything is just fine, shuffleboard league is going okay and the 'boys' are doing the same." He laughed and patted her on the shoulder when he walked by. "What are you doing?"

"Getting ready for our Christmas dinner. We're going to have a magnificent meal for our celebration."

"That's good; just as long as you're making oyster stew."

"Dad! No, not oyster stew!" Kim looked up from the computer and shifted her body so she could look directly at him.

"It's not Christmas without oyster stew," he told her.

"Ugh; Dad, I hate that stuff. Mom doesn't like it, either. You'd be the only one eating it."

"It's not Christmas without oyster stew," he repeated.

Kim jotted down a few notes on the pad next to her and did a search for oyster stew on the computer.

CHAPTER THIRTY

The sun beamed into the window and flooded the spot where Kim slept. She had forgotten to close the shade the night before, due in part to the fact that she had had one too many glasses of wine. Since they were not doing anything for Christmas Eve, Sam Corley had invited the three of them over for some Christmas cheer. He said he was having just a few people, but when she arrived with her parents, Kim thought that most of the park had to be there. The senior citizens and their interactions with each other thoroughly entertained her; Kim decided that it was just like a college fraternity, only with much older students, and these students had money.

Camilo had called to wish her a Merry Christmas and laughed at her, saying that she must be having fun, commenting on how her words sounded funny when she wished him a Merry Christmas.

"I am," she slurred. "And you? How is Mexico?"

"My *nijas* are doing fine. They are excited for Santa Claus to come. I can't wait to see you again. Are you coming for New Year's?" he'd asked. Kim nodded. There was silence. "Kim?" Camilo said after a few seconds.

"Yes," she softly said.

The next morning when Kim got out of bed, she remembered that Camilo had called. Had she told him that she was going to meet him for New Year's? She couldn't remember; she hoped not, because she hadn't talked to Nita and Jack about it yet. She thought she would bring up the idea today, perhaps during dinner.

Kim spent most of the morning in the kitchen, preparing their meal. They decided to eat early, so they could take a walk around the park to give Jack some exercise and visit friends. She made her planned meal, along with Jack's oyster stew. And as she had predicted, he was the only one who ate it. But she didn't care; he was pleased.

After dinner, Kim brought up the idea of her spending a few days with Camilo. Jack raised his eyebrows. "And spend time with him where?" he asked. He was eating the crème brûlée Kim had set in front of him.

"He has a home across the border, in Mexico. It's somewhere south of Matamoras."

"You have to be careful over there," Jack interrupted. "There's a lot of drug stuff going on—shootings in the streets, I hear."

"It'll be okay," Kim reassured him. "I'm sure Camilo will not put me in any danger."

"And about Camilo," Jack said as he took another bite. "Are you jumping into things too fast?" His stern tone startled Kim. "I know Alex broke your heart, and I know your marriage may not have been a good one, but you should take things slow," he cautioned.

"Dad, I'll be fine." Kim felt like she was beginning to sound like a broken record. "I know what you're saying, and I'll be careful. He is a nice man and easy to talk to. I enjoy my time with him, but I also know I'll be going home and that will be that. Don't worry," she assured him again. She got up from her chair and picked up her plate. She walked past Jack, picked up his plate, too, and kissed him on the cheek.

"I just don't want you to get hurt again. Plus, you need to be careful about how you throw yourself around these days."

"Dad! I don't throw myself around. How could you say that?" Kim was disappointed that he even thought that she would do anything risky. Then her face suddenly turned red as she put the dishes in the sink. *Thank goodness Dad can't see me*, she thought. *I am doing something risky. How close had I been to getting into bed with Camilo the other night?*

During their conversation, Nita had sat in silence. Kim couldn't tell from the reaction on her face what she was thinking, and then she finally spoke. "I think it is perfectly okay for Kim to spend time with Camilo. His company has been doing work for the park for quite some time now, and everyone at the office knows him and his reputation. He is a good man. I don't think he will do anything to hurt Kim," she said and looked at Jack, her eyebrows knitted together.

Kim was surprised at her mom's support. She hadn't been used to that kind of support from her in the past, but things had changed lately and she welcomed it. "Thanks, Mom," she responded. Jack scowled and got up from the table. Kim followed him to his chair and sat down on the footstool in front of him. She hated for him to be displeased with her. "Dad, please don't be mad," she whispered.

"Just be careful," he said, scowling at her again and then smiling. "You know I can't be mad at my little girl."

Kim motioned her parents toward the Christmas tree. They pulled their chairs in front of the tree and opened their presents. Nita liked the necklace and Kim could see tears in her eyes when she opened it. "I told you, the only present we needed was your visit."

"I know, Mom, but I wanted to get you something nice."

Jack lit up when he opened his gift. "How did you know I wanted one of these? I saw them on television the other day and thought how nice it would be when I sit in my chair. Your mother didn't think I needed it," he said and winked at Nita.

"I didn't say that," she said, frowning at Jack and then turning and smiling at Kim. "I'm glad you got if for your dad. He will use it a lot; he always gets cold. Thank you."

Jack wrapped himself in his new blanket and grinned as he stroked the soft material. Nita got up, walked over to the tree, and picked up a gift the size of a shoe box and handed it to Kim. "Here's your present."

"I thought we weren't going to exchange gifts?" Kim questioned her.

"It's nothing; just a little something." She sat back down in her chair and watched as Kim opened the package that was wrapped in newspaper. Newsprint was staple gift wrapping at the Whitman household, a tradition Jack had started years before.

"How did you guess I wanted a new pair of shoes!"

Kim said before she took off the paper, giving her mom an impish smile. What she opened was not shoes at all, but a bottle of wine, a red zinfandel.

"I know you like wine, so I had dad go to the liquor store and ask the clerk what would be a nice red wine. You know, I usually only drink Lambruso or white zinfandel, but they tell me that's not true wine."

"Who tells you that?" Jack asked.

"Sam or Bob or one of the ladies in the office—I'm not sure which one it was. But they know wine and I don't," she said and looked embarrassed.

"It's very nice of you, Mom; thank you. And Dad, too. Thanks to both of you."

"You have another one," Nita said. She got up from her chair again and picked up another package from underneath the tree.

"Another one? You guys didn't have to get me anything, let alone two presents."

Nita handed her the package wrapped again in newspaper. "Careful; it's heavy. Your dad wrapped it," Nita said as she sat back down.

Kim grabbed the present; it *was* heavy. "What did you get me, bricks?"

"Almost," Jack said under his breath.

Kim took the paper off the box and opened it. Inside she found a pile of rocks that appeared to be from Jack's garden in the back of the house. "Very funny, Dad," she said as she cocked her head and gave him a sarcastic smirk.

"Do you like them?" he asked and laughed. Kim started to put the box aside, thinking that the rocks were one of Jack's jokes and that there was nothing else in the box. "Don't you want to look further at what's in there?" He grinned.

Kim dug deeper and discovered a small box underneath the rocks. She pulled out the package. This time it was wrapped in bright red paper. "I took that from the hall the other day. They were going to throw it away, so I told them I wanted it," Jack said.

Kim gave him a puzzled look. "Okay . . ." she said. She opened the package and to her surprise, found a bracelet.

"It was your Grandmother Sadie's bracelet," Jack told her. "Your mother had it in her drawer for years and never wore it. We thought you might like it. You seem to wear those kinds of things."

Kim picked up the bracelet from the box. It reminded her of something Sadie would wear. She had had a flare for style and had always accessorized her outfits, even when she was working around the resort. Kim turned the bracelet over and over in her hands, surprised at how heavy it was. It was made of solid gold and silver links intertwined together, creating the look of a heavy chain.

"Thank you very much. I love it!" Kim got up and gave them both a hug. "This means a lot to me; thank you." She put the bracelet on her right arm and twirled it around, marveling at how beautiful it was and, more importantly, the fact that it had been her grandmother's.

While Kim admired her new bracelet, her phone rang in the distance. For a minute, she didn't remember where she had put it. Then she realized it was on the shelf next to Nita's computer.

"Hello?" she answered.

There was silence.

"Hello?" she said again. This time she could barely make out a whimper on the other end. "Who is this?" she snapped.

She could just make out another whimper. Then a soft voice said, "It's me."

"Connie?" Kim asked, her voice softening. "What's wrong?"

"I don't know what to say." Kim could hardly hear Connie. "I put myself out there and thought that finally I understood that relationships are good and that I need to be in one, then whammy; I get punched in the stomach."

"He hit you?"

"No, no," Connie replied. " I mean, just when I thought things were going so well, I find out something that took the air out of my sail.

"What happened?"

"Juan, Juan is what happened—or didn't happen," Connie sobbed. She was silent before she continued. "I was sitting in my house, sipping a glass of wine by myself when I thought, I should just give in and go be with his family and spend Christmas with him. He said they would all be together, so I figured they were at the condo where he took me the first night we met."

Connie hesitated again. Kim could hear another sob then a sniffle. "The condo is not far from this house, so I decided to take the boardwalk there. When I got closer, I could see all kinds of people on the patio and balcony and thought it was his family gathering—his brothers, sisters, and their children."

She stopped and blew her nose. "That was not the case. I let myself in through the patio door and mingled in with the many guests, looking for Juan. I made my way to the kitchen and when I got there, I saw Juan embracing a beautiful dark-haired woman. I stood in the doorway, watching, while they kissed. Then he noticed me. I turned and left as quickly as I could—"

"Oh, honey," Kim interrupted. "I'm so sorry."

"Turns out he *was* spending Christmas with his family: his wife and children! Kim, he's married—married, can you believe it?" She started crying again and Kim could hear Connie's hand cover the phone's mouthpiece.

"How do you know that was his wife?" Kim asked. When she got no answer, Kim pleaded again. "Connie, Connie, can you hear me?" Kim waited for her friend to respond. She wished she could snap her fingers and be by her side. *She should not be alone,* Kim thought. "Connie," she said again.

Connie answered in a soft voice, "I'm here." She paused, and then continued. "When he followed me, he stopped me at the boardwalk and told me who the woman was. He said he had meant to tell me and that he hadn't wanted to lead me on, but there never was a good time."

"Hmm, that's funny," Kim said with a cynical laugh. "That's exactly what Alex told me. What is wrong with these men? Where are you? Are you back at your house?"

"Yes," was the faint response.

"I should come out there," Kim blurted out. She wasn't sure how she would do that, but at that moment she didn't care; Connie needed her.

"No, that's not what I want. That would only make me feel worse, to have you ruin your vacation, too."

"You shouldn't be alone," Kim coaxed.

"I'll be fine; please don't come. You need to stay there and take care of your parents. I just need a night for the shock to wear off, then I'll be back to my old self by morning. And I mean my old self, Kim. I'm swearing off relationships because see what happens?" Kim could hear her softly crying softly again. "I'm going to hang up now, Kim; I'll call you in the morning."

"Wait!" Kim insisted, and then she heard a click.

CHAPTER THIRTY-ONE

After she hung up with Kim, Connie poured herself a glass of wine and headed outside. She stopped when she got to the glass doors, went back inside, grabbed the bottle, and went back out to sit on the porch. She could hear music playing all along the boardwalk, some of it Christmas music, some just plain old rock and roll. With each sip of wine, it all became muddled together in one big blare of sound.

She was displeased with herself, first for calling Kim. Now she has ruined Kim's Christmas as well. But she was more displeased with herself for falling for Juan. She should have known better. Hell, she *had* known better. How did she miss the signs that he was married? She never needed men in the past, and always did just fine on her own. Why did she have to change that now?

Connie sat for an hour watching the people strolling along the beach. She heard chatter and laughter floating in the air and tried to imagine what the conversations were about, even making up possible scenarios, anything to take her mind off of Juan and her broken heart. *This is the perfect place to spend Christmas—or at least I thought so a few hours earlier.*

She poured more wine into her glass and looked at the bottle; it was almost empty. "Looks like I need to go get some more supplies," she said to herself. She made her way down to the first level and searched the cupboards for another bottle of wine. She opened every door, but found nothing more than a half-empty bottle of Diet Coke. She then remembered that there was a liquor store down the way, but she wasn't sure it was going to be open on Christmas Day. She grabbed her purse and opened the door to the patio, turning to flip the lock.

"Hello," a voice said behind her.

Connie jumped and spun around to find Juan standing there. "What are you doing here?" she yelled at him, her face turning hot with anger.

"Connie, can we talk?" he asked and stepped toward her.

"Talk about what, the fact that you're married?"

"I didn't want you to be alone after you ran out like that. You left without giving me a chance to explain."

"What more was there to explain after you said that the woman you were kissing was your wife? You can't possibly tell me you're getting a divorce and that you don't have much of a marriage anymore," she said and then gasped for air. "No, that's not what I saw back there. I saw you passionately kissing your wife! And you know what? I feel sorry for her, but I really feel sorry for you. I may go from one guy to the next, but at least I am not living a lie."

Connie moved toward him. "Get out of here," she said through gritted teeth. When he didn't move, she screamed, "Get out of here!"

"Connie, wait."

"Get out of here!" she screamed louder. A dog started barking next door and someone yelled from the loft across the street to shut up. After a few minutes, Juan walked away. "Good riddance," she said under her breath.

Connie finished locking the patio door and waited until Juan was out of sight. Then she walked down the boardwalk in the opposite direction, toward the liquor store. When she got there, she smiled. She was in luck; it was open. *That's California for you*, she thought as she wiped the tears from her face and walked in.

—•••—

Connie slept poorly that night, tossing and turning, trying to calm her mind and clear her head. Her thoughts were not necessarily of Juan as much as how she had been so stupid. She just couldn't forgive herself. When dawn came, panic set in. The thought of spending New Year's alone frightened her. Back in North Carolina, she always had a party to go to and always had someone to kiss at midnight.

When the sun came up, Connie had a plan. Jim had always been a good friend, listening to all her escapades and hearing about the trouble she got into. He had even held her hair back while she got sick from drinking too much at a work party. He had helped her into the bathroom and sat with her until she felt better, then took her home, all the while not trying to maul her or get into her pants.

He was then—and always remained—a true gentleman. She didn't find him attractive in the least, but she did like him, sort of like a brother. From dawn until morning, his image kept popping into her head. It seemed to be a good plan. She would call and invite Jim out to spend New Year's with her. The house had two bedrooms, so that wouldn't be a problem. If he hesitated, she would agree to pay for his ticket so he couldn't have any excuses. *Of course, he may already have a date,* she thought, *but not likely*.

Connie waited until it was nine o'clock in the morning, Eastern time. She sat on her porch sipping coffee, watching the clock until the big hand clicked on the twelve and the little on the six. Then she pulled her phone out of the pocket of her robe. She flipped through her contact numbers and came to Jim's.

"Jim," she said when he answered after five rings. "Did I wake you?"

Jim's voice was groggy on the other end. "What?" he asked. "Who is this?"

"Oh, I did wake you; I'm sorry."

"Connie?"

"Yes," she said softly.

"Connie, what's wrong? Is everything okay?" His voice rose in pitch as he spoke.

"Sorry Jim; I didn't mean to wake you."

"Look, you didn't wake me."

"Yeah, right," she said and smiled to herself. He was such a sap. She knew he would do anything for her. "I was wondering . . . um . . ." she stammered. "What are you doing for New Year's Eve?"

Jim's voice calmed. "What do you mean, what am I doing for New Year's Eve?"

"It's not that hard of a question," she replied. "I was just wondering if you wanted to spend it with me?"

"Connie, you are, what, maybe five thousand miles away from here. Spending New Year's with you is going to be tough, don't you think?" She could hear the sarcasm in his voice.

Perhaps this is a bad idea, she thought. She had imagined that this would be quick and easy, but he was making it very difficult. "I mean, I was thinking, if you wanted . . . you could fly out to San Diego." She waited to hear his response. When she didn't hear one, she said, "Jim, are you there?" The hand with which she gripped the phone was getting sweaty. *What am I thinking?*

"I'm here," he finally said. "Why do you want me to come out there?" His voice was accusatory. "I thought you were trying to get away from all of North Carolina, including me."

"That's not true," Connie said, stiffening. "I never said I was running away from anything. I just wanted to get away from the cold and dreariness. Why are you sounding so condescending? I just called you to see if we could spend New Year's together. You are a good friend and I thought it would be fun."

"What, your California boys didn't work out?"

"What?" Connie asked indignantly. Then she hung up. She got up from her chair and, out of frustration, threw what was left of her coffee over the railing. Only then did she look down to make sure she didn't hit anyone. "Bastard," she hissed.

It took Connie three hours to finally call Jim back. He had called her several times, but every time she saw his number, she hit the hang-up button. She really didn't know what she was going to say to him. The invitation was out there, but it was clear to her he didn't want to come. How was she going to take it back?

"Hi," she said when she finally got the nerve to stay on the line when he answered. Her voice was barely a whisper.

"Hi back," he said.

"Sorry I hung up on you, but you were really being a bastard. I was just trying to be nice and wanted to know if you would like to spend some time with me."

"That's just it, Connie; I don't want to be your consolation prize—"

"Wait a minute," Connie interrupted. "I never said anything remotely close to the fact you were a consolation prize. Now you are being a bastard again."

"Don't hang up!" he quickly responded. "I'm sorry; it's just that, if I fly out there, am I going to play second fiddle to some young surfer boy?"

Connie lowered her voice again. She paused and then told him the story about Juan. "That does not mean you are a consolation. It's just that when I was agonizing over everything last night, your face kept popping into my head. You are a stabilizing figure in my life and I think that's what I need right now. How about it? I'll buy the ticket and I have this big house—two bedrooms—so it won't be awkward. What do you say?"

Jim was silent on the other end. He finally said, "I'd like to come, yes, but somehow I think I'm making a big mistake." He was silent again. "Connie, I'm coming only as a friend. I think you and I both know that I'd like it to be much more, but I'm not going to let myself feel anything else right now.

"Thank you," she sighed.

CHAPTER THIRTY-TWO

Kim's phone rang as she zipped up her running jacket. She looked around for it, then remembered it was in the bed. She had kept it by her side that night, in case Connie called.

"Hello?' she answered.

"Hi, it's me." Connie was on the other end.

Kim sighed. "Hi; how are you?"

"I'm better today, thank you. I had a rough night, but I made it through. I finally decided to forgive myself and then I came up with a plan. Don't be mad at me, but I made a phone call last night."

Kim pressed her brows together. "What?"

"I called Jim. He's going to fly to San Diego to spend New Year's with me."

"What?" Kim said again, raising her voice. "How did that happen?"

"I called him, Kim. Don't be mad," she said again. "I panicked at the thought of being alone on New Year's and I kept thinking about it and I think right now what I need is Jim—"

"You had better not hurt him," Kim interrupted.

"I'm not going to hurt him. He's concerned about that

as well. We had a long talk this morning; we're all good. Please, Kim; this is what I need right now."

"Why are you concerned about what I think, Connie? You're a grown woman."

"You know you are my best friend and I care about what you think."

"Yes, I know. I'm sorry. You do what you need to do. I won't be mad and I'll help you anyway I can. So when is he coming?"

"He's going to try to get a flight out tomorrow and spend the rest of the week here."

"Boy, that's going to be expensive," Kim said, shaking her head, thinking Jim might not be coming out just as a friend. "That's a lot of money for him to spend." Then she paused. "Okay, I'll change the subject. Did you talk to Juan again?" Kim cringed. *Nice way to change the subject*, she thought. "Sorry."

"In fact, he came over and tried to talk to me, but I made him leave."

"Good for you . . . men!"

"Men," Connie repeated.

Kim clicked her phone shut after they said their goodbyes. She reached for her running shoes and sat down on the airbed. *Poor Connie,* she thought, *and poor Jim.* She hoped she was reading the situation wrong. She didn't want to see her two friends get hurt.

"Good morning," Jack said as he came around the corner from the bedroom. "Boy, did I sleep good last night. I think I may even play a little shuffleboard today."

Kim stood up and leaned over to stretch her legs. "Are you sure that's such a good idea?"

"Yes; the more I stay active, the better. That's what Dr. Lopez said, anyway. You should ask him. Aren't you going out on a date with him?"

"Dad! Aren't you the one who said I should be careful and not throw myself around?" she said and smiled as she stood up.

"Kimberly, you knew what I was talking about."

"Not really, but I love you anyway," she said. She kissed him on the cheek and walked out the door.

CHAPTER THIRTY-THREE

A few days later, Kim decided to call Connie again. She had waited to make the call, trying to avoid any judgment that she would project toward Connie and her situation. She wanted her friend to be happy, and she felt guilty that she couldn't be there, so she was more than grateful that Jim could step into the picture and take care of her. But at the same time, she didn't want Connie to use Jim and ultimately hurt him.

She had the haunting feeling that Connie only invited Jim to make sure she didn't spend New Year's by herself. She thought this whole thing was a bad idea and imagined what was going to happen after the holidays were over, when they were all back at work. Things for sure would never be the same.

Kim opened her phone and pressed three. After the second ring, Connie answered.

"Hi, honey!" Connie's voice was vibrant on the other end, a far cry from how she had sounded a few days earlier.

"Hi," Kim said. "Sounds like you're feeling better."

"I'm much better. Jim flew in late last night. He's out

getting us some breakfast now. I know you don't approve, but really, Kim, this is exactly what I need."

"It's not that I disapprove; it's just that I don't want you to use him and I don't want you to get hurt, either. You know how he feels about you. Don't string him along."

"Did you decide to spend New Year's with Camilo?" Connie said, changing the subject.

"Yes I did. I leave tomorrow."

"Good for you. Call me when you get back and tell me all about it," Connie said cheerfully. "Say, I have to go; Jim has just gotten back—and he's got breakfast," Connie told Kim.

Kim heard Jim's muffled voice in the background: "Say hi to Kim!"

—•••—

"What did you get us?" Connie asked, grabbing the paper bag from Jim.

"Boy, the fresh fruit is fabulous out here. I couldn't decide what to buy, so I bought a little of everything," he said and laughed.

"Of course it's fresh; this is California. It's not like the frozen crap we get back home," she said and grinned at him. Connie emptied the contents of the bag onto the counter. Jim had purchased oranges, a pineapple, a quart of strawberries, and some small green things. "What is this?" she asked as she held one up.

"Those are kumquats," he said. "I've never had them, but the lady said they were good, so I thought what the heck, we'll try them."

Jim had also picked up a loaf of nut bread and some

cream cheese. "Perfect," Connie said. She scrounged through the cupboards looking for a platter to serve their breakfast on. After finding one in the top cupboard above the refrigerator, she sliced the bread and laid it on the brightly colored plate, along with the cream cheese. Then she prepared the fruit, cursing when she tried slicing the pineapple.

Jim sat on the stool at the kitchen bar looking on with amusement, not budging. When Connie scowled at him and threw down the knife, he came to the rescue and finished where she had left off. He put everything on the plate and handed it to Connie. She examined the creation and smiled. "I'll pour us some coffee and we can sit upstairs on the porch," she said with approval.

The sun was midway in the sky, shedding its heat on the upstairs balcony. The boardwalk was already full with people either running, walking, or skateboarding. Connie pointed out the familiar character who made his way by the house every morning. He wore Rollerblades and skated as if he were ice dancing on the asphalt. He had a speaker strapped to his waist, which blared classical music. The sight of him made Connie laugh.

"There are some real doozies out here," she said, turned to Jim, and smiled. "Thank you for coming. I know I sounded like a mess on the phone, but I really needed the company of a friend, and you were so kind to be that friend."

"Connie, why can't I be more than a friend?"

Connie's hands flew up in a shield in front of her. "Oh, no let's not start that. Let's just take it for what it is. Deal?"

"Deal," he replied.

—•••—

Connie and Jim spent the day walking the beach. Connie wanted to avoid going past Juan's condo, so she and Jim explored the other section of the ocean walk. When the boardwalk ended, they walked along the street and ended up at a small café overlooking steep cliffs that dropped straight down to the ocean. They could hear the thunderous sound of the crashing waves from the deck on which they sat. When the waiter came over, Connie took charge and ordered a loaf of French bread, a chunk of Havarti cheese, and a bottle of wine.

"I don't have a say?" Jim asked and then smiled at her.

"Ah, I know you don't mind," Connie said and batted her eyes. She knew she was being silly and flirtatious.

They talked all afternoon and into the early evening, sharing two more bottles of wine. Jim wanted Connie to tell him all about Juan and what happened. At first Connie refused, but then gave in when Jim kept insisting and wouldn't let it go.

"I decided that relationships were not such a bad idea. Actually, it was Kim's persuading that convinced me," she said, pursing her lips together. "So I can blame her, right?" She laughed, looked out over the ocean, and then turned back to Jim.

"I want to know about you; what are you all about?" she asked. She pressed him about his family, where he grew up, who his parents were. "Funny," she said. "I've known you what, seven years, and never once did I ask where you were from."

"I know," he answered. He picked up his glass of wine,

finished the last of it, and motioned to the waitress to bring another bottle. "Wisconsin," he turned back to Connie.

"What?"

"Wisconsin. That's where I'm from."

"Oh, and where in Wisconsin?"

"My parents lived on a farm in southern Wisconsin, just outside of Milwaukee. The farm's still there, but they're not. They moved to a small house in town five years ago. The farm was getting to be too much for them to keep up. My dad still hasn't gotten over the fact that they had to sell it, and now all he does is sit in front of a TV all day; it's pretty sad, actually."

"And siblings? Do you have any brothers or sisters?"

"Just one brother, two years younger than me. He lives in Milwaukee."

"Do you see them often?"

"Not often enough; the job gets too demanding."

"Tell me about it!"

"What about you? Where are you from?" Jim asked. The waitress came over with their bottle of wine. Connie waited for her to uncork it and pour them each another glass.

"I'm from all over," she replied slowly. Jim leaned closer and cocked his eyebrow.

"You see," Connie continued, "my father left my mother when I was two years old. My mother couldn't keep a job for very long, so we were forced to move from one town to another so my mom could seek out new work. She was a very vivacious woman and made friends easily, so it was not difficult for her to acquire a new network of people in each place we lived. She made up a new story about her past every time she met new friends, pulling people into her web. They thought she was a sincere and trustworthy person. But after she settled in and revealed her true self, her friends figured out who she really was, and it wasn't the sweet, innocent person she portrayed." Connie paused and looked at the ocean for a minute, then lifted her glass and took a sip of wine.

Jim had been listening carefully to her every word. "What was she really like?" he asked.

Connie looked up at him, puzzled, then cringed when she realized what he was asking. "She had trouble with the booze,'" she said, smiled, and pointed to her glass. "Not only that, but I suspected she suffered from depression. Of course, back then it wasn't widely recognized or diagnosed."

"Where is she now?"

"She died a few years ago," Connie sighed. "We had grown apart, so I didn't see much of her most of my adult life," Connie said and shifted in her seat. "We'd better get back before it gets dark," she said.

CHAPTER THIRTY-FOUR

Kim packed the small backpack she borrowed from Nita. The day before, Camilo had called to discuss how she was going to get to Mexico and then to his beach house. "I don't want to drive over the border. I'm much more comfortable walking across," Kim told him.

"Good, then I can meet you in Matamoras. Or would you rather that I come get you at the home of your *padres*?"

"No, I can do it by myself. It'll be an adventure. Where should I meet you?"

"There is a little *restaurante* on the corner as you cross over the border. You can't miss it; it's a white brick building with a courtyard in front. I will meet you there, *si*?"

They had agreed to meet at noon. Kim finished stuffing her clothes into the backpack, which now contained a bathing suit—Camilo had assured her it was going to be warm enough on the beach to wear it—a pair of jeans, shorts, two shirts, and the black dress she wore when they went to dinner. She imagined New Year's was going to be more formal.

Her plans were to stay until the day after New Year's Day, which meant she would be with Camilo for three nights. She wasn't quite sure that was such a good idea. After all, if things didn't work out, she was pretty much held captive, since she'd have no car. She suddenly wished that she had dusted off her diaphragm and packed it in her suitcase. Then she laughed out loud, so loud Nita peered around the corner.

"What's so funny?"

"Nothing," Kim snorted. She put her hand over her mouth to stop herself. *Why in the world would I have thought there was even a remote possibility I would need it?* She smiled to herself again and went back to shoving clothes into the backpack. But then she thought, *What happens if we do have sex? I'm not about to get pregnant at forty-three.* The fact that she was even considering sleeping with Camilo made her nervous. If she had it in her head, she was afraid she was not going to be able to stop herself—if the opportunity arose.

Jack had warmed to the idea of her staying in Mexico for a few days. Kim knew it must be hard for him to see his little girl live a lifestyle that appeared to him to be promiscuous, so she was sensitive about what she told him, making sure he knew Camilo had three separate bedrooms and three separate baths. "It's a big house, with plenty of room for guests," she told him.

When she finished packing, Jack and Nita drove her to Brownsville. She had planned on getting a ride from someone in the park who was headed in that direction, but at the last minute, Jack insisted on taking her, making the excuse that he wanted to go to his favorite place for lunch anyway. They arrived at the parking lot adjacent to the border crossing at eleven thirty. "You need two pesos to cross," Jack told her. "And don't forget your passport. They will need to see it when you cross back over the border."

For an instant, Kim stood frozen. She thought about what Beth told her about being afraid to go to Mexico because of the possibility that the Mexican border guards were corrupt and would recognize her name from some sort of hit list. She then thought back to Mark's testimony, and how Javier Perales had had his men spy on every aspect of Mark's life, which at the time included her. *Nonsense,* she thought. *My name is totally different and I'm sure I don't look at all like I did when I was nineteen.* She let out a little laugh. "Yes, Dad, I have my passport."

Kim looked at her watch when she crossed over to Mexico. It was already five minutes after twelve. She hoped the restaurant Camilo was talking about was not far. She hated to be late. What if he thought she wasn't going to show? The line for the entrance into Mexico was long and the streets were crowded with tourists. *Probably more than usual, due to the holiday*, Kim thought.

She made her way through the crowd and spotted a white brick building with a courtyard, thinking it must be the one he was talking about. When she got closer, Kim saw Camilo sitting at a small bistro table. There were two glasses of wine in front of him and in the middle of the table sat a red rose. "Oh, how sweet," she said softly to herself.

"*Hola*," Camilo said as he stood up when Kim entered the tiny courtyard.

"*Hola*," she said. "This is such a cute place; I love it!" He grabbed her hand and gave her a soft kiss on her cheek. She felt like turning her head and planting a full, long kiss on his lips but thought better of it.

"Is that all you have?" he asked when he took her backpack from her.

"Yes; what else do I need?" she said and smiled.

"Oh, you know, women, they always seem to pack three times more than what they need—and all that washing stuff," he said as he waived his hands in the air.

She laughed. "Washing stuff? What do you mean, like shampoo and makeup?"

"*Si.*"

"I'm a pretty simple girl. I can consolidate when I need to." Kim sat down across from Camilo. She was glad she had worn a tank top; the midday sun was hot as it beat down on the black wrought iron table. "It's warm," she said as she sipped the glass of wine in front of her. "Thank you," she said and lifted it up to Camilo.

"*Si,*" he replied. "I did not lead you wrong?" he asked, then looked up into the sky. "It's going to be beautiful on the beach!"

"No. I mean yes," Kim said and pointed to her backpack. "I brought my swimsuit."

Camilo raised his eyebrows. "I hope it's one of those, ah . . . bikinis?" he said and smiled. Camilo ordered lunch for the two of them: seafood crepes and chicken quesadillas. They finished their first glass of wine and ordered another while they ate. "This does not taste like Mexican food," Kim commented.

"Not like Taco Bell?" he said and laughed.

When they were done with lunch, Kim followed Camilo to his truck, which he had parked a block away. He grabbed Kim's backpack, flung it in the back, opened the door for her, and then got in on the driver's side. When he pulled away from the curb, they made their way through the dusty streets of Matamoras and headed south, toward the Gulf of Mexico.

Camilo explained that the place they were going was not very populated. "That's why I love it so much," he said. They traveled for about half an hour on a single-lane highway before they came to Fraccionamiento, a little village situated in what Kim thought was the middle of nowhere. They had barely entered the town before they were out of it.

The only buildings in the town were a bar, an old gas station, and a church. Off the highway, fingers of small side streets stretched out to tiny hut-like houses. The streets were brown and dusty and very much in need of repair. Kim bobbed up and down in her seat as Camilo steered the truck over the bumpy road.

"It's a small, poor town, but don't worry; where we are going is not like this," Camilo said and laughed when he saw the look on Kim's face.

They traveled for fifteen more minutes before they came to a driveway that was blocked by a heavy black metal gate. Camilo got out of the truck, unlocked the gate, and swung it back away from the driveway. Kim noticed a big ornament on the top of the gate; it appeared to be some sort of family crest. Making the top of the crest was a castle tower, and below that, a knight's helmet. The most prominent piece of the crest was a square piece with a cross in the middle. Around the sides of the entire emblem were swirls of vines. And on the outer most part, on either side of the vines, were two letters, P.S. When Camilo got back into the truck she asked him about it.

"My family symbol, from hundreds of years ago."

"It's beautiful."

The truck made its way down the long palm tree–bordered driveway. When Kim stepped out of the truck, she peered at the massive, sprawling home in front of her. It was enormous in comparison to the houses they had just passed, and much bigger than what she was expecting.

She walked up the stairway into an open courtyard while Camilo unpacked the truck. The porch was built out of red and orange tile. The tile came up to form a solid wall around the entire house, and above it sat wrought iron fence, which gave the house the appearance of a small fortress. Pots of cacti were scattered about, some of the plants with bright yellow blooms, some with white, and some with red. The sun beat through the wrought iron posts and cast shadows, making a striped pattern on the floor.

Kim took a deep breath in and smelled the salty water of the Gulf. "This is magnificent!" she exclaimed.

"Glad you like it," Camilo said. He had walked up behind her with the backpack in one hand a brown bag in the other.

Kim grabbed her backpack and noticed the bag. "What's that?" she asked.

"I picked up some fresh shrimp before I came to get you. It's been in a cooler in the truck. I thought we could make a fire on the beach tonight and cook some shrimp scampi."

Camilo opened the two wooden doors that led into the house and they stepped into an open tiled area. A love seat and two high-backed wicker chairs that looked like thrones created a small sitting area. The formal living room was to the right, and beyond the foyer she could see the kitchen. Past that, glass doors led out to a patio, which had the most spectacular view of the beach. Everything in sight had a Hispanic motif. "Very Mexican," she said.

Camilo laughed. "We are in Mexico, you know? Come, I want to show you where you are going to stay." Kim followed him down a long hallway until they came to three doors. Camilo opened one of the doors. "This is your bedroom," he said, "and this is the bathroom." He opened the next door and walked in. He turned around and looked down the hall to the other side of the house. "The master bedroom is down there," he said and pointed.

"I want to make sure you are as comfortable as possible," he told her. She knew what he meant. "Put on your bathing suit and meet me on the beach," he said and winked. "Towels are in the bathroom. Don't be long." He closed the door behind him and Kim plunked herself down on the bed.

What am I doing here? she thought. *Having fun.* She sat up, grabbed her backpack, and fished for her swimming suit. She had brought three for the trip to Texas and selected the sexiest of the three for the occasion. She slipped into a black two-piece halter and examined herself in the mirror. *Not bad,* she thought.

Kim went to find a towel in the bathroom and was amazed at the size of the space. It was almost as big as the living room in her apartment. It was entirely done in tile, like the rest of the house, and in the corner sat a free-standing claw-foot bathtub. A mosaic-tiled countertop surrounded two sinks, and gold-plated fixtures matched the gold frames around the mirrors. "I wonder what the master bath looks like if this is the one for the guests," she said softly. She grabbed a towel and went to find Camilo.

CHAPTER THIRTY-FIVE

Kim and Camilo spent most of the afternoon on the beach. Camilo had set up two lounge chairs, side by side. He placed a table between them and on the table he set two full hurricane glasses, both with umbrellas. "What's this?" Kim asked with a laugh.

"I thought we would have something other than wine this afternoon."

The sun was high in the sky and beat down on the sand, heating everything, including Kim as she sipped the concoction Camilo had made her. The warmth was a welcome change for Kim. She didn't think she ever wanted to go back to cold, dreary North Carolina. They sat in silence for a while. Kim enjoyed her drink while Camilo dozed. "What's in these drinks?" Kim asked when she took the last gulp from her glass.

"Rum," he said without opening his eyes.

"May I have another?"

"How about water first?"

"Camilo! Are you cutting me off already?" Kim sat up in her chair. She looked at him, not knowing if he was serious. He still had his eyes closed, but was smiling.

"They are strong drinks; I don't want you to get tipsy, otherwise I might take advantage of you." He opened his eyes and winked at her. "Okay, I will get you another."

"Thank you . . . and a water, too," she called after him.

—•••—

Later that evening, Camilo built a fire on the beach, right near the water's edge. He laid down a big red blanket and motioned for Kim to sit. "Since you were so good as to listen to me earlier and have some water with your rum, how about a glass of wine, señorita?"

Kim *had* felt tipsy after the second rum, so she had done what she was told and switched to water. She didn't want to have to be in bed by five o'clock. "Yes, wine would be nice. Do you want some help?"

"No, you sit. I will be right back."

Kim looked out over the water. She had her back against the sun as it was getting ready to set for the night, but before it did, it left shadows in its wake. Kim listened to the waves move onto the shore and back out again, lulling her into a peaceful state. *This truly is heaven,* she thought.

When Camilo came back out, he carried two glasses of wine and a shawl for her. "It gets cold out here when the sun goes down," he said. He set the wine in the sand next to her and wrapped the shawl around her shoulders. When he did, he kissed her softly on the lips and smiled into her eyes. He kissed her again on the neck and brushed past her ear. "Señorita, thank you for coming," he whispered.

Kim sighed and closed her eyes. "Where have you been all my life?"

"What?" Camilo said and sat on the blanket beside her.

"It's an expression. But really, why are you not with a woman your own age celebrating New Year's?"

Camilo groaned. "Kim, I tell you, age does not matter. Now you have to stop talking about it. You promise?" he asked. He leaned over and kissed her again before he stirred the fire. They sat in silence for a while, watching the waves fade into the dark as the sun set. "Hungry?" he asked, breaking the silence.

"Let me help you," Kim volunteered and rose when Camilo stood up. They started for the house and Camilo grabbed her hand and squeezed it. She squeezed back, then starting running for the patio. "Bet I can beat you!" she yelled over her shoulder.

When they both stumbled into the kitchen, Camilo gathered all of the ingredients needed for their beach snack. Kim looked in the refrigerator for a bottle of wine. "Never too much vino," she said and laughed.

"*Si*," he responded. "Let's go and enjoy."

Back on the beach, Kim watched as Camilo stirred the shrimp in the pan he had set on the fire. In it was shrimp sizzling in a sauce of butter, garlic, and freshly squeezed lemon. When it was done, Camilo took the pan off the heat and set it on the sand. He picked up a plate and spooned shrimp onto it. "It's hot," he said as he handed Kim the plate. After she took it, he lifted her glass and filled it with wine.

Kim took a bite. "Oh . . . Camilo," she groaned. "You spoil me."

When they finished their meal, they sat on the beach for a while. Camilo had run to the house to turn on some soft jazz music that flooded the evening air from speakers that sat on the patio. They danced slowly in the moonlight before they decided to call it a night.

— ••• —

The next morning, Kim awoke when the sun came up. She purposefully left the curtains open the night before so she could wake up to the rising sun. The guest room had an attached patio, which overlooked the beach and the water. She slid open the glass doors and walked outside wearing a white terry robe she found in the bathroom.

The robe had the same crest embroidered on it that was on the entrance gate. *He thinks of everything here,* she thought. She hadn't asked many questions of Camilo the day before about all of this. Was this where he grew up and where his mother had lived? She remembered him telling her that his mother had lived near Matamoras and hadn't gone to the United States much. She made a conscience note to find out more today.

Camilo came around the corner as Kim was looking out toward the water. She jumped when she heard his voice.

"Sorry, señorita; I did not mean to scare you," he said and handed her a cup of coffee.

Kim felt self-conscious about her appearance. She hadn't even run a brush through her hair yet. "You should let a lady make herself presentable first," she said, but then smiled, taking the cup.

"You are beautiful any time of day."

"Thanks, but I feel like a mess. Stay here; I'll be right back." Kim ran into the bathroom, quickly put her hair in a ponytail, and threw on some blush and mascara. She was back on the porch in a few minutes. "Thank you for the coffee. How did you know that I can't function in the morning without coffee?" She took a sip, looked back toward the water, and sighed. She looked down at her robe. "And thank you for supplying the robe; it came in very handy." She ran her hand along the sleeve.

"Come, let's go sit by the beach," Camilo said, motioning her to follow. They sat in the lounge chairs they had shared the day before. They laid back and closed their eyes. Kim sat for a minute listening to the sound of the water before she spoke.

"Is this where you grew up?" she asked. Her eyes were still closed. It took Camilo a minute before he answered.

"Yes, for the most part. This is where I spent most of the time with my brother and sister and my mother."

"So this is where she lived? Did she die here?"

"*Si*," he said softly.

"What about your father?"

"He lived here on and off," Camilo said, his voice indifferent.

"It's so far from everything. Did you have many friends to play with?"

"My father brought home many business acquaintances and their families. We always had people around and things to do," he answered.

"And did you go to school here?"

Camilo shifted in his chair. "We had tutors. Why all the questions, Kim?"

"I just want to know more about you. I'm sorry if I am making you uncomfortable. You are a mystery to me, but a very nice mystery." She smiled and got up from the lounge chair and leaned over to kiss him. He pulled her on top of him and wrapped his arms around her. He kissed the nape of her neck and then laid his hands on both sides of her face and gently pulled it toward his lips. At first he lightly brushed her lips and then his kisses became more intense, the passion building between them.

"So early in the morning," she said and laughed. Kim was glad she took the time to brush her teeth earlier.

They spent the day walking the beach. The complex was very secluded, so they saw no one else. Kim was amazed at the serenity of it all. She wore the black halter suit again and wrapped a sarong around her waist. She felt very alive and free, thinking to herself how thankful she was that she decided to come.

Camilo showed her where he used to hide from his mother. It was inland and away from the beach, but still in view from the house. He told Kim that he felt safer that way; he was hiding, but he knew he was never far from home. She reached over and brushed a strand of his hair away from his face. "Did you have a good childhood?" she asked.

"Yes, I did. *Mi madre* saw to it that we had a good life."

"That's good, because I did as well and I think that's important."

When they got back to the house, it was time to start dinner. Kim excused herself to freshen up and clean the sand off. "I'm going to dress up, since this is a special occasion," she told him.

"And what is that, Kim?" Camilo asked and winked.

"New Year's Eve," she said as she laughed at him.

An hour later, Kim had showered, thrown her hair

into a tousled bun, and put on her black halter dress. She entered the kitchen where Camilo had already started the preparations for the evening. He was wearing a white button-down shirt made from cotton gauze. The buttons were only buttoned halfway up, leaving most of his chest exposed.

"Señorita, you look beautiful." He kissed her as he set a piece of paper on the counter.

"You don't look so bad yourself," she responded.

"This is going to be the meal for our celebration," Camilo said and pointed to the paper. Kim picked it up to look at what appeared to be a detailed menu, outlining what they were going to eat for the evening. It started with a soup, a starter, followed by the entree, and then dessert.

"Where did you learn to do all this?" Kim asked him as she studied his handwriting. It was very precise.

Camilo was emptying ingredients from the refrigerator. "I studied cook," he said.

"You studied cook?" Kim said and laughed. "What? Were you from some royalty or something?"

Camilo scowled at her and she wished she could take her words back. "It's the way we lived down here," he said and frowned.

"Sorry," she said and kissed him on the cheek.

Kim helped Camilo in the kitchen, even though he insisted that she sit down and relax. She told him that she liked to cook as well, and was very interested in what he could teach her. He wrapped an apron around her, set a bottle of wine on the tiled counter, and started in on the process. "We are going to stretch dinner out all night," he told her.

Most of what they were going to eat Camilo had prepared ahead of time. The soup was a fresh Mexican-style clam chowder. He told her, "I get the clams from the river." They stood in the kitchen while he heated up the broth. "Kim," he said and motioned to a cutting board at the end of the counter, "you can slice up some of that fresh cilantro for the garnish." When she was finished, he dished the chowder into shallow bowls.

Kim followed him as he carried the bowls into the next room. She hadn't noticed, but he had set up the dining room table with a white tablecloth and white napkins. The place settings consisted of white china and sterling silver flatware. Kim was amazed again at his exquisite taste.

"The soup was excellent," Kim said when she finished the last spoonful.

"Good, I am glad you liked it. We will sit for a while until the next course."

"Sounds good to me," she said and lifted her glass up in a toast.

They made their way out to the porch. The sun had already set, but the evening was much warmer than the night before. They stood side by side against the railing. Camilo had his arm around Kim.

"It intrigues me to see your many different talents and how you appear to live a very fine life," Kim said as she looked up at Camilo.

"*Mi madre* had very good taste; she liked the fine things in life. But that was okay; she did not have much else to look forward to. I don't think it was a bad thing."

"I wasn't saying that, but it's just that . . . well, it just doesn't add up. Okay, I'm sorry, and I seem to be saying that a lot. I will shut up. Maybe it's the wine talking."

"Just enjoy, Kim; not so many questions," he said and kissed the top of her head.

The next course consisted of fresh crab cakes. "I know how much you enjoyed them the other day, and so I want to make them for you again."

"Perfect."

They spoke little as they ate the crab cakes. Camilo moved his chair closer to Kim's. They gazed into one another's eyes, kissing intermittently between bites. At one point, Camilo took Kim's hand and kissed it, then proceeded to kiss her arm from hand to shoulder, stopping there before he lightly traced the base of her neck. Kim moaned at his touch.

"Camilo, we'll never get through dinner at this rate," she whispered. "Let's get some fresh air before we have the next course. I need to settle my stomach." She moved her chair back from the table and brought her plate into the kitchen. She knew what she was doing: delaying the evening's inevitable conclusion. Kim opened a cupboard door, looking for a glass. She desperately needed some water. When she found one, she called to Camilo, who was clearing the dishes from the table. "Where do I find some water?" He came into the kitchen and moved directly behind her, brushing up against her backside.

"Water is in the bottle in the refrigerator," he said as he placed the dishes he was carrying in the sink. "Can you pour me a glass, too, señorita?" They took their glasses and ventured out onto the patio. The moon was full in the sky and shone brightly across the water. "Good luck, that means," Camilo whispered. Kim didn't respond.

"Camilo," Kim said, breaking the silence. "What are we doing?"

"What do you mean?" he said, turning toward her with a puzzled look.

"Where is this going to lead us? I'm really struggling with this . . . us," she said and pointed her finger back and forth between them.

"Why must you always label the situation?"

"That's just me." She turned, snuggled close to him and he put his arm around her. "I'm so confused," she whispered. They stood there for a while without talking.

After a few minutes, Camilo went inside to get the next course started. "Kim," he called out to her, "I won't feed you seafood anymore; I am putting filets on the grill."

She laughed. "Good."

They enjoyed the next course with a bottle of cabernet. Kim was glad she had taken a break from the wine earlier, but it didn't take long for the wine to go to her head again. She felt herself staring at Camilo more than once, and when she did, he winked at her and laughed. "Señorita, you are beautiful," he would say each time. The only talking they did were romantic quips about how wonderful each thought the other was.

When they had finished dinner and the bottle of wine, Camilo suggested they go into the living room and enjoy a glass of port. Kim agreed, and followed him to the next room. She sat on the couch while he went to the bar, took two small glasses from the shelf, and set them down.

Kim couldn't resist, so she joined him at the bar, sitting on a stool across from him. She leaned over the bar and he leaned closer to her, giving her a kiss. She could feel the effects of the wine and knew her guard was down— way down. She giggled. "Camilo, I think I'm drunk."

"Do you need some water?"

"No, Camilo, I don't need water." She got up from the stool and walked around to where Camilo stood. "You is what I need," she said. She stood on her tiptoes and put her arms around his neck. He untied her dress and it fell to the floor, revealing her half-naked body. She stood in front of him in just her black lace panties. Camilo leaned over and kissed her neck; all she could do was let out a soft moan.

Camilo picked her up and laid her on the couch. He kissed her forehead, then her lips, lingering there for a while before he moved to her neck, kissing her softly all the way down to her shoulders. Kim sighed softly. Before she knew it, Camilo had picked her up and carried her toward the bedroom. She noticed they were not going to the guest room, but were making their way back to the master suite. He had not shown her that part of the house and she had not asked.

He laid her on the big poster bed. He stood back and took off his shirt, showing his muscular chest. His pants were next, then he laid down next to her. Kim snuggled closer to him and soon they were both naked under the sheets. Kim was glad it was dark in the room when Camilo slipped her panties off. *After all,* she thought, *I am forty-three and he is only in his twenties.*

When their lovemaking was done, they lay together, holding each other while Camilo whispered Spanish words into Kim's ear. She didn't know what they meant, but they sounded nice. Soon they were both asleep, still holding on to each other. They stayed like that and missed ringing in the New Year altogether.

CHAPTER THIRTY-SIX

Kim opened her eyes the next morning to the sun peering through the curtains. Camilo's arm was draped across her and she gently lifted it up so she wouldn't wake him. She slipped out of bed and wrapped herself in a blanket, covering her naked body, and tiptoed into the kitchen to make some coffee. *First,* she thought, *I need a glass of water.* Kim ran her tongue across her teeth and scrunched up her nose. *Boy, how much did I drink last night?*

After she put on a pot of coffee, Kim walked back to the guest room to get her robe. She passed the doorway to the formal living room and noticed a baby grand piano she had not seen the night before. She walked over and sat on the overstuffed seat, which was covered with burgundy crushed velvet, and opened the cover and touched the keys. She tapped lightly and the sound rang out louder than what she anticipated.

She waited for a minute, but it didn't appear that she had woken Camilo, so she tapped the keys again and smiled as memories of her childhood flooded back. She had not laid her hands on the ivories in years. She stopped playing and leaned away from the keyboard, looking around the room, again surprised at the elegance.

She sat there for a moment, taking in the unique smells of her surroundings, and then took a deep breath, detecting a hint of musk. She heard the coffee finish brewing, got up, and started to walk back to the kitchen when something caught her eye. Next to the piano was a bookshelf built into the wall, but instead of holding books, each ledge held a number of different sized picture frames.

She stepped toward the shelf and picked up one frame and then another, examining each subject in the picture. One appeared to be Camilo's mother and father in front of an old Lincoln Town Car. His mother was a very beautiful woman and his father had a distant look in his eyes. The two stood side by side, but it looked as if there was an invisible wall between them.

The next picture Kim picked up looked like it was of the entire family. It was a formal picture that seemed to have been taken at a studio. The girl in the picture was just as beautiful as her mother, and the two boys had similar likenesses. Kim could make out the older one as Camilo. The father gazed directly at the camera, but again had that distant look. His thin mustache made him look much older than Kim suspected he was.

Kim looked through the other pictures, moving them around, examining each of them before putting them back into their places. She reached her hand all the way to the back of one of the shelves and pulled out a black and silver-plated frame. When she saw the image in the picture, she let out a gasp.

It was a picture of a group of people standing in front of a house. It appeared to be the house she was in. She took another look, then sunk to the floor, dropping the picture. She reached for the frame to look at it again, and couldn't believe what she saw. The image staring back at her was that of Mark. He was standing next to the same woman in the previous pictures. Kim stared at the picture for a while, not believing it could be Mark. But the more she studied it, the more she was convinced it was Mark. But how and why . . . why? She was so confused. Why was Mark's picture in Camilo's house?

Kim realized she had dropped the blanket she had held around her, so she was left sitting naked on the floor. She picked it up to cover herself and walked back to the guest room, all the while her head spinning. When she got to her room, she put on the robe and walked out to the patio. She felt nauseated and confused. She stood there for a while, collecting her thoughts. *There must be an explanation.*

Kim put on the robe, then returned to the kitchen. She paced the kitchen floor with the photograph in hand, waiting for Camilo to wake up. When she heard him stir, she went down the hall to the master bedroom. She stood by the door, watching him, her anger welling up inside of her. *But why am I so angry?* she thought. *Camilo has Mark's picture—so what? There could be a logical explanation.* Kim stepped back into the kitchen to wait for Camilo. When he came in, she didn't hesitate. "Do you know him?" she asked as she thrust the picture at him.

"What?" Camilo asked and rubbed his eyes. "I smell coffee. Did you make some, señorita?"

Kim waved the picture in front of him again. "Do you know him?" she asked again, trying not to shout.

Camilo looked at the picture. "Yes, I do. Do you know him?" he asked, reaching for a cup.

"Camilo, Camilo, Camilo . . . do I know him? This is insane. Yes, I know him, but more importantly, how do you know him?" Now she was yelling.

Camilo stopped and stared at her, seemingly catching on to her mood and realizing who she was talking about. "Kim," he said slowly. "What are you talking about? How do you know this man?"

"Oh, no; don't you turn it back to me," she said. She was hysterical now.

Camilo grabbed her shoulders and drew her into him. She sobbed for a while, not really knowing why she was acting as she was. She had not let Camilo explain, and was uncharacteristically acting like a lunatic. After a few minutes, she calmed down and stopped shaking. "I'm sorry," she whispered.

Camilo poured them both a cup of coffee and guided Kim out to the patio. The sunshine instantly calmed Kim down, and she sighed, taking a seat on one of the patio chairs. She drew her legs close and took a sip of coffee. Camilo sat next to her. "Now Kim, how do you know this man?" he asked calmly.

"I knew him from many years ago. He actually was my grandmother's nephew." She remembered the gift from her parents and showed Camilo her wrist. "This bracelet was his aunt's, my grandmother's," she explained.

Camilo looked confused. "So was he your cousin?"

"Not really; my grandmother married his father's

brother." Kim went on further to explain the relationship between the two families, including Sadie and Alexander's affair and marriage. "He and his family owned the resort I told you about where I spent a lot of time when I was young. It was a big part of my life."

She turned to the picture. "He was a very good friend of mine," she continued. She was cautious before she let him know the whole story. She first needed to know more about why Mark's picture was in this house. "I grew up with him; he was a family friend," she told him. "We became close. I could really trust him." She was stalling. Kim stretched out her legs and stood up. "He lived in Texas for many years and had a few different businesses. Maybe that's how you knew him?"

"Really, *mi madre* was friends with him; this was from her collection," he said and picked up the picture. "I did not move very many of her things when she died."

"Do you know why she knew him?"

"Yes, I do, but I would like to know more about how you knew him."

Kim told him of the time Mark and Maite came to northern Maine and she decided to follow them to Texas. She told him about how she had lived and worked in the valley for a year and a half before she left to go back home. She paused to look at Camilo, who looked at her intently. Then she continued to tell him about what she had discovered that past week, about Mark's past and what he had been caught up in.

"I may have been very close to the drugs and the danger," she said. "There was this man, this drug lord who, before he went into business with Mark, had him followed, investigating all of Mark's life, including everyone he knew. I was living with them at that time." Kim stopped and looked at Camilo, who had a puzzled look on his face. He got up, reached for her hand, and led her back into the living room. He picked up one of the pictures and pointed to the man in the picture.

"Do you know him?" he asked her.

"No, but isn't that your father?"

"Yes . . ." He hesitated. "The only father I knew." He set the picture back on the shelf.

Kim sat down on the couch. "What do you mean, the only father you ever knew? He was not your real father?"

"Kim, does the name Perales mean anything to you?"

"Yes, you said that was your name. Perales is your last name."

"*Si*, it is. This man was Javier Perales," he said and pointed in the direction of the picture.

Kim flushed at the mention of his name. "I was reading about him, in the articles I told you about . . . he was the drug lord," she said and stopped. "Camilo, was your father a drug trafficker?" She thought back to the accounts in the articles. The author had said that Mark had become good friends with Javier Perales and his family. That must be how Camilo's mother knew him. "That's how your family knew Mark, from the relationship they had through the drug dealings?" It was more of a statement than a question.

Camilo sat in silence. Kim noticed he was only wearing a pair of white pajama bottoms and no shirt. The muscles in his arms contracted and she noticed his jaw tightening. She remembered him telling her that his father was not a nice man; now she knew what he meant. *Poor Camilo; this must be hard for him. To be tied to a past such as this must be devastating.*

Kim reached for his hand and squeezed it. "This has to be tough for you," she whispered. They sat for a few minutes in silence. Kim's thoughts went back in time to when she was eighteen and in the relationship with Mark. She thought about Javier Perales and his family, Camilo's family. Kim jerked her head toward Camilo. "How old are you again?" she asked.

"Why?" he asked, looking at her.

"You are twenty-six, right?" Kim quickly did the math. "That means that I was seventeen when you were born and I was eighteen when I lived in Texas. Mark must have visited here when I was living with him in Harlingen." She paused; she was thinking now how ironic it all was. "He knew you. Wow, the world can be so small sometimes," she said with a tired laugh.

"Kim," Camilo said softly. "Come, I want to show you something." Kim followed him to the master bedroom. He sat down on the bed and pulled her next to him. "This was my mother's room. This is where she died." He patted the bed.

"I'm sorry, Camilo," she said quietly.

"I was with her when she died. She was a beautiful woman and I loved her very much. She had a hard life. It was not easy living with Javier Perales and the life he created for her. There was so much bad going on in her life. She did not like it, but she had nowhere else to go. That is why she spent most of her time here and kept the family here; it was away from most of the dangerous things."

Kim nodded but was unsure why he was telling her all of this. Camilo got up and went over to the nightstand by the bed. He pulled opened the drawer and paused before he pulled out a picture. He looked at it for a minute before he brought it to Kim. He sat back down on the bed and handed it to her. Kim took the picture and looked at the two figures looking back at her. It was of Mark and he had his arm around a woman, Camilo's mother. She squinted her eyes and looked over at Camilo. "I don't understand," she said.

"That picture was special to *mi madre*. I did not know it until she was on her deathbed."

"I don't understand," Kim said again as she looked at the picture.

"She had a fondness for him." He paused. "Much more than a fondness. When *mi madre* was on her deathbed, some of the last words she spoke, she spoke only to me and she spoke about him," he said and pointed to the picture. Camilo turned to Kim. "*Mi madre* did not speak English; she spoke only Spanish, so I will translate." Kim nodded.

"She told me how much she loved me and that she wouldn't do anything to hurt me, that I must trust her and forgive her. She reassured me that I was a good person and that I should not let the things from the past hurt me." He paused. "At that time, I could barely hear her, her words were so soft. She had me pull this picture out of the drawer so she could hold it. She pointed to Mark. He was a good man, she told me. She then told me he was my *padre*."

"What?" Kim jumped up from the bed. "Camilo, what are you talking about?" she screamed.

Camilo had a painful look on his face. "Kim, please,

please sit down," he said and reached for her. "I am not understanding all of this myself."

Kim sat back down, her heart pounding. She sat next to him for a minute, then got up and went into the bathroom. She felt nauseous and wanted to throw up. She looked in the mirror at her reflection. She was as pale as the white towel next to her. She turned on the faucet and splashed cold water on her face over and over, until she heard a knock on the door.

"Kim, please come out," Camilo coaxed.

She slowly opened the door. Camilo tried to hold her, but she brushed past him and sat back on the bed. "Camilo, this is all too much for me to handle." She got up and walked into the kitchen. She stood for a moment looking out the window then slid the door open and went outside. Camilo followed her.

They sat side by side on the patio chairs. Kim was the first to talk. "Camilo, Mark was much more than a friend to me. I know I explained the family relationship and I know it's hard to understand. As I said, he was not really related to me."

"Yes I know, I understand," Camilo replied.

"Mark was special to me as well." Kim was cautious as she continued. "One of the reasons that I came down to Texas so many years ago was because Mark asked me to. Not as a friend, but as a lover." Camilo did not say a word. "I was a young, naïve eighteen-year-old. I didn't know what I was getting into. At first, after my move, we remained friends, but then it grew into a love affair." She turned to Camilo. He had his hands in his face.

Kim continued. "I had put the affair out of my mind

all these years. I hadn't thought about Mark until my flight down here. And when the memories flooded back, I felt nothing but shame. I was the other woman in an affair. I was no better than the woman Alex had an affair with." She turned again to Camilo. He had lifted his head and was looking at her. "Are you sure he is your father?" she said softly.

Camilo cleared his throat. "After she told me who my real father was, I tried to question her. She was so weak at that point that I wasn't sure if she even knew what she was saying. I let her rest and did not push her anymore. When I returned to her room a few hours later, she was awake again and seemed to be more alert. I did not want to upset her but I needed answers, so I asked her again, '*Madre*, who is my real *padre*?' She was more coherent then and told me, 'Don't be afraid; Mr. Carson is your *padre*.'

"I asked her where he was. She paused and replied, 'They think he is dead, but I know that is not true.' I questioned her about who 'they' were, but she closed her eyes and would not talk anymore. That night, she died in her sleep." Camilo closed his eyes and let out a sigh. "I believe that Mark Carson is my father. What would *mi madre* have to gain by not telling me the truth?"

Kim got up from the chair and headed down the stairs to the beach. When she reached the water, she stooped down and submerged her hand in a wave. Her head was swirling so much that she became dizzy. Mark was her long-ago lover. Mark was Camilo's father, and Camilo was her current lover. She sorted her thoughts out again; the two men for whom she had felt the most passion in her life were father and son. She felt sickened. *Oh my god, I could be Camilo's mother,* she thought.

Camilo walked onto the beach and stood behind Kim. "How long did your love affair last?" he asked.

"Camilo, why does it matter?"

"It matters because I need to know if he was having an affair with you the same time my mother was in love with him and if she knew about you. Could you have caused her pain?"

Kim cringed and shut her eyes. She couldn't look at him. She hadn't thought it through, but it seems that because of her relationship with Mark, she actually had betrayed more than one woman and one of those women was Camilo's mother. "Camilo, I . . ."

He didn't let her finish. He walked past her and headed back to the house. She stared in his direction until he was out of sight.

Kim sat in the lounge chair on the beach for the next hour. She tried to sort her feelings out. The fact that she had had an affair with father and son was strange, but shouldn't be horrible. After all, the affairs were many years apart from one another. The fact that she hurt two women *did* matter, especially if one of those women was Camilo's mother. And if it meant that Camilo thought she had caused his mother pain, that she couldn't bear.

Even though in a week she would be gone and *could* forget about this whole thing, she knew she wouldn't do that. She wouldn't forget Camilo that easily. She had already been thinking of how they might possibly have a long-distance relationship, now that appeared to be impossible. How could she continue an affair with Mark's son? And Camilo—he probably wanted her out of his life for good. Over the past hour, he had not come out of the house at all to check on her.

Finally, Kim got out of the chair and walked up the stairs to the patio. She peered inside the window to see if she could see Camilo. He was nowhere in sight. She slowly slid the glass door open and walked inside. Camilo was neither in the kitchen, nor in the living room, so she tiptoed down hall to the master bedroom. The door was slightly cracked and she pushed it open to find Camilo on the bed, fast asleep. He had the picture of Mark lying next to him. Kim slipped back out the door, letting Camilo sleep, and went to the other side of the house to the guest bedroom to pack her things.

CHAPTER THIRTY-SEVEN

Later that afternoon, Kim sat on the porch with her backpack sitting next to her. She was waiting for Camilo to wake up. She assumed that he was going to want to bring her back right away because of everything that had happened. She looked at her watch; it was noon in California. Connie and Jim should be awake by now, so she hit Connie's button on her phone and let it ring four times before she hung up. She clicked her phone shut and sat for a minute looking at it. She turned her head to see if there was any sign of Camilo. There wasn't.

Kim's phone rang. She opened it up and saw it was Connie.

"Did I wake you?" Kim asked. She forced her voice to sound cheerful.

"No, we were up. We were just coming in from the beach. How about you? How was your New Year's?"

"That's what I called to ask you, so you tell me first," Kim said, stood up, and walked toward the beach. "What did you guys do?"

"Jim made a fabulous dinner for us and it was such

a nice night that we sat on the upstairs deck and ate by candlelight."

"Hmm, sounds romantic." There was uncertainty in Kim's voice. She reached the beach and started walking along the water.

"It was," Connie said, catching on to her concern. "Don't worry; we didn't do anything," she said and laughed. "But we did kiss," she whispered into the phone.

"What?" Kim asked and stopped walking. "Connie, what are you doing?"

"We kissed at midnight, honey. Quit being so paranoid," she said and laughed. "But I would've liked it to be much more," she whispered again. "We talked all afternoon and into the evening and talked throughout dinner, really getting to know each other. I have known him for years but never *really* knew him. He's a nice guy."

"I know! Just don't hurt him."

"I won't. I think I may be able to date him," Connie said. "I have made a New Year's resolution. I've decided to change my lifestyle. I'm tired of one-night stands and jumping from one man to the next," she confessed.

"Good," Kim said, turned around, and started to walk back to the house. She was preoccupied. *Camilo must be up by now,* she thought. She brought her attention back to her friend. "I thought you were swearing off relationships. Remember what you told me on Christmas?"

"I know what I said and I meant it, at that time anyway. Jim made me realize that relationships are not a bad thing."

"Oh he did, did he?" Kim interrupted.

"It's just that I have to be more careful about who I fall

for. I'm so used to one-night stands that I never recognized the difference between a decent man and a scumbag. I didn't have to; they'd be gone the next day anyway. But enough about me, how was your night?" Connie continued.

"Everything was wonderful—until morning came," Kim said and stopped walking. "Bizarre things have happened here," she said softly. "I'm only going to give you an overview; I'll fill you in on details when I get back," she explained. She started walking again and told Connie about Mark, his past, her relationship with him, Camilo's family, and how Mark might be . . . she paused. "Mark is Camilo's real father," she said.

Connie didn't say anything until Kim said that Mark was Camilo's father. "So you've slept with father and son?" Connie cried out. "Wait, did you sleep with Camilo yet?"

"Yes," she said softly. She was back in front of the house; Camilo was standing on the porch. "Connie, I have to go. This isn't funny." She had heard the amusement in her friend's voice. "It's much more complicated than you can know."

"Sounds pretty complicated to me right now," Connie replied.

"I have to go," Kim said. "I'll talk to you later." Kim clicked her phone shut. She looked in the direction of the house. Camilo motioned for her to come closer as he stepped down the stairs and onto the sand. "I see you are packed," he said. Kim could see the hurt in his eyes.

"I am sorry, señorita," he said. "I know I have acted badly and mean you no harm. *Mi madre* suffered so many things. I don't want to think of any hurt that she felt. I can only imagine the pain she would have felt if she knew she was not the only one for him, for Mark Carson."

"Camilo," Kim whispered. "I don't think I was the only one. Neither was your mother."

He stepped farther away from her. "What do you mean?" he asked.

"From the articles I read, it appears that Mark Carson was a womanizer. He had many love interests while he was married, and not married, and sometimes more than one at the same time."

Camilo cringed and turned away from Kim. All she could see was his back. His usually meticulously styled hair was tousled from the last few hours he spent sleeping. She heard him let out a soft sigh. "You must have been, what, four when Mark died?" she asked.

He stood silent for a minute before he spoke. "Before he supposedly died," Camilo told her, "but yes I would have been about four when you say this body was found." He turned back toward Kim but looked beyond her toward the water. "I searched all the papers I could find of my father's, but mostly they were taken by the police and the United States government when they arrested him. I found very little about Mark Carson. I only found the same court documents that you discovered, his testimony . . ." Camilo's voice trailed off. "I never understood how she could keep that secret from me all those years, but I only imagined she had her reasons."

"Was your father—Perales—sent to jail?"

"*Si*, but he got out five years later after he negotiated a plea bargain by testifying against another drug cartel. They must have thought that that ring was much more of a danger than my father's business and more important to get off the streets. I don't know how he got away with it, but he went right back to his old ways, right back to the drugs."

"He's no longer alive, right?" Kim remembered him telling her that his parents were not living anymore.

"He died two years before my *madre* did. I saw him very little in his later years. I already had started my business in the United States and obtained my papers to work over there. He thought I was of no use to him. The only time I would come to Mexico was to see my *madre* here at this house. He got cancer of the pancreas and spent his last weeks here. Despite all of the hard times and life she had to put up with, my *madre* was there by his side all through the sickness and was with him when he died." He looked into Kim's eyes. "Love is a funny thing."

Kim let out a small chuckle. "I think that's a song or something." When Camilo did not laugh, she lowered her eyes. "Sorry; I didn't mean to make a joke of this." Just then, a wind came up that sent chills down Kim's back. She hugged her arms around herself.

"Let's go back into the house," Camilo said. "I'll take you back to Texas." The tone in his voice was sharp.

Kim put her hand up to her mouth to smother a cry. "I know you must have so many thoughts going on inside your head. I can only imagine what you must be thinking about me and I don't blame you," she said. "I'm sick to my stomach about this whole thing. Camilo, this is all so bizarre!" She sat down on a patio chair. Camilo continued to stand on the top step. His eyes were sad as he looked at her.

"I don't know what I feel," he said. "I think I am falling in love with you. I was making plans for us to see each other after you left. . . ."

"Me, too," Kim whispered.

"And now I am so confused. I don't blame you. I don't have ill feelings about you, Kim. It's just that if you and my mother were . . ." He looked away. ". . . with Mark at the same time, I just could not bear that."

"Camilo, let's try not think about the past. Can we just believe that your mother and Mark's affair ended before I came to Texas?"

"I don't know," he said.

CHAPTER THIRTY-EIGHT

Later that day, Kim helped Camilo close up the house. She took one more walk on the beach before they left. She wanted to burn into her mind the beautiful scenery, which she hoped would overcome memories of the revelations of the last day.

On the way back to the border, Kim looked out the window as they passed through the small towns and thought about the poverty of so many people. It was something she thought very little about, how so many people in this world lived and how lucky she was. They rode in silence for most of the way. Kim was trying to sort out her feelings about the situation. She was mad at herself for even getting involved with Camilo. She should have followed her instincts about the age difference between the two of them. *But now that I've met Camilo and have gotten to know him, how can I possibly forget him so easily?*

Kim turned to Camilo. "Why do you think your mother said she believed that Mark was still alive?"

Camilo did not speak for a minute, then looked over at her and shook his head from side to side. "I don't know," he said quietly.

Kim looked at him, her eyebrows knitted together. "Aren't you curious?" she asked. Camilo just shrugged his shoulders.

— •••—

That afternoon, Kim started to gather her things together to get ready for her return to North Carolina. She was back a day earlier than expected, but was grateful for the extra time she could spend with her parents.

When Camilo had dropped her off, they exchanged a hug first, then he bent down and kissed her on the lips. "I don't want this to be goodbye," he had said. She hadn't either, but the situation had become awkward and neither knew how to proceed. Jack came in from his usual afternoon walk to the recreation hall. "Kim!" he said, surprised to see her.

"And how was your celebration?" Kim asked him. She wanted to change the subject and was feeling guilty for not calling them on New Year's Eve.

Jack didn't press her any further about why she was back. "Your mother and I had a great time," Jack replied. Kim could hear a sparkle in his voice. "We went to the recreation hall and I even danced!"

"Mom must have been very happy that she didn't have to find someone else to dance with."

"Oh, she did plenty of that, too; I don't think she sat down the whole night. I couldn't keep up with her!"

"Dad, how're you feeling?" Kim again felt guilty for not paying more attention to his health battles.

"I feel great, Kim. I feel like I have a new lease on life. We went for another visit to the doctor yesterday morning, and he gave me a thumbs-up. The treatment is doing just what they want it to do. I think everything is going to be just fine, Kim. Don't worry about me. I'm going to be around for a long time," he concluded and laughed. Then he lowered his voice. "I think your mom was so happy, she had one too many glasses of wine last night," he said and laughed again.

Kim smiled. She was glad her mom felt relieved.

"Did *you* have a nice time?" Jack asked. "I thought you weren't coming back until tomorrow."

"Yes; it was beautiful there." Kim paused, trying to think of an excuse about why she returned a day early. She tried as best she could to conceal the anxiety in her voice. She had already decided she was not going to reveal to her parents what she had discovered, not now and perhaps not ever. "Camilo ended up having to work tomorrow, so I told him to bring me back today," she said. She spoke quickly as she lied to her dad. "Besides, I wanted to spend some extra time with the two of you."

Nita came through the door just as Kim finished speaking.

"Kim! What are you doing back so early?" she asked.

"I wanted to spend time with you and Dad," Kim told her. "I'm told you had a nice time on New Year's."

"What?" Nita asked.

"Dad said you two had fun on New Year's Eve. I'm glad he is feeling better."

"I am, too," Nita said and sat down next to Kim on the couch. "I'm so glad you came to visit us, Kim." She put her arm around her daughter. "I know that I may not be a very emotional or doting mother, but I want you to know how much I really love you. Even though I may not admit it, I needed you here for support through all of this, and you gave me that."

Kim leaned closer to her mom and gave her a hug. "Mom, I feel the same way. I'm so glad I was here. We have not been able to spend much time together and I felt that over the past several years we've drifted apart. But now I feel differently. I feel that we've gotten a chance to reconnect. So thank you."

"Thank me for what?" Nita asked as she pulled away from Kim.

"Thank you for letting me get close," she said and smiled.

Kim walked outside and lifted her head toward the sun. She had checked the weather that morning; Raleigh was only going to reach a high of forty-five over the next few days. She hated the thought of going back, but it was inevitable. She needed to get on with her life. She thought about her life back in North Carolina: divorced and alone and no Camilo. She knew she wanted to stay in touch with him, but didn't know when she would see him again. She wasn't going to let herself get frustrated with the uncertain future. She needed time to think things through; then she would see where things would end up.

Her thoughts turned to Mark and his death—or his presumed death. Camilo seemed convinced that his mother had known that Mark was still alive, but Kim wasn't quite sure what she believed. She had one burning question that she needed answered before she left. Kim reached for her pocket and took out her phone and dialed Beth's cell number.

"Beth?"

"Yes?"

"This is Kim." She paused. "Kim Thompson."

"Yes, I knew it was you. You caught me in the middle of something; sorry."

"No, I'm sorry. I don't mean to bother you, but I have to ask you something." Kim paused and there was no reply. "Did you ever bury . . . I mean," she stammered. "Where did you bury Mark?" There was another pause.

"We never did," came the answer.

Kim gasped under her breath. "You never did?" she asked.

"No, since we never got a death certificate and because Violet thinks he is still alive. They cremated the body that was in the trunk and gave us the ashes, but she stuck them somewhere in a closet. She didn't want to bury someone she didn't know."

"Oh," was all Kim could say. She thanked Beth, told her goodbye, and hung up.

CHAPTER THIRTY-NINE

The next day, Kim was up early. The sun was just coming up over the horizon and the air was already thick with humidity when she stepped out the door for her morning run. She thought she would clear her head before Jack and Nita woke up—that, and she wanted to plan the day with her parents. She wasn't sure when she would get the chance to spend time with them again.

Kim wondered if Camilo would call, or even if she wanted him to. She had spent most of the previous night in a fretful sleep, thoughts of Camilo and Mark occupying her mind. Early that morning, before she got up for the day, she had decided that she should not pursue any type of relationship with Camilo. It was way too complicated and Camilo might not even forgive her for having an affair with Mark, his own father. Kim shook her head. *Wow, does that sound absurd,* she thought.

Kim ran the rows and rows of streets; each time she turned a corner, her gait got faster. She couldn't slow herself down; something was gnawing at the pit of her stomach. She thought about her conversation with Beth. They had not even buried the remains. Then it hit her:

Why had she not put it together before? Camilo has family right in his backyard. She needed to tell him about Violet and Beth—he had a grandmother and aunt living right here in Texas!

When she finished her run, Kim took a shower and dressed, all the while pondering what she was going to say to Camilo. Would he even talk to her? *Of course he will,* she thought. She remembered what he had told her in Mexico: He was not mad at her, just confused. She picked up her cell phone and quickly called his number.

"Hi Camilo, this is Kim," she said into her phone.

"Kim . . . hi." Camilo sounded better than he had the day before. "How are you?"

"I'm good, Camilo," Kim said. She was trying hard not to bring her emotions into the conversation. "Can you meet me for coffee?" she asked.

"Yes—sure," he said. "When do you want to meet?"

"Can you meet me in an hour? There is a coffee shop on the Expressway and 83. I drove past it the other day. Can you meet me there?"

He agreed, and soon they were face to face in the bustling shop.

When they ordered their coffees and found a table, Kim got up enough nerve to tell him what she had been contemplating all morning. "Camilo," she said, her voice just above a whisper, "I . . . want to tell you something that I think is very important."

"What is it?" he asked. "I sense that you are nervous about something, and you shouldn't be. You can tell me anything." Camilo sounded like his old self. He grabbed Kim's hand and she pulled it away.

Kim looked down at the table and at Camilo's hand. Without looking up, she said, "Camilo, you have a grandmother and an aunt living right here in Texas." She waited for a response before peering into his eyes. She wanted to see what he was thinking. Camilo didn't answer. His eyes looked puzzled as he stared at her.

"I don't understand," he finally said and shrugged his shoulders.

"I'm talking about Mark's mother and sister. The family I was telling you about, who owned the resort in northern Maine. They still live here in Texas, over by McAllen." Kim looked at Camilo. She could see sadness in his eyes. "Camilo, this is a good thing. You have family and they are so close."

"Kim," he said and put his hand on his forehead. "I cannot know this family. I am sure they are good people, but under the circumstances, I cannot know them." He looked down.

"I think you are wrong. You owe it to them."

"What?" he asked, his voice louder.

"I didn't mean it like that. It's just that you are family. Shouldn't Violet know that Mark's son lives so close by? I think it would make her very happy. She still holds out hope that he will come back."

"You have spoken to her?" he asked. He looked confused.

"Yes, but not about you. Jack and Nita still stay in touch with them. In fact, they were the friends we went to see a few days after I arrived, the night you wanted to take me for wine."

"Yes, I remember."

"I then met with Beth right before Christmas, when Jack was in the hospital. Camilo, Mark's mother, thinks he is alive, too." She gave him a pleading look. "Please, think about it."

"How do you think she would feel if I went to her and said, 'Hi; your son had an affair with *mi madre* and I am your grandson'?" Camilo said and laughed. "No, Kim. I don't think that is such a good idea."

Kim reached for her purse. She took out a piece of paper and a pen and then searched for her phone. She opened it, found Beth's number, and wrote it down. "Here," she said as she slid the paper across the table. "Think about it."

"I will," he said, then added, "Kim, should we try to figure this out?"

Kim shook her head. "Camilo, I wish we could, but you know how I was worried about the age thing between us?" She pointed her finger back and forth between the two of them. "I'm very fond of you, but from the beginning, this was a wrong thing. Now it's gotten even worse."

"You don't love me?" Camilo asked.

"I don't want to believe that I do," she responded. "I can't let myself."

"It's hard for me as well," Camilo said. "You had an affair with my father." His words were sharp and Kim cringed.

"Yes, I know," she said softly. "I think we need time to think this through." She reached for his hand and let her grab hold of it.

CHAPTER FORTY

Kim's plane was scheduled to leave at eleven o'clock in the morning. She finished packing, poured herself a cup of coffee, and headed out to find her parents, who had already gone to the recreation hall. When she stepped off the step, she stopped and breathed in the fresh air. Her mind was spinning, and she used her long, slow breaths to calm down. Just before she got to the door of the hall, she spotted a lawn chair by the door and sat in it instead of going inside.

She laid her head back and closed her eyes. *I don't want to go home,* she thought. She let out a sigh and opened her eyes. She thought about the past month and the funny turn her life had taken. She wished she could convince Camilo to call Beth and Violet, but she knew why he had reservations; it would be an awkward call. Kim thought about Mark and where he may or may not be at that very moment. She didn't know what else she could do to solve the mystery about Mark, or how to go about finding him. But what if they did find him? What would happen then?

Jack came out of the door. "Are you ready?" he asked.

Kim got up from the chair. "I guess as ready as I'll ever

be. I don't want to go, but I know I have to." She followed him back to the house. Two hours later, she was on the plane headed east. This time, the plane was only half full and Kim had the whole row to herself. So after the seatbelt sign was extinguished, she stretched out her legs, closed her eyes, and let her mind drift.

—•••—

The next day, Kim was back to work and fell quickly into her usual routine as if she hadn't missed a day. She parked her car and headed into Wicked Manufacturing, unconsciously taking her usual path. She stepped of the elevator onto the seventh floor, and when she did, Jim was rounding the corner from the exit door.

Kim jumped when she saw him. "What are you doing coming from that direction?" she asked without even saying hello.

"The stairs do wonders," he said as he smiled a long, slow smile. "Your friend got me into the fitness thing."

"Now about that," Kim said as they walked to the break room. "What are you two doing?"

"What do you mean, Kim, what are we doing?" he asked.

"I better not have to pick up the pieces," she replied, and then smiled as she poured herself a cup of coffee. Just then, Connie came into the room.

"Kim, you're home! I was worried about you. Why didn't you call me?"

"I got in late last night and I didn't want to bother you," she lied. Her mind had been so preoccupied that she totally forgot about Connie, Jim, or anyone other than

Camilo and Mark. "When did you guys get home?" she asked, quickly changing the subject.

"We came in on Friday," Jim answered.

"And what's this health-and-fitness thing that Jim's talking about?" Kim asked as she turned to Connie. "That's not like you!" She rolled her eyes at her friend.

"I really got into running. We'll have to go together sometime," Connie responded.

"Okay, I would love to see this," Kim said and laughed. "Let's talk later, you two."

Jim reached over and squeezed Connie's hand and she smiled.

With coffee cup in hand, Kim headed to her office to start the day and to dig into the enormous pile of work that was waiting for her.

CHAPTER FORTY-ONE

Two weeks went by fairly quickly. Kim settled into her same old routine. After one particular trying day, Kim finally was able to plop down on her couch, glad it was the start of the weekend. She looked at the clock on the wall; it was nine thirty. She hadn't had time to check her personal phone all day, and wondered if Camilo had called. She had checked her phone each night over the past two weeks and each time found there were no messages. But then again, she hadn't called him either.

Before she checked it yet another time, she went into the kitchen, found a bottle of wine, and poured herself a glass. Then she walked over to the stereo and searched through her collection of CDs. She found what she was looking for—her favorite jazz tunes—and popped the CD in the player.

Kim looked out the window at the rain pounding on the sill. The weather had not changed during the month she had been gone. She was right back to where she left off a month ago. *But no,* she thought. *It's not in the least bit the same.* She paused and took a sip of wine. Kim closed her eyes, then reached for her purse to find her phone.

She opened it up and saw she had three missed calls. The voice mail icon was blinking back at her. She pressed the number to listen to her messages. She heard Jack's voice on the other end. "We miss you," he said. "We love you and are so happy you came for a visit. Come again soon." Kim heard a click and then a dial tone.

She scrolled to the next message; it was from Camilo. Before she listened, she scrolled down and the next message was from Camilo as well. *Hmm . . . I wonder why he is so persistent?*

She pressed the keypad and heard Camilo's voice. Kim let out a sigh. "Call me, señorita," he said. She smiled at the sound of his voice. She erased the message. She had tried hard over the past few weeks to sort out her feelings for him. She knew she loved him, but she also knew she couldn't have a relationship with him. She was old enough to be his mother, and it was too complicated and weird to have an affair with him when years earlier she had had an affair with his father.

She pressed the one key again and listened to the next message. "Señorita, please call me." This time he sounded more urgent. Kim got up from the couch, concerned about his urgency. She looked at her watch; it wasn't too late to call him. She dialed his number but after a few rings got his voice mail. She left a message, telling him that she received his call and to call her. Camilo never returned her call that evening. She checked it several times and finally went to bed at midnight. She tried to squelch the feelings of jealousy, thinking he must be out somewhere—and with whom, she didn't know—but was not able to.

—●●●—

When Kim had not heard from Camilo by the next afternoon, she decided to call Connie for advice. She and Jim had been spending a lot of time together since they came back from California. Kim was happy for them, especially for Connie—she seemed like a different person. Connie always tried to carry an aura of confidence, but Kim could always see right through it. Now the confidence seemed real.

"Hey, girl," Kim said when Connie answered the phone. "Do you feel like a glass of wine?"

"Buglios? Of course," Connie answered.

An hour later, the two were sitting in their favorite wine bar.

"Camilo left me a few messages yesterday. I called him back, but he hasn't returned my call," Kim said, taking a sip of her wine.

"Did you try this morning?" Connie asked.

"No."

"Why not?"

"I don't know," Kim said. She wondered that herself.

"Can I give you some advice?" Connie asked. "You need to embrace this relationship—this man. I know you don't like that you're old enough to be his mother, but honey, who cares?" Connie paused. "I can't believe I'm giving you relationship guidance, but look at me: I broke out of my shell and finally found happiness. Who would have known that I could be so content with straight-laced, boring Jim?"

"Connie!"

"You know what I mean. He never seemed my type, but I was able to look past that—I'm happy, Kim. I want you to be happy as well," Connie said, taking Kim's hand in an uncharacteristic gesture. "Listen to your heart . . . please."

"Okay," Kim said, hesitating. She looked down at her hand, which Connie still held.

"Then you have to call him."

"Okay," Kim said again.

—•••—

Kim waited until the next morning to call Camilo. She wanted her head clear when she talked to him. "Camilo," she said when she heard his voice.

"Señorita!" he said, his voice cheerful.

"You sounded like it was urgent," she said. "What's the matter?"

She heard Camilo sigh on the other end. "I am back to the beach house," he told her.

"Yes?"

"I wanted to search for more papers of my *madres*. I got to thinking of our last conversation about Mark, and I needed to see if I could find out more about why she told me she thought he was still alive. I have found nothing significant. I have not been able to sleep or eat or think about anything else but him and my *madre*. I don't know what to do."

"Okay, so where are you now?"

"I am sitting on the beach. I wish you were sitting next to me. I have also been thinking a lot about you, Kim."

"We can talk about that later, but for now, concentrate, Camilo. Where would your mother keep her most personal items?"

"I don't know. I searched the attic but only found boxes of old clothes, mostly baby clothes of mine and my brothers and sisters. Not much else other than business papers of my *padre*, things from his office. I did find a small brown wooden box. Its cover was carved with the family seal. At first I thought it was locked, but when I examined the box further, I found a secret panel on the bottom and inside it was a key," he said and chuckled. "When I opened it, I was amazed at what I found: items from my childhood. These were things my father kept, Kim," Camilo's voice broke. "I found the box among his things. It was his box." There was silence.

"Camilo?" Kim whispered after a few seconds.

"I am just surprised that he cared to even take the time to keep mementos from when I was a child."

"But none of these things were your mother's?" Kim questioned.

"No, I found nothing personal of hers."

"Where would your mother keep her most personal items?" Kim asked again.

"I don't know, Kim. I am so confused."

"Where was your mother's favorite place there? Where did she like to spend some alone time?" Kim's questioning was deliberate but caring.

"That's easy," Camilo answered. "There is a small building to the right of the house. A small brick path leads to its door. The brick came from deep in the heart of Mexico. It was from my *madre*'s childhood church where she attended with her *padres*. She made my *padre* transport it here when the church was torn down."

"And what is the building?" Kim asked.

"It was one of my *madre*'s most favorite places to be. My mother was a very religious woman, a very faithful Catholic. She had my *padre* build a chapel so she could pray when she was unable to make it to town. She sometimes let us children inside, but mostly this was her private area."

"Camilo, that's it!" Kim exclaimed. "Her most treasured items must be in that building."

"I have not set foot in there for years. I don't even know if I know where the key is to get inside."

"Think hard, Camilo. You must find the key and get into that building. I'm positive you will find your mother's things there."

"Okay, Kim. Wait a minute. I'll start walking to the house. I will call you right back when I find the key."

Kim stood up from the couch and walked to the window. She looked at the rain falling outside while she waited for Camilo to call back. After what seemed like an hour but was really only five minutes, her phone rang.

"Hello," she answered.

"I found it," Camilo said. "Remember the table next to the bed where Mark's picture was?"

"Yes."

"I looked in the drawer and at first there was nothing. Then I brushed my hand all around the inside and came across a piece of tape. Under the tape was a key, which I hope will unlock the door to my *madre*'s sanctuary."

"Did you try it?" Kim asked, her voice anxious.

"No," Camilo said and laughed. "I was waiting for you. You will take this journey with me." A few minutes later, Camilo announced he was in front of the door and ready with the key to open it. "I hope this will work," he told her. A few seconds later, he was inside. "Señorita," Camilo's voice was shallow, "I forgot what this place looked like."

"Tell me about it, describe it," Kim urged.

"It is beautiful, Señorita. I have to stop a minute to let my eyes adjust."

He paused before he continued. "It's a tiny room with one pew and right beyond the pew is a small altar. A statue of the Virgin of Guadalupe is on the right and on the left there is a smaller statue of Jesus. A cross is hanging on the wall just above the altar. A single stained-glass window faces the pew. Right now, the sun is streaming through the window, lighting up the inside as well as the dust particles swirling through the air."

"Do you see anything else? Perhaps a chest of some sort?"

"Slow down, Kim," Camilo said and laughed. "I haven't had a chance to look. I am still admiring the beauty and—what do you say?—peacefulness of it. I can see why my *madre* loved it here." Camilo paused again, then Kim heard his voice. "This statue of the Virgin of Guadalupe is so wonderful." Kim could hear his steps, then a loud gasp. "Oh, she moves!" he exclaimed. "Kim, there is a hole in the floor! I'm going to place the phone down for a minute," Camilo told her.

Kim paced back and forth in her tiny living room while she waited for Camilo to continue his search, occasionally taking a sip of wine. She could hear the sound of objects being dragged across wood and then a banging noise. She looked at the clock on the wall. Ten minutes had passed since Camilo set the phone down. She walked back to the window and then to the kitchen, all the while keeping the phone pressed against her ear. Then she heard footsteps become louder.

"Kim?" Camilo was out of breath. "My *madre* sure had a secret way of hiding things. Below the Mother Mary, the floor was hollowed out and there was another key. It's a small key with a bright red ribbon tied to it. I had to search the room to find out what the key was for."

"Yes, I heard a lot of movement," Kim said.

"Of course she wouldn't make it easy. I studied the room from top to bottom and in the corner by the window there was a panel close to the ceiling. When I looked closer, I could see a slight outline of a keyhole. I had to use the bench to reach high enough to place the key in. I felt as if I was dishonoring my *madre*, as I knew this was the pew she used to say her prayers."

"And what did you find?" Kim pressed him, ignoring the sentiment for his mother.

"A box," Camilo softly replied.

"Did you open it?"

"Not yet. But I will now." Kim could hear Camilo set the box on wood, possibly the pew. Then she heard paper rustling. During this, Camilo said nothing. "There are pictures in here," he finally said. "And letters. The letters are from him."

"Him who?" Kim asked.

"Mark," he replied. She heard him open one of them.

"Listen to what he wrote," Camilo continued. "'Don't worry, sweetheart. I am safe, but you must not know where I am. Please don't try to find me. Just know that I love you and that I will always love you and will always keep you in my heart.'"

"When was it written?" Kim interrupted.

"I don't know. There is not a mark from the post office."

"We have to find out!" Kim insisted. She paused before she continued. "If we can find out when he wrote the letter, we can compare that date to the time the article said that the body was found in the trunk."

"I don't know how we can do that," Camilo told her.

"Dig deeper; open all of the letters and see if you can find a date," she said even more insistently.

"Señorita," Camilo said with a laugh, "slow down and take a breath."

"You look, I am going to get the articles. I'll be right back." Kim set the phone down and went to the bedroom, where she had the stack of papers that she had brought home from Texas. She practically ran back to the living room and was out of breath when she picked up the phone. "Did you find anything?" she asked Camilo, but there was no answer. "Camilo?" She heard nothing. "Camilo?" she said again.

"Kim," he finally replied. "I am going to call you back tomorrow. It's going to take me a while to go through all these letters."

"But Camilo—"

"I'm sorry, Kim; I must take my time. I will read these letters and then I will call you tomorrow. *Si*, Señorita?"

"Yes," Kim said, with a hint of protest in her voice.

———— ••• ————

When Kim got off of work the next day, she quickly went to work reviewing Jake Michaels's articles, searching for dates and details. She scanned the piece until she found the part about the body found in the trunk, and found the timeframe that the journalist stated it was found. It appeared that Violet reported him missing in June of 1983 and the body was found six months later. Now she had a date. She hoped Camilo had found something on his end.

She picked up her phone and dialed his number. When he didn't answer after five rings, she hung up. She found herself wondering where he could be, then she shook her head. *Oh no you don't; you're not going to do that again!* She scolded herself for her brief jealous thoughts.

She walked into the bedroom to find a sweater. The cold rain of the day had chilled her to the bone and she needed to warm up. She pulled a sweater out of the drawer and then went into the bathroom and turned on the water for the tub. She poured vanilla cream bubble bath under the running water. She went into the kitchen, found some candles, and carried them back into the bathroom. She lit all six of them, quickly slipped out of her clothes, and slid into the warm, bubbly water. She laid back and closed her eyes and thought of Camilo.

A few minutes later she heard her phone ringing in the other room and her eyes flew opened. She cursed herself for not bringing it into the bathroom. She quickly got out of the tub, wrapped a towel around her soapy body, and ran into the living room. "Hello?" she hastily blurted out.

"Kim." It was Camilo. "What did I catch you doing? You sound like you have been running."

"No, I was just taking a bath and didn't want to miss the phone."

"Hmm, you are naked, no?"

"I have a towel around me," she said and laughed.

"Kim, I found more letters," he said.

"You did? And can you tell when they were written?"

"He wrote more telling her that he was safe. One of them was still in the envelope; it was dated January 6, 1984."

Kim walked over to the couch where she left the article and searched for the page she was reading earlier; she found the page where she highlighted the dates. She scanned it again.

"The article says the body was found in December of 1983 and that Violet reported him missing six months earlier." Kim paused. "Camilo, do you know what this means?"

"*Si*," he said softly.

"Those letters were written after the body was discovered. That means it can't be Mark's body. Camilo, he must be alive!" she screamed. Camilo did not say a word. "Camilo?"

"*Si*, I am here." Kim heard nothing but silence again. "Deep down, I never knew if I believed my *madre* or not. Not that I didn't think she was not telling the truth, but I was not sure if she really knew the truth. Now I know she did and now I know he must be alive. My real father must be alive."

"Oh, Camilo," Kim sighed. "You have to talk to Mark's mother and sister now. You must tell them what we know."

"I can't do it without you, Kim. When can you come back?"

"Camilo, I've been thinking about us—the two of us together."

"Yes?"

"I know it will be scary, tough, and at times awkward, but I want to stay in touch with you, try to have some sort of relationship."

"Yes," Camilo said. "I, too, want that. I don't want to forget about you, Kim. So when can you come back?"

"I don't have any time off until spring."

"Then I will wait for you."

After Kim hung up with Camilo, she opened her calendar to April. She had marked her next holiday with Xs. She closed her planner and opened her computer. Before she knew it, she had a flight booked to Harlingen for three months later.

Photo by Misty Moments Photography

ABOUT THE AUTHOR

Deborah Jensen was born and raised in Minnesota. Writing has been a lifelong passion for Deborah although she spent most of her career in the finance world. *Beyond Escape* is her debut novel, inspired by real life relationships and circumstances. Deborah currently lives in Northern Minnesota with her husband. They have two grown children.